STRANGER RANGER

PARK RANGER SERIES BOOK #2

DAISY PRESCOTT

WWW.SMARTYPANTSROMANCE.COM

COPYRIGHT

DEDICATION

"The truth about who we are lives in our hearts."

— BRENÉ BROWN

CHAPTER ONE
DAPHNE

"*I*'m going to hell."

"What is it this time?" Kacey repeats her typical response to my declaration.

"Impure thoughts." I sigh and stare up at the sky.

Taller than I am by half a foot, she scans the crowded farmers' market. "Which guy are you thinking about? The tall one with the blondish hair or the grumpy-looking guy loudly talking about his sausages? I can see this going either direction."

"The tall one." I've been trying not to stare and failing miserably —like a belly-flop-instead-of-swan-dive level of failure.

"Ooh. He's a living, breathing advertisement for eating your recommended daily servings of vegetables." Kacey sighs, and I find myself doing the same once again.

Across the community center parking lot is what I can only describe as a fever dream crossed with a hallucination, sprinkled with fantasy, and a dash of what-the-ever-loving-hell-is-he-doing-here-in-Green-Valley-Tennessee mystery.

The six-foot-something bearded man—or perhaps demigod is a

better description—stands behind a table loaded with wooden crates and baskets full of vegetables.

Wholesome farm boy comes to mind, but that's not quite right. He's all man, from the light brown beard to the wide spread of his shoulders, from the muscle-corded arms to the flat planes of chest and abs, right on down to his long, strong legs. To clarify, he's not hawking his wares naked. I'm certain public nudity is frowned upon by the good citizens of this fine town, but my imagination is happy to conjure up a visual of what's beneath his long-sleeved T-shirt and jeans.

The demigod is currently chatting up a customer, completely unaware of me—which is exactly how I prefer it. Gives me a chance to observe him like he's in a nature documentary narrated by some impossibly stuffy British man.

Great, now I have David Attenborough from the *Planet Earth* series in my head narrating the scene:

The farmer has a habit of brushing his hands through the messy waves of dark blond hair that nearly reach his shoulders to keep them out of his face. As he moves and gesticulates while speaking, a lock flops over his eyes and he sweeps it away. It's mesmerizing and draws attention to his tan forearms and the stretch of white cotton around his bicep and shoulder.

Then there is his face, chiseled by the gods themselves. Angular, but not harsh. The hard cut of his cheekbones and broad forehead are softened by large eyes and a slightly-too-wide mouth. From afar, his eyes look brown, but they are probably pools of molten chocolate up close.

If I had a fan, I'd use it to temper the flames of lust heating my face.

Tearing my attention away from cataloging his features, I take in the rest of his setup. Tables. Vegetables. Open-sided tent. A black and white pig sleeping in a pen.

My mouth drops open and a puff of disbelief escapes.

"What now?" Kacey asks.

"I know that pig," I whisper.

"Did you just call that fine-looking man a pig?" Unlike me, she doesn't lower her voice. In fact, she raises it in shock. "Did you date and he dumped you?"

"Shh." I reprimand her and flap my hand to remind her we're in public.

"It's fine. He's too far away to hear us."

Making sure she's looking at me, I glare at her.

"It's fine," she says in a normal voice before whispering, "*Fine.*"

We both stand as still as fence posts, staring across the market.

"Damn, why do the good-looking ones always have to be terrible humans? What a waste." Resigned disappointment tinges her words.

I take a step to the left and face her. "What are you rambling about?"

"The cruelness of handsome men always being pigs. Looks versus decency is a dilemma for the ages. For once, I'd like to have the complete package." She softly snorts. "Yeah, I stand by that statement."

Ignoring the familiar diatribe, I correct her. "It isn't a metaphor. The actual pig in the pen behind him—I recognize it."

"Does that mean you know him? Because if you do, you should go over and say hello."

"Weren't you bemoaning the cruel imbalance of looks versus substance not ten seconds ago?"

"There's only one way to find out if the hypothesis is true." Pressing her hand between my shoulder blades, she gives me a soft push.

"I doubt he's your type."

"Who said I'm interested?" She pretends to be offended, but her smile betrays her.

I pretend to wipe drool from her chin before she swats my hand away. "For one thing, he's a farmer."

3

She scoffs. "I like food, so we already have one thing in common. Two, we share a love of plants. I own a fiddle-leaf fig."

"A fake one," I remind her.

"You're one to talk. The only vegetable I've ever seen you eat is a potato, preferably fried or formed into a tot."

She speaks the truth.

"I'll eat salad," I say in my defense.

"You eat ranch with iceberg as the vehicle because it's not appropriate to eat dressing with a spoon. At least not in public."

"You forgot the grape tomatoes and cucumber—if it's peeled—thank you very much. Oh, and I'll also eat raw carrots with ranch. Cooked ones taste like old people." I stare at my feet, because if I glance at Kacey, I'll make a weird face. Knowing my past luck around guys, that will be the exact moment the hot farmer glances in our direction and notices me.

Kacey is on the move, and I follow. Sticking close is better than letting her roam off on her own.

Continuing our conversation as a means of distraction, I ask, "Does popcorn count as a vegetable? It's corn—comes from the same cob as sweet corn. The corn lobby would argue it's an important part of the standard American diet, and kettle corn must count, too. Being made in an old-fashioned pot means it's wholesome, which equals healthy." I'm breathless from trying to keep up and share random thoughts about corn at the same time.

I don't think Kacey is even listening to me because she's making a beeline for the row of tables on the far side of the lot.

"Look, apple butter!" Pointing at a stand decked out in red and white gingham with green accents, I try to throw her off course. "Is that apple cake? There are free samples. Bet they'd be nice enough to let us have more than one."

Her steps falter as she swivels her head, pausing and sniffing the air like a velociraptor. "Ooh, cake."

I know my best friend's weaknesses and I am not afraid to use this knowledge to my advantage.

While Kacey loads her palm with free baked goods, I sneak a peek over my shoulder.

Farm boy has his head thrown back, laughing at something an older woman is saying. The way she's gripping the cucumber in her hand, I'm assuming something inappropriate has been said. She's old enough to at least be his mother and is probably related to him, by marriage if not blood. In Green Valley, everyone is connected somehow.

I'm one of the few exceptions. Recently hired seasonally as an interpretation specialist for the park's visitor center, I've only been in the area since April.

Kacey picks up a small paper cup and hands another one to me. "Have some cider."

Happily distracted, she appears to have forgotten about the demigod.

After blowing on my cup, I take a sip.

"Where should we go next?" Kacey's attention swings from table to table.

In the opposite direction from Vegetable Thor is one of my favorite vendors. "Let's go look at that one."

"I thought you were self-banned from buying any soap or soap-based products." She sounds suspicious.

I refuse to meet her eyes. "Who says I'm purchasing it for myself? Handcrafted items make thoughtful gifts, and your birthday is coming up."

"First, who says I want soap?" She wrinkles her nose. "Second, when is my birthday?"

"November," I mumble.

"Which is three months from now."

I give her a full smile. "Never too early to be prepared."

"Is it time for an intervention?" She removes the stack of bars from my hand.

"I'm trying to support the local economy," I complain as she returns my collection to the table.

"Then buy some veggies or alpaca socks, or one of those weird-looking carved wooden spoons."

"I already own seven pairs and two spoons. I barely cook." Casting a loving glance at the bars, I sigh. "You're right. No more soap. I already have half a dozen bars waiting in the cabinet under my sink. How many soaps can one single woman use in a year? Three? Four? I can't be allowed to buy any more."

Eyeing me with suspicion, Kacey sips her beverage. "You could always put them into your drawers to freshen your clothes. That's what my grandmother did."

"I'm not sure I want to smell like your grandmother. Plus, my work is kind of a scent-free zone. Don't want to attract bears or other wildlife."

Kacey wrinkles her nose. "Please tell me you at least wear deodorant."

"Natural." Took me a while to find one that works, but I now smell like roses and sage instead of lavender and B.O.

She lifts my arm and sniffs close to my shoulder. "Not sure that counts."

Squealing, I try to escape her grip.

"Stop!" My voice comes out louder than intended, and I sense the people around us directing their attention our way.

I lift my gaze to see who is staring. Across the crowd, my eyes catch those belonging to the farmer I'm not supposed to notice. His brow wrinkles and his head cocks to the side, like he might recognize me but isn't sure from where. Or maybe he just thinks I'm a nut because he witnessed Kacey sniffing my armpit in public.

As soon as he realizes we've locked stares, he breaks the eye contact by dipping his chin and focusing on his table.

Not for the first time in my life, I debate whether it's better to be invisible or seen but judged.

"What else do you want to get this morning? Honey? Jam? Crocheted pot holders? Vegetables? The hot farmer guy?" Kacey singsongs.

"What? No. I wasn't staring."

"Never said you were," she says with a knowing lilt.

"Even for Green Valley, seeing a pig hanging out at the market is unusual."

"Right, the pig is what caught your attention. You were practically licking him with your eyeballs."

I groan. "Ew. Never use licking and eyeballs in the same sentence again. Promise?"

She holds up her palms. "Okay, okay. There was a line there and I crossed it."

"Was it that obvious I was staring?"

"If he were a bullseye and you were throwing lust axes with your eyes, I'd say you hit your mark . . . or something like that. You get my point."

"I'm definitely going to hell." I groan again.

"It's not a sin to appreciate beauty."

I huff out a laugh. "Not sure my thoughts were focused on his beauty."

"Daphne!"

"I know, he's a wholesome farmer and I'm having all the dirty thoughts—definitely going to hell."

"Then I'll be sitting next to you in the handbasket." Kacey grins. "This is going to be so worth it."

Before I can react, she's wrapped her hand around my wrist and is tugging me forward through the crowd.

"What will be worth it?" I ask, attempting to drag my feet enough to slow her pace.

"You'll see."

7

"Stop. This isn't college! You can't make me do embarrassing things just for the hell of it," I plead. "I'm a park ranger—I have a certain reputation to uphold. I've taken a *vow*."

"Whenever you say that, I feel like you've decided to become a nun."

"I'm not even Catholic, or Buddhist. Anymore," I add half-heartedly.

"I know. That's why it always confuses me."

"Trust me, I have no plans to join a convent or cloister myself off from society."

"Good to know." She gives my hand another yank and returns to her mission. Acting as a human icebreaker ship, she parts the crowd, making her way through the various clumps of people. A former college lacrosse player, she makes an imposing first impression, especially with her height and nearly black hair. As if sensing her determination, people instinctually move out of her way.

"Kacey." I wriggle my arm free from her grasp.

She pauses, turns. "What?"

Her face glows with false innocence.

"I don't need you playing matchmaker. You're only in town for the weekend and I want to spend time with you." There are exactly zero lies detected in my statement.

She's not buying it. "Don't you want to meet the hot farmer?"

"When have I ever been into ditching a friend for a guy?"

"Never. That's part of your problem. I'm not actually advocating for you to ditch me, but why not at least talk to him? You never put yourself out there to meet anyone. I worry about you."

"No need to do that. I'm great. I love my job. My co-workers are awesome, and my boss is amazing."

"How many dates have you been on since moving here in the spring?"

I hold up a circle with my index finger and thumb.

"Exactly. I doubt you have a lot of options around here." She glances to the left and right.

"I don't need options, plural." I sneak a peek at Vegetable Thor and sigh. "He'll probably be here again next week. If it's meant to be, it can wait seven whole days while I spend time with my best friend."

"Nice try." She grins at me.

Without giving me the chance to change her mind, she walks over to the table.

"Wait, Kacey," I softly call after her, sounding lame even to my own ears.

I have two choices: let her go off on her own and observe her from a safe distance, or join her and attempt to prevent any meddling on my behalf. From prior experience, I know both possibilities come with their own risk.

By the time I catch up, she's parked herself right in front of his display of brightly colored and, frankly, weird produce. I recognize a few things, but most are only vaguely familiar. Oddly shaped and strangely hued, some look straight out of a Dr. Seuss book.

"Welcome." He greets us with a warm smile, sweeping his hand through his hair. "What are you looking for today?"

"Tell us about your bounty," Kacey casually says to the demigod like he's a normal man.

Lord of the Vegetables gazes down at me, a tiny smile curving the corners of his mouth. "What do you like?"

If she picks up the extra-long carrots, I'll pretend I don't know her and walk away. Simple as that.

His large eyes are more melted caramel swirled in milk chocolate. A dark ring at the edge of his irises gives way to warm amber surrounding his pupils, all framed by dark lashes. I'm staring again.

"Umm . . ." I scan the display, willing myself to ignore the carrots. "Lettuce?"

"What kind?" He cocks his head to the side, indicating the bins of colorful leaves and small heads of green and red.

9

"Iceberg," Kacey answers for me.

"Boring," he says. "That's like saying your favorite beverage is water."

"Don't knock the old H-two-oh. It's magical. You can make tea or coffee or lemonade with it, or drink it on its own, or add bubbles and call it seltzer." After I finish my defense of water, we all stand in awkward silence for a beat or two.

"Tell us about these." Kacey pinches my side while using her other hand to point at a neat pyramid of green balls next to the carrots.

"Japanese turnips." He picks one up, tosses it in the air, and catches it.

I make a face and don't bother hiding it.

"Not a fan?" His voice loses its friendly tone and he eyes me challengingly.

"They smell like feet." My nose wrinkles at the memory of my grandmother's boiled turnips.

"Have you ever tasted this variety?" he asks. "I promise there's nothing remotely foot-flavored about them."

I shake my head. "I'll pass."

He pulls a small blade from his back pocket. It isn't the typical Swiss Army style, more like a fancy hunting knife with a bone handle, worn smooth from use. There's something old-fashioned and rugged about it.

Using the flour sack towel resting on his shoulder, he wipes the turnip clean before cutting a paper-thin slice. Extending the knife toward me, he implores, "Taste."

I really don't want to eat a raw, unwashed turnip, but Kacey elbows me, doing so neither gently nor subtly.

"Come on." He wiggles the knife back and forth. "Trust me."

He's a stranger. I'm not going to trust him.

However, it would be rude to reject his offer and walk away.

"Fine." I slide the slice from the knife and lift it to my nose. "It's peppery."

"You sound disappointed it doesn't smell like old shoes." He's clearly amused by my reluctance.

"Has anyone ever called you a food bully?" I retort.

He laughs, though not the head-back guffaw from earlier. More of a chuckle, and it feels authentic and less staged. "Yes, but not for a long time. I won't force you, but you'll never know what you might be missing out on if you don't give things a chance."

His knife pauses near the turnip as he waits for me to make my decision.

I take the tiniest bite possible. A mouse would take a bigger mouthful. A wave of spicy pepper hits my taste buds, but it's not like hot sauce. This is followed by an unexpected sweetness, and I take another bite, wondering if I imagined the combination.

"Good, huh?" He offers a slice to Kacey.

"Amazing," I mumble as I crunch the rest of mine.

"So, I was right?" He offers me another piece, which I happily accept.

"It isn't polite to say I told you so or gloat."

"I've never been a fan of being polite." He sets down his knife. "How do you feel about kale?"

"Isn't everyone over kale? It's all about the cauliflower now." Kacey laughs. "Don't you follow the food fads?"

His face tightens and his mouth narrows into a thin line. "Can't say that I do. I prefer to eat what I enjoy and leave the trends to people who need to be told what to like."

She's hit a nerve, and we stand around in another awkward silence. While friendly on the surface, I get the feeling Vegetable Thor isn't a real people person.

"What's this?" I point at a pale, yellowy-green cluster comprised of tiny triangular towers.

"Romanesco. Italian cousin to the cauliflower." He eyes Kacey. "Incredible roasted and drizzled with fresh olive oil."

"And these?" I point at the white version of the turnips.

"Ah, these have a surprise inside." He cuts one in half, revealing the fuchsia center with a pale green outline. "Watermelon radishes."

"Do they taste like the fruit?"

He chuckles and flashes his small smile again. "No, but they're delicious."

I take the piece from him and bite into it.

"Good, right?" he asks.

I nod. After swallowing, I say, "They taste similar to the turnips but different."

"They're from the same family. Kind of like cousins."

"Makes sense." I finish the radish, surprised by the kick of heat on my tongue.

"Better than iceberg?" He tilts his head back, and the posture feels intimidating, like he's sizing me up.

"Don't hate on the 'berg. It serves a purpose."

Kacey laughs—or more accurately, snorts. I'm surprised his pig doesn't confuse her for one of its own. "Don't try to convince her otherwise. You won't win this battle."

He crosses his arms, forcing his muscles to bunch in a rudely distracting way. "Is that so?"

When he directs his attention at me, I can't decide if I should feel flattered he's so interested or perturbed he's judging me.

"Life's too short to be boring or eat boring food," he declares, still focused solely on me.

"Let him who is free from sin cast the first stone," I retort, the words flowing from deeply ingrained memory.

"Did you just Bible-verse me?" His steady gaze falters.

"Sorry. Slips out sometimes." Out of habit, my teeth find my lower lip and chew the smooth skin.

"What's up with the pig?" Kacey breaks through the weird tension surrounding us.

"That would be Patsy Swine, finest sow in the land." He points at the black and white pig asleep in the shade of the tent. "She was supposed to be a miniature pot-bellied, but as you can see, she's an overachiever."

"Is she a pet?" I ask.

"Sure is. House-trained and everything. Her manners are impeccable—except when she naps on the job."

"Nice to meet you, Patsy." I give her a wave.

"We didn't catch your name," Kacey interjects.

"Odin Hill." His grin returns as he stares at me "And you are?"

Are you freaking kidding me? Odin? God of thunder? Father of Thor? Of course, he's a Norse god.

"I'm Kacey, and this is Daphne. She works up at the national park."

"Do you?" he asks. "Are you new?"

"Four months next week." I hold his stare.

He makes a humming sound but doesn't comment. Like he's making up his mind about something, he bobs his head once. His demeanor shifts and he takes a step to the side. "Well, nice to meet you. I have other customers waiting. Let me know if you decide to buy anything."

I meet eyes with Kacey before weakly saying thanks.

We shuffle out of the way of the line that's formed behind us.

Once we're a few yards away, near a table crowded with jars of honey, I stop and face Kacey. "What happened back there? Did it get weird or was it just me?"

Crinkling her nose, she confirms my observation with a nod. "He was flirting with you until you went all biblical on him over lettuce."

"That makes it sound like I sent a plague of frogs or lightning to smite him. You'd think a man who loves turnips so much would be more accepting of differing tastes."

"I'm teasing. He was still chatty until I mentioned you work at the park. Did you notice that?"

"Weird. Who hates national parks?" Not sure why, but I feel

deflated by how our encounter ended. What do I care if the weird farmer judges me? Or has a weird grudge about rangers?

"Guys with pet pigs?" Kacey offers in response to my question. "Do you think he lets it sleep in the house? Or in his bed? Why do all the gorgeous ones have to be freaks?" She sighs.

"Better to be appreciated from afar, I guess." I take one last glance over my shoulder at Odin. The name suits him even if he's not an old man with one eye. Smiling and laughing one moment, serious the next, he's as unpredictable as a summer thunderstorm.

"You sound disappointed." Kacey links her arm with mine. "Sorry we had to ruin your impure thoughts with reality."

"No need to apologize. I'm happier to spend time with you before you head back to Greensboro." I force myself to focus on the positive.

"Lies, but I'll take the compliment." Kacey gives my wrist a squeeze. "Let's buy you some consolation soap to cheer you up."

CHAPTER TWO
ODIN

*B*y early afternoon, the crowd at the farmers' market fades, leaving only stragglers, bargainers, and tourists sampling the charms of small-town life.

I've had enough people for the week, and I'm looking forward to the quiet of my own company. All the talking and friendly chatter exhausts me. You'd think vegetables would sell themselves given they're pretty self-explanatory, yet folks wanna hear a story about a carrot being grown from the guy who pulled it out of the dirt himself. So, I play my part of the happy farmer at the stand. It's my bad luck I've always been charming. Part of my DNA.

My family has lived in the mountains surrounding Green Valley longer than anyone around here can remember. Before there was a national park or even a Cades Cove, the Hills established a homestead in the Smokies straddling Tennessee and North Carolina.

Because our last name is Hill, some people like to joke that we put the hill in hillbilly. Some people think they have a sense of humor when they're just being mean-spirited. As my Nannie Ida always says, glass houses provide good views, but then again, so do mirrors.

This is why I prefer the company of Patsy over most folks. She's smart, a good listener, tidy, and doesn't give a damn about my family and reputation. She has more class than a lot of the gossips and Sunday churchgoers around here.

After I consolidate the remaining produce into crates and load them into the van, I fold the tables and collapse my tent. While I work, the face of the brunette ranger floats through my mind.

She looked familiar, but I didn't recognize her name. It isn't likely our paths have crossed. I don't get out much, and I'm not hanging around the bars or the visitor center in Cades Cove. Normally, one of my cousins covers the stand at the weekly farmers' market and I can avoid the crowds, but this week everyone had other obligations. This is what happens when I let my guard down and am forced to engage with the public. I get iceberg and Bible quotes. I've never been a fan of either.

Bothered I'm still thinking about her, I close and lock up the van.

"Come on Patsy. Let's go for a walk."

She gives a happy snort and steps closer to where her leash hangs on the top rail of her pen.

When the two of us stroll through town, folks stare. It's worse when they insist on sharing an observation, tell the same old joke, and, in general, make a fuss. Honestly, at this point I'd think people seeing the two of us together would be old news around here.

Guess some folks don't have enough going on in their lives and they need to make commentary about people minding their own damn business.

I don't understand what the big deal is about a man walking his pig.

Patsy's excellent on a leash. Doesn't pull. Has never instigated fights with dogs. Hasn't bit anyone. Doesn't do her business in the middle of the sidewalk. In my mind, she's much better mannered than any old hound dog.

She's pretty darn perfect in every conceivable way.

There was the one time she trampled Mrs. Simmons flower bed, but even that was my fault for not paying closer attention to where we were walking.

If I had to find a fault in her, it would be that Patsy thinks she's in charge. She's also a little more than spoiled. I only have myself to blame.

"Clarice, please tell me you see that man walking his pig." A woman shouts to her friend and points from about three feet away.

"I'm not invisible," I tell her with a flat smile.

"Oh dear." Her companion rolls her eyes. "You're a tall drink of cool water, aren't you?"

The question is rhetorical. Being compared to a refreshing beverage doesn't require a response, so I remain quiet. Patsy tugs on her leash and releases a frustrated snort that we've stopped walking.

"You two have a nice day, m'kay." I step off the sidewalk to pass them.

I'd like to say their behavior is atypical, but if I hear "You're like the Jolly Green Giant, only less green" one more time . . .

For the record, I am not jolly.

There must be something in the well water around here. We grow 'em tall in Green Valley.

Does a pig need to be walked on a leash for health and exercise? No.

I'm the only weirdo in the area who likes to take my daily constitutional accompanied by a sow. Not even Cletus Winston is as much of an oddball as I am, and that's saying something.

He's only interested in pigs and boars in terms of sausage. In my opinion, he's missing out. If we were friends, or even friendly acquaintances, I might suggest we partner up. Truffle salami can be incredible—or so I remember. I don't eat pork anymore, not since I've had Patsy. I'd be offended if she ate human body parts around me, so it only seems fair.

Hogs will eat pretty much anything you give them. A few years ago, a pig farmer went missing. Wife said he ran off with his mistress, and everyone believed her until his gold tooth turned up in the muck and mud of their hog pens. Macabre, but true.

I don't eat pork, and Patsy doesn't eat me. It's an unspoken pact between us.

Not that she's some sort of demon-pig crazed with bloodlust. Not at all. She's the best pig in eastern Tennessee. Don't need a blue ribbon from the state fair to make it true.

This leisurely stroll around town is all part of my ruse.

If someone sees us ambling someplace we don't belong, they'll leave us alone, which is the entire point.

There's freedom in being a weirdo. Folks keep their distance. Sure, there are the asinine comments, but for the most part, they assume I'm dimwitted or crazy. Fine by me. With or without my porcine sidekick, I've always been different. I learned early on that people like to form and hold onto their own opinions. It's pretty pointless to try to change someone's mind and what they think of me is their problem, not mine.

On my way out of town, I drop off the majority of unsold produce at the back door of the food pantry. Sure, I could keep it and try to sell it next weekend, but I'd rather people get fresh vegetables instead of sad leftovers. In my opinion, food insecurity shouldn't equal puny carrots and wilted lettuce.

After knocking to let them know the crates are here, I climb inside the van and turn the key, only pausing to make sure someone opens the door.

A curly-haired woman wearing a volunteer smock over a red and black buffalo-plaid dress gives me a friendly wave. She says something and I roll down the window, gesticulating that I can't understand her. Shouting her words of thanks, she braces the door open with a wedge of wood.

"You're welcome," I say loudly enough to be heard over the engine.

I don't need to stay for more chitchat and praise. If I could donate anonymously, I would. Accolades aren't the reason for my generosity. Words and awards won't fill your belly if you're hungry.

A notification flashes on my phone and I catch the name of an old friend in the text, someone I haven't thought about in a long time, not since I left my old life behind to return to Tennessee. Ignoring my phone, I swing a wide left across traffic and onto the road that will wind its way up into the hills and take me home. Whatever is within that message can wait.

Long after commercial buildings give way to houses and the neighborhoods transition to farms, fences fading into trees, I realize today's date. The farm and my other projects have successfully distracted me from the outside world this month.

Another August is almost over, and I survived.

Four years ago today, my mentor and one of my best friends skipped out on this life and changed the course of mine.

A mix of anger and sorrow blur my vision as I slam my hand down on the steering wheel. *Goddamn you, Tony.*

The van swerves into the gravel shoulder and the pull on the tires draws my attention back to driving. I roll down the window and let the warm, humid air fill the van. Using the side of my hand, I swipe away the tears on my cheek. Nothing would piss Tony off more than knowing I was upset. He'd slap my shoulder and remind me there's no use crying over the dead or burnt toast. Tears won't fix anything.

Antoine "Tony" Beard was one infuriating fucker, one of the biggest assholes and egos I've ever met. He was also one of the best chefs who ever stepped into a kitchen. If I let myself, I would miss him every day. Instead, I try to forget he's gone by pretending he's off doing his thing in some remote pocket of the planet while I'm doing mine in this forgotten corner of the country. Sounds crazy, but most days it works.

I make a plan to cook something tonight in his honor, maybe even open up one of the few bottles of wine I have tucked away in the cellar. I'm not saving them for special occasions so much as times like today when I need to remind myself I'm alive, and living means indulging in the best this existence has to offer.

My shoulders relax when I spot the mile marker right before my road. Past the pavement's end, I navigate the van around the dips and ruts in the dirt. The old house sits with her back to the hill, the view from the porch looking out over the gardens and fields encompassing the valley below. The location is as close to ideal as I could imagine, and I have my great-great-grandfather to thank for building his homestead here.

Patsy grumbles and snorts as she walks down the plank into the yard. I have a fenced area around her house, but we both know she spends most of her time acting as my second shadow. Where I go, she follows, unless she's found a shady spot for a nap and can't be bothered with my constant productivity nonsense.

My dog, Roman, leaps off the side of the porch, ignoring the steps. His curly brown and white coat gives him the appearance of a poodle mix.

True to my word, once I've unloaded the van, I head for the old root cellar's entrance on the outside of the house and use the flashlight on my phone to pick out a bottle of wine.

The open kitchen and living room take up the first floor. Hand-hewn boards cover the exterior, but the original logs are exposed in the interior. Ceiling beams of sturdy, local hardwood have withstood storms and wars for centuries. Worn floorboards don't mind new scratches from boots, claws, or hooves.

My restorations and additions to the original structures have been minimal. Among the modernizations required to make the cabin inhabitable in this century, my favorite is the professional gas range, powered by a large propane tank I buried in the yard. A bonus is that I never have to worry about running out of hot water in the shower.

I grab a glass and the bottle opener before returning to the porch where the afternoon breeze carries the scent of rain and the promise of storms. As I open the bottle, distant thunder echoes through the valley. Patsy lifts her head and sniffs before trotting up the steps. I keep one of her beds next to my chair, and she settles in it while Roman chases something in the yard.

I pour the deep claret into my glass. French wine for a French bastard.

Giving the glass a swirl, I inhale the scent of the fine Bordeaux. A gift from someone who tried to impress me, I'm certain the bottle cost half as much as the old church van I bought to haul cargo for the farm.

I take a sip, swishing the liquid in my mouth, rolling my tongue through the expensive wine like I'm savoring the taste of a first kiss.

Thunder crackles across the dark sky to the west, and the boom of sound takes five seconds to catch up. Roman gives up the hunt and joins us on the porch.

Lifting my glass, I toast to the storm and the memory of my dear friend.

By the time I pour a refill, fat drops of rain have turned dirt into mud. The wind bends the skinny trees and flattens plants in the field. On the porch, Patsy and I remain dry.

As soon as the downpour begins, it ends. All that blustering and blowing are forgotten as leaves unfurl and trees return to stillness.

I raise my glass to the sky. "Thanks for the show, Tony."

Standing, I carry the half-empty bottle to the railing. As a curtain of rainwater drips from the roof onto the ground, I pour the remainder of the wine over the pebbles, watching as it swirls with the clear water before disappearing.

Feeling melancholy yet satisfied, I head inside to make dinner.

Patsy relocates from her bed on the porch to her bed in the living room.

Instead of something fancy, I decide to make a pot of broth beans using Nannie Ida's recipe.

I might not have everything I've ever dreamed of or wanted, but I have what I need.

CHAPTER THREE

DAPHNE

*M*onday morning, Gaia finds me at my desk in the ranger station. We chat about our weekends for a few minutes and then she gets down to business.

"Daphne, I want you to take over social media for the GSM. There are a couple of private accounts tweeting about the park, so we need to have an official one. We gotta gear up for the fall visitor season."

Normally, I'm happy to take on any project she brings to me. As a seasonal employee, I want to prove myself in hopes of getting promoted. I need a good recommendation from her to be considered for full-time, year-round positions in any of the national parks.

Problem is I hate social media and sharing about myself. A support group is basically my worst nightmare—too close to my past. This might explain why I personally have zero social media presence. I can also proudly confirm that online photos of me don't exist. Occasionally, I search for my name and I'm always relieved when nothing directly related to me shows up on the first couple of pages.

My life is better without too many people complications, but I'm not foolish enough to believe living is easiest without anyone else in it. I have zero desire to live off the land in isolation like a doomsday prepper, stockpiling canned meat and pickling anything semi-edible, but on a scale of social butterfly to hermit, I probably lean toward the latter. I do have friends. Besides Kacey from college, there's Isaac, my best friend from childhood. Throw in the rangers, campers, hikers, and visitors, and I have more than enough social interaction.

I'd like to continue flying under the radar, so I deflect with the first thing that comes to my mind. "Ranger Lee is a much better writer than I am. He's great at quips and pithy commentary."

Bus, thy name is Daphne, and this route runs express to Deflection Town.

Gaia's mouth bends into a frown. "We don't need quippy. What we do need is updates on road closures and parking being maxed out at the visitor center, bear safety reminders—things like that. This isn't a popularity or personality contest. We're federal employees. No one expects us to be pithy."

"Which is a shame," Griffin grumbles from his desk across from mine. "No reason we have to be boring. Nature is hysterical—ask Jay and his bird puns."

"No," Gaia and I both groan together.

"Hey." Jay's head pops around the divider. "I will try not to take your bad attitudes as personal insults. Et tu, Daphne? If I'm not mistaken, you used one of the owl jokes in the campground not even a week ago and received loud laughter and hearty applause."

"The audience was mostly twelve-year-old boys." I defend myself. "*Smelt it, dealt it* got an even bigger guffaw."

"I can appreciate a fish pun. I'm not as bird-obsessed as y'all make me out to be." Jay huffs with inflated disappointment.

The three of us stare at him in silence.

"Whatever." He sighs and disappears behind the partition. There are times when I think we're a colony of meerkats or prairie dogs, popping out of our various holes before quickly disappearing again. This visual is typically followed by imagining us all trapped in a human-sized whack-a-mole game. My mind can be a strange and sometimes terrifying place.

We all have our distinct roles. Jay is the bird guy, aka an avian specialist. When not playing the clown, Griffin works in operations. He's great at systems. For some reason, he prefers to act like a doofus instead of the smart person he is.

Gaia is our head ranger and therefore everyone's boss. After ancient Ed retired earlier this year, she took over as the interim chief before getting the official promotion over the summer.

As for me, I work in education and interpretation, which means I'm the front line of visitor interaction both in the park and the community.

Want to know more about the history of the Great Smoky Mountains National Park? How long do ya got?

Curious about bears? I have stories.

Nervous about skunks? Let me tell you more about this misunderstood animal.

Want to bring home that cool rock you found as a souvenir? Drop it and leave it for the next visitor to enjoy.

Thinking about eating those berries or mushrooms you found on your hike? I'm probably going to tell you not to forage without being informed.

I'm full of fun sayings like "Leave it better than you found it" and "National parks are for everyone."

If I were a cheerleader, I'd be yelling out, "Give me a P! Give me an A! Give me an R!" (You get the idea.)

And yet, I'm probably the least outgoing and social among the rangers, except maybe Jay—although he has loosened up since he's been with Olive.

Gaia prompts me about the account again. "Just give it a go. Type up information from the daily bulletin into bite-sized morsels that can be fed to the public in a few hundred words."

"You can do it!" Griffin gives me an enthusiastic thumbs-up. "I believe in you."

"You're only saying that because you're glad this isn't your assignment."

His grin reveals more teeth. "Yep."

"Be sure to follow the other parks, including state and local ones. Build a community. Have fun!" Gaia smiles before returning to her office.

I spin in my chair with my head tilted back, which I'm pretty sure is the universal posture of someone who doesn't wanna do something.

"What's worse?" Griffin asks. "School visit or typing a bunch of stuff on your computer in the silence of your own cubicle?"

He makes an excellent point.

"School visits."

"Change your attitude, change your life," he offers as a bit of random Griffin wisdom.

I spin myself so I can stare at him upside down. The effort to lift my head is too much on top of my existential angst at the moment.

"That's kind of deep," I tell him, actually meaning the compliment.

"I have my moments." He gives me a genuine smile before spinning my chair with his foot. "Back to work. We have a school visit this afternoon. First one of the year. Aren't you excited?"

When I sit up too quickly, my head pounds as blood returns to my brain. I can't fake enthusiasm to cover my nerves, muttering, "Yippee!"

* * *

My job requires me to visit local schools to encourage kids to enter the junior ranger program and Ranger Lee accompanies me on many of these presentations. He's charming and goofy. The kids always love him, and I'm grateful to have him take the lead.

Honestly, a crowd of children still freaks me out. The staring and the questions—so many questions. How. When. What. Why. Always with the why.

They may act innocent and sweet, but I believe deep down they are completely aware of what they're doing—especially the younger ones. People think the tiny humans aren't fully developed, aren't smart enough to figure out the ways of the world. To which I say, "Ha!"

Children have one foot in this world and one still in wherever souls come from before they are born. They know things. They see ghosts. This is a well-established fact. Fairies and magical bunnies and the bearded guy with his sleigh and presents all exist in their version of the world because magic is real. Anything is possible, so therefore, everything is possible.

This is why kids freak me out. Unlike adults, their world involves an irrational and fantastic existence not yet bogged down by science, logic, and facts. Part of me is jealous. I want to believe in their world.

Meeting eyes with these beings is like staring into the sun or the dark void; it's as terrifying as it is fascinating.

Griffin thinks I'm weird when I mention any of this to him. Most people have the same reaction as he does.

"They're just kids. Don't you remember when you were young and curious about everything?" he asks, parking our official NPS vehicle in the school visitor lot.

I haven't told him anything about my childhood. I rarely disclose the reality of my upbringing and family situation to anyone. Opens the door for questions I'd rather avoid.

Thankfully, when most people around here learn I'm from far away, they're not interested in hearing more. It's enough of a relief that they don't have to figure out how I might be kin with them or their neighbor or the organist at their church. Familiarity kills curiosity. In my months in the Smokies, I've learned that around here community is one giant game of six degrees of separation.

I meet Griffin at the back of the white SUV where our presentation supplies are stored. "Speaking of curious, I wanted to run something by you before we do our presentation."

"Shoot." He slides my plastic bin toward the edge of the cargo area.

Before I can muster the nerve to ask him about Odin Hill and his weird attitude about the park, Griffin continues speaking. "I've been hoping to discuss something with you as well."

I chicken out. "Really? You go first."

Happy mischief sparks in his expression. "I've been thinking we need a salamander costume."

My own eyes blink rapidly as my brain tries to process his suggestion. "Why?"

"Well, the Smokies are the salamander capital of the world. I keep telling Gaia we need to highlight our best assets, amphibian and otherwise. What size do you think you'd need? Medium?"

"Size?"

"For the salamander costume. Ideally, we'd get you one of the inflatable kinds like those T-Rex that are so popular. If we can't find one of those, we can probably locate the high school mascot kind. Think of all the hysterical videos we could film for the social media accounts you're managing. This is going to be great." Wide-eyed and smiling, he shoulders the supply bin and closes the hatch.

Typical Griffin: he's gone off on a ridiculous tangent. I never know if he's serious or seriously wrong in the head.

"I'm not wearing one of those."

"Fine. Suit yourself. I'll do the research and see if I can find one in my size." He continues walking toward the school entrance like I've agreed to his crazy idea.

I appreciate his enthusiasm, but there's no way Gaia will approve the purchase of a costume. He keeps suggesting wild schemes for park activities and she always turns him down. For fall, he thought the history docents at the farm museum should wear zombie makeup along with their period costumes. Vetoed.

Bless his heart for still trying.

Sometimes I think he does it just to get a reaction out of Gaia. He's a little boy pulling her braids or putting a frog in her desk. Even I know that's the wrong way to express his interest—if that's his intention.

When I first started, I thought he was handsome and funny, and I did consider the possibility of liking him in a romantic sense. I've had crushes on coworkers before and even dated a few, which hasn't always been the wisest decision. While Griffin is nice, he's too goofy for me. If I have to talk myself into liking someone, he's probably not the one for me.

CHAPTER FOUR

ODIN

I have buyer connections in Asheville, Knoxville, and Nashville. Basically, all the villes. Depending on the season, I drive to all three cities several times a month, the demand always outstripping my supply. Great for prices as long as I can provide top quality and my source remains a secret.

A friend from my old life has tried to persuade me to go in with him on a new venture in Asheville. No matter how many times I tell him I'm not interested in working in that world anymore, he keeps asking. We do this dance every time we see each other. He inquires and cajoles. I dodge and decline. I'm happy to be his supplier, not his business partner.

As a reward, I often treat myself to a fine meal whenever I have to drive into the city. The more froufrou and fine dining the better. Throw in a Michelin star, and I can't stay away. Great food is my weakness.

Today, I'm making the three-plus-hour drive to Nashville with a couple crates filled with mushrooms. It's me, Roman, a bunch of fungi, and a podcast on foraging.

The best part of a solo road trip is there's no one complaining about my taste in podcasts. An open window, heat blowing up from the floorboards, and nothing but winding roads ahead of me make for a nearly perfect day. Roman rides shotgun, either curled up asleep or hanging his head out the window, ears flapping.

Alone time was in short supply growing up with so much family around. Generations of kin living under one roof and more within a few miles, so many cousins and second cousins and cousins by marriage that I couldn't keep track even if I were inclined to try. Somebody's always having a birthday, getting married, giving birth, or dying.

Growing up, pretty much every weekend of the year was some sort of familial obligation. Holidays spent trying to remember the names of distant cousins, their spouses, and their progeny. Hundreds claiming each other as family when most of them wouldn't give me the time of day should we pass in the street.

Being named for the god of thunder pretty much sealed my fate as being an outcast, made me stand out as different from the rest. Guess that was Momma's plan. Maybe she thought she could save me, change my path in life. I think she was secretly happy when I left.

Always being told I was a black sheep just because of some family legend about firstborn sons, I couldn't wait to get away from here and left a week before high school graduation.

Can't pretend I wasn't pleased that some of the Hill folks disowned me after I bailed on high school and moved to the big city. If they could've afforded pearls, they'd have clutched them while they whispered their opinions. *Who does he think he is? Full of himself. Uppity. Arrogant. Entitled. Thinking he's better than all of us for leaving the Smokies.*

And my favorite: *God bless his heart.*

When I arrived in Atlanta, I lied about having my diploma. Turned out, working as a dishwasher didn't require proof I'd finished high school.

Keeping a job was less interesting than having fun, and a fake

ID and an attitude got me into any bar or club I wanted. Partying and drinking evolved into missing shifts and eventually getting the boot. Thing about being the lowest grunt in the kitchen, there's always another place needing a body to do the work no one else wants.

If I kept moving around, my bad reputation took a while to catch up with me.

Blessed by good looks, I knew how to work with my natural talents to talk my way out of trouble and under skirts. The world owed me and I was there to collect. With sweet words and a slow smile, I could be allowed or forgiven almost everything.

In other words, I was born a fool, unable to realize the difference between a blessing and a curse.

Three years ago, no one seemed all that surprised when my rental car pulled up to my parents' house, dust billowing down the road in my wake. Dad gave me a nod over Momma's shoulder while she hugged me tight. The prodigal son had returned home.

Nannie Ida greeted me with a wary glance and asked if I was done being a fool. I told her I couldn't make any promises. Her narrowed eyes studied me and her thin lips pressed together so tight they disappeared as she made up her mind about me.

Woke up the next morning, stepped outside into the mist, and knew for once in my life I didn't have to second-guess my decision.

I belong to these mountains. I can breathe deeply here in a way I can't anywhere else. Took me a decade and a half to realize it, but I'd rather have this dirt under my nails than concrete beneath my boots.

Angry, seventeen-year-old me swore he'd never set foot in a holler again. Anywhere in the world had to be better than getting stuck in the shadows of the Smokies.

I'm here to say I was wrong—about many things, but mostly about random places being better than right here. Guess that's called perspective. With age comes hard lessons and sometimes, if we're lucky, wisdom.

Funny how the shit we swear we'll never do when we're teenagers we end up doing at some point as grown-ups.

I read somewhere that the "universe" doesn't hear the negative in a sentence. Saying "I won't turn out like my parents" is pretty much the same as declaring you will. In other words, we're all doomed to keep repeating our patterns, which is the same as saying we're fucked. Nihilistic, sure, but also liberating.

Once I stopped rebelling against everything, I had enough energy to figure out what I wanted to do with my life.

CHAPTER FIVE
DAPHNE

*T*ucked into the narrow point of a small valley sits a white, one-room church, its steeple jabbing into the sky. Having more in common with a chapel in a fairy tale than today's mega churches, the building dates back at least a hundred and fifty years.

Long gone are the echoes of sermons warning of fire and brimstone, and a bird's nest above the door is the only ornamentation in the otherwise bare interior. Other than two rows of pews, their wood soft and smooth from years, there isn't much indication inside of what was once an active house of worship. No altar or cross. No hymn books or donation cards tucked into the carved pockets on the backs of the benches.

No stained-glass colors the windows. The clear glass isn't original, but a small church like this was probably never able to afford fancy decorations.

And yet, this is where I come to think and sometimes have conversations with myself and sometimes God, or whatever higher power I imagine might listen. More *Are You There, God? It's me, Daphne* and less *Forgive me Father, for I have sinned.*

When I went through my "experimental" phase, I briefly explored

Catholicism, thinking I needed more structure. The saints and their stories of martyrdom appealed to me. I always liked the story of Saint Lucy plucking out her eyes to deter an over-zealous suitor. Even with the cool stories and all the miracles, turned out I needed less organized religion, not more.

Unitarians and their songs to the trees should've been a good fit. I've dipped a toe in Buddhism and even sat in on a Wiccan circle or two. Alas, nothing has been quite right. I've tried on a lot of religions like a spiritual Goldilocks. Too structured. Too scary. Too big. Too woo-woo. Too . . . weird.

I've finally accepted I'm not really a joiner.

I'm more agnostic than churchgoer, even though I still feel a microscopic dose of guilt if I sleep in on a Sunday morning—at least until I snuggle under the covers and enjoy the quiet of a lazy morning in bed.

Deconsecrated years ago, this tiny chapel suits me fine, and I come here often to enjoy the quiet. Some people like hanging out in clubs or bars, bowling alleys or arcades. I've always found those places to be loud and crowded, the opposite of what I crave.

If anyone ever asks, I can tell them I'm in here on official park business. Security, or perhaps maintenance. Slightly outside of my official duties, both are still viable explanations.

Along with abandoned moonshiner cabins and the restored settler buildings at Cades Cove, the Smokies are dotted with old structures held together by a few rusty nails and stubbornness.

I swear some of the local residents share the same composition: rust, reluctance, and pure obstinance toward anything, or anyone, new. If I hear "That's the way we've always done it around here" one more time, I might scream.

That reminds me—I need to make an appointment to see the dentist. My jaw has been bothering me, probably from all the clenching to swallow words I should not say out loud. I'm almost positive I've begun grinding my teeth in my sleep again.

There isn't one particular reason I'm internalizing stress; nothing I can put my finger on specifically. Job is good. My boss, and newly appointed chief ranger, Gaia, is both a friend and mentor. I get along with my co-workers, and I'm enjoying teaching my classes. I feel useful and needed. The park is beautiful and the local small towns are charming. As a bonus, I have a small cabin to call my own.

None of the above is reason for me to be grinding my teeth.

Cloven hooves flash to mind. No, not the devil, nor is it an adversarial goat I'm picturing. They belong to a certain pig, one owned by a certain local.

My jaw tenses.

An unfamiliar warmth settles low in my belly.

My heart contracts with a delicate squeeze of anticipation.

Clearly, it doesn't understand that sometimes fear and excitement are the same sensation and would be the idiot who runs toward danger like a tourist snapping a selfie with a bear at close range, or climbing a sheer cliff for the adrenaline rush.

Acts of defying death come with great highs, but they also sometimes end in death.

Tell that to my heart.

Inhaling through my nose and then unclenching my jaw, I blow out a slow exhalation while counting to seven. I press my hand to the center of my chest the same way a parent might rest their palm on top of their child's head, indulgent and firm and filled with calming energy meant to soothe wayward emotions.

"There, there," I tell my body. "Nothing to get worked up about. Odin Hill is nothing more than a strange farmer, most certainly not our type and definitely not the right man for us. Stop with these delusions you're having just because a man with symmetrical facial features and more than his fair share of muscles smiled at us."

My heart flips and flops around like a trout in a net at the visual memory of biceps, reminding me it, too, is a muscle, as if sharing something in common is proof of their entwined destinies.

"He's not our type. We want a good man, a decent and kind person. Gainful employment and clear life goals would be nice. Truthful and trustworthy. Intelligent and ethical. Funny—definitely funny. Nowhere on this list is cheekbones or a classical nose or a well-arched eyebrow. Yes, a heart is necessary. No vampires. Adequate arm strength to at least hold a fork or a glass, or my hand, but we don't need to go overboard and get greedy with those bulging globes of overworked flesh. Nothing in excess. Avarice is a sin."

I feel the urge to say amen to this list. Feels appropriate given my current location.

"Amen," I whisper.

"Amen," a male voice echoes.

Holding my breath for a beat, I freeze as I strain to hear footsteps or other movement. There's nothing but the faint chirp of crickets and the wind brushing through the gaps in the clapboards.

Behind me, a floorboard squeaks, or maybe the door creaks on its hinges. I can't be sure. My head spins around faster than a doll possessed by the devil himself, but there's nothing in the empty room.

Dust dances in the triangle of sunlight brightening the old floorboards where the door is wedged slightly ajar. I swear I closed it behind me when I entered; it's habit after the time Oscar the donkey wandered inside and scared the bejeezus out of me.

No sign of man or beast.

It's possible I imagined the second amen, or it may have been a previously undetected echo. I test this theory.

"Amen," I say, louder than the first time.

Silence.

Perhaps the wind blew the door open and my brain translated the sound into a word. There are other possible explanations involving the voice of God or angels. Those are silly, particularly given my pseudo-prayer was more a shopping list for a man—hardly the subject matter to warrant an in-person visit from the holy.

Although I might need a miracle to help my romantic life.

"Only the wind," I declare, standing and brushing the dust from the pew off my pants.

* * *

Beyond the heavy wooden door, the sounds of the world return, loud against the silence within the chapel. Birdsong repeats through trees and a breeze rattles the first fallen leaves of autumn, distance muffling the white noise of a small waterfall. Inhaling, I try to decipher the scents of the upcoming change in seasons. Warm earth. Harvest. Rain. The return of cool, misty mornings.

I've only been here a few months, but I feel more at home than I have in a lot of my other jobs. Right out of college, I got a seasonal gig at the Grand Canyon. Not as a ranger; I worked in the gift shop and laughed at the same joke about a big hole in the ground over and over every day for an entire summer.

Turns out, there are a lot of things in the desert that want to kill us. Dying from venomous creatures is one thing, but even the plants are hostile to humans. Openly aggressive, with sharp spines ready to draw blood at the slightest touch—nope, not interested. Beyond the reptiles and plants, the sun itself is deadly. It is entirely possible to be scorched to death.

Yes, there are dangers in the Smokies, too, yet something in these foggy valleys resonates with me. Standing in the thick, humid air, I lift my gaze to the mountains across the valley.

Movement at the tree line catches my attention. In the shadows between the thick trunks, a large, dark shape slips in and out of the dappled light. A bear? Too low to the ground and the gait isn't right, not even for a cub.

"Boar," I whisper.

I know there are wild hogs in the park, but I've never seen one with my own eyes. They tend to be nocturnal and avoid populated areas. If it's prowling around in the middle of the afternoon, it might have rabies or swine flu, or some other porcine ailment affecting its behavior. In other words, this is not good.

I press the button on my radio, ready to call in a report.

One of the shadows among the trees takes on the shape of a man . . . a tall, lean man. Facing the sun, I lift my hand to my forehead to shade my eyes. Where the man-shadow stood is empty sunlight.

Obviously, my mind is playing tricks on me. The boar has disappeared too—if it was a boar at all. Probably nothing more than the play of shadow and light.

Static crackles near my ear, indicating my radio is still on and waiting. I release my finger. There's no imminent threat or emergency. No need to alert anyone about a shadow.

After double-checking that the door to the church is locked, I make the short walk back to my official vehicle. The drive from the chapel to headquarters is less than half an hour and I'll have plenty of time to report the possible sighting to the team before leading the evening nature talk.

CHAPTER SIX
DAPHNE

*a*fter our quarterly meeting with the federal game warden, Dr. Runous, I find myself in the lounge with his brother-in-law Cletus Winston. I don't quite know what to make of the guy, but he seems friendly enough. Could be the baked goods. Sometimes he shows up with donuts from Daisy's Nut House or muffins from his wife's bakery, along with a thermos of his special coffee.

Curious, I sniff the mug of dark brew, an unexpected sourness prickling my nostrils. "Is it spiked?"

"No," Cletus declares with a huff. "Why would I put alcohol in your coffee?"

"The question you should be answering is why would anyone put apple cider vinegar and molasses in a cup of perfectly adequate coffee?" Jay removes the beverage from my grasp and sets it on the table.

"You sound backed up." Cletus apprises him with narrowed eyes, as if Jay were one of those plastic models of a human where you can lift off the skin and then remove muscles and bones to reveal the major organs.

X-ray vision doesn't exist outside of fiction, and even Cletus Winston isn't an exception to this rule.

"Are you going to let someone else decide for you what you like and don't like?" His eyes dance with judgment the way some people have kindness shining in theirs. The man has judgy eyes.

"No, I make up my own mind." I wrinkle my nose at the thought of vinegar, molasses, and coffee. Acidic, metallic, and bitter is not my favorite flavor combination.

"Don't knock something until you try it," he tells me, continuing with his challenge. It isn't exactly a dare, but he's definitely not backing down. "Some people hate mushrooms while others are willing to spend exorbitant sums on a sliver of an exotic fungi. One man's fungus is another man's joy, or pizza topping." He emphasizes his insouciance with a shoulder shrug.

Along with the beard and the baked goods, I suspect the gesture is a practiced part of his persona. There's more to the man than he lets people see. He's a closed book, kind of like me. I think Odin Hill might be the same.

"You don't have to drink it." Jay reminds me.

I eye the steaming liquid that began this discussion on free will and personal preferences. There are a lot of the old-time recipes in Appalachia that are back in vogue. Apple cider vinegar is probably the most popular but molasses does contain a ton of vitamins and iron. He might be onto something.

Griffin strolls into the room, taking one look at Cletus and another at the cup in my hand before he shakes his head. "Don't drink that."

"Why is everyone acting like I'm trying to poison them?" Clearly offended, Cletus crosses his thick arms and widens his stance.

"Drinking Cletus's 'coffee'"—Jay puts air quotes around the word —"is a rite of passage around here."

"Hazing is more like it." Griffin gives the mug back to Cletus. "What brings you to the station?"

With a disgruntled sigh, he pours the liquid back into his old-fashioned thermos. "Ranger Baum said she recently had a wild boar sighting near one of the old churches. I was curious if there had been more."

"Sausage on your mind?" Griffin asks

"Always." Cletus gives him a serious look.

"I'm not sure what I saw. Could've been a bear." Thinking about Odin and Patsy, I don't want to narc on them, especially if I'm not even sure of what I saw.

Cletus squints to study me. "If you can't tell the difference between the two, you might need to get your eyes checked. Have you needed prescription lenses in the past?"

"No, I don't need glasses. Honestly, I didn't get a good look because I was facing the sun and the forest was in shadow. I doubt whatever it was is hanging around waiting for Sunday services."

Cletus wrinkles his brow. "Why would you assume the boar was a Methodist?"

Thank goodness I'm not drinking anything because I'd turn into a human fountain.

"Excuse me?" I manage to sputter.

"Rather presumptuous of you." He doesn't back down.

"More like preposterous." Griffin takes my side—at least I think he does until he adds, "Everyone knows black bears in Tennessee are Baptists."

I've stepped into another dimension. "Right. Got it."

When I glance at Jay for back up, he just lifts his shoulders in a silent *don't involve me* gesture.

"I'm going to go." I try to think of a reason I suddenly have to leave. "My bins need organizing."

A bald-faced lie. I'm type A when it comes to neatness and being prepared.

"Keep me apprised of any more boar sightings," Cletus hollers after me.

He should really hang out with Odin Hill. The two of them are weirdly obsessed with pigs.

* * *

I keep all my supplies for my nature talks in two large, plastic bins. One has pelts, bones, teeth, and skulls. That's the fauna box. The flora box is filled with pressed flowers and leaves laminated for eternity, lichen-covered rocks, various pinecones, and illustrations of mushrooms. Not nearly as exciting, but the flora box is my favorite.

Ranger jobs are difficult to come by. No way was I going to let my fear of kids stop me from accepting this position. So far, so good. I've only cried twice.

During the summer season, I've been hosting multiple talks and hikes daily for visitors in the campground. Spring and fall have more school trips. Those are also the most stressful days even though I technically have backup from the teachers. Hordes of kids are terrifying.

Over the months, I've developed a sixth sense about who will be most likely to cry, vomit, pee their pants, start a fight, end up bleeding, or not follow directions. The last one tends to be eighty percent of the population, both kids and adults. I'm now a pro at anticipating most inappropriate jokes and talking over the talkers.

When I feel like I'm losing their attention entirely, I bring up skunks—or snakes.

I really hate snakes.

The fauna collection includes several snake skins, which are almost worse than actual snakes. Almost. I blame my dislike toward the slithering creatures on a guy I briefly knew in college for forcing me to visit the reptile house during a date at the zoo. He said my phobia was ridiculous and reminded me they were behind glass, thus unable to hurt me.

Obviously, he had never read *Harry Potter and the Sorcerer's*

Stone. We only went on the one date. Unsurprising to anyone who knows me, I'm a proud Hufflepuff. I'm hard-working, loyal, and sometimes patient. Definitely have a strong sense of right and wrong. Truth is important to me. I like rules and fairness. In other words, I'm never the life of the party, but I'll stay and help the host clean up after.

After working at the Grand Canyon, I also learned never to tell my coworkers about my snake phobia. If I do, they may take it upon themselves to help me get over it by hiding a fake, rubber snake anywhere I might discover it. I'm surprised I haven't died from a shock-induced heart attack before the age of thirty-two.

Ixnay on the akesnay alktsay.

That's Pig Latin, not parseltongue.

Here's a fun fact: a badger will kill and eat a snake.

I always save the snake skins for emergencies.

Stacking the plaster molds of various animal tracks, I busy myself with tidying the bins for tomorrow's sessions. The material may be the same, but I never have the same experience twice because my students are always changing. Some have a ton of questions. Some want to show off their own knowledge. Others are reluctant attendees. I've learned to recognize the blank stare of indifference versus boredom.

The forecasted rain has created puddles and pools along the road, and today's activities have been relocated to inside the visitor center due to the threat of thunderstorms. We like to avoid park patrons getting struck by lightning. If it were just rain, we could gather under the roof of the pavilion in the campground, but I'm happy to stay inside. It's better to keep the skunk pelts dry.

Hosting programs in the visitor center also means my coworkers can observe and give feedback. Most of the time, they're constructive.

I'm finishing up the talk to a small group of about a dozen people when I spot Griffin leaning against the door jamb.

Squaring my shoulders, I prepare to close out the session. "If there aren't any other questions . . ." I pause, internally bracing myself as I give Griffin an opening.

"I have one." His voice is loud, but friendly. Heads turn in his direction.

"Yes, Ranger Lee?" My smile is warm but if you look closely, you can see trepidation in my eyes.

"What do you call bears without ears?"

Softly, I groan.

"I know!" A boy raises his hand over his head, waving it enthusiastically so I don't miss him.

I don't dare glance at Griffin.

"Yes?" I ask the kid.

"Bees!" he shouts, adding a fist pump in triumph.

Everyone laughs except for the girl next to him. She makes a point of waiting for my attention before rolling her eyes in a dramatic fashion. I'm guessing she's his sister, and I know how she feels. I want to tell her to ignore boys being loud and silly.

Griffin snorts and slips through the door back to our offices. I'm not sure if he does this in hopes of tripping me up or if he simply can't help himself.

"On that note, I think we'll end there." I thank everyone for attending and remind them to check out the exhibits and the gift shop.

Griffin Lee is in rare form today. Makes me wonder if something's up or if he drank too much of Cletus's coffee.

Most of the small crowd leaves immediately, but a few families linger among the permanent exhibits. A woman with the same dark curls as the eye-roller approaches me with both kids in tow behind her.

"Sorry to bother you as you're tidying up," she apologizes, "but my daughter has a question."

"No worries. How can I help you?" I focus on the girl.

"How do you become a ranger?" she asks in a quiet voice.

Her mom gives her shoulder an encouraging squeeze. "She's always loved the parks."

"I have an official map in my room." Her excitement and pride are palpable.

"I have a map in my room too. How many parks have you visited?"

"Twenty-two. We visit them every summer."

This is why I love this job: encouraging girls and young women to explore their passion for nature and conservation. My ultimate goal is to spark curiosity in the parks. If we can get people interested, especially kids, they may turn into lifelong visitors, or become junior rangers and work for the NPS themselves someday. I never believed I'd be a role model; it's hard to have that kind of faith in myself after being told countless times I'm going to hell.

And by people, I mean girls and kids from diverse backgrounds. I'm tired of looking at staff pictures and seeing an ocean of white men smiling back at me.

We chat for a few more minutes before her brother whines he's hungry. I recommend they get the brownies at the snack bar.

Right before they walk away, the girl comes over and hugs me.

"I want to be you when I grow up," she whispers.

My heart melts.

* * *

Gaia asks me to join her in her office after I finish my last talk for the afternoon.

"Have a seat." She gestures to the pair of chairs opposite her desk but doesn't sit down. "I wanted to speak with you privately."

"Is everything okay?" Nervous, I remain standing too.

"Everything's great. I have good news—your promotion has been approved. You're now a full-time NPS employee, Daphne." Gaia shakes my hand, making the moment official. "How do you feel?"

After years of bouncing between parks and working seasonal gigs for low wages, I'm thrilled to have a permanent job. "If I say ecstatic, would you judge me?"

"Not at all. I remember when I got my first full-time position." Her hazel eyes are warm, friendly. "These jobs aren't easy to come by, and you've worked hard to prove yourself this summer. I'm thrilled you're going to stay on with us."

"Speaking of promotions, should I call you Ranger Abbott now that you're chief ranger?"

She laughs. "You can if you want, but Gaia or Guy are still both fine."

"How'd you start going by Guy?"

"It's always been a family nickname. Back when we started, Jay liked calling me that because he thought it was funny because with me being the only full-time woman on staff here. Another one of the guys."

"I know that feeling. Most of my ranger jobs have been three to one men to women."

"Yep, we're still outnumbered." She glances out the window for a beat, but when her gaze settles on me, it's happy. "At least there are two of us here now."

"And now you're in charge. The big boss." I smile, proud of her.

Gaia is a big part of why I accepted this job.

First time I've had a woman as the chief ranger of the park where I'm working. If it can happen here, in the hills and valleys of Appalachia, progress can happen anywhere. Actually, women were instrumental in the formation of the Great Smoky Mountains National Park. I guess it's fitting there's a woman in charge now.

"At least you didn't call me a girl boss." She makes an exaggerated scowl and then laughs. "I hate that expression. Nope, not a girl, just a woman in charge, thank you very much."

"I agree." I don't tell her that the very concept of working, let alone being management, is outside the scope of possibility my childhood self could have imagined. None of the women I knew growing up worked outside the home. It simply wasn't done. Going to college and getting a degree was an act of rebellion for me.

"Speaking of the guys, they'll want to take you out to celebrate the promotion. It's tradition around here. Are you up for that? If not, we can get a cake from Donner Bakery or something and have a party here. No pressure." Gaia gives me a sympathetic look. "I know you're not into big social events."

Pushing myself out of my comfort zone, I decide to go with the first option. "I'm totally down for going out. What did they have in mind?"

"Let's go ask them." Gaia leads the way down the hall.

Friendly chatter among our colleagues fills the front office. It's the end of the shift and the crew is gathered at the station. When we enter, Jay and Griffin are talking with a couple of the part-timers about the road project starting soon.

"If they wait for the leaf peepers and foliage creepers to all leave, winter weather could be an issue. Can't pave if there's snow or ice on the ground." Jay tells one of the guys. "Remember last year? We had heavy snow in October."

Gaia clears her throat. "Sorry to interrupt Jay's climate report, but I wanted to make a plan for Daphne's promotion party."

After a round of congratulations, handshakes, and pats on my shoulders, they bring up the topic of what we should do and where.

"My mom owns Genie's. Good food, good drinks, and a dance floor. I practically grew up behind the bar." Griffin's brow furrows. "Not as an underage bartender, nothing illegal or against child labor laws. Genie's abides by all ATF regulations."

Gaia sighs from behind me. "Is there a point to this lecture about your family's business?"

He narrows his eyes at her. "You said you wanted to get together as a group to celebrate Daphne's new permanent status. I was merely making a suggestion on location."

"It's a bar." Gaia's voice reveals her lack of enthusiasm for his suggestion. Then again, she often has that tone around Griffin. "I was thinking more like dinner, or a group activity."

"Like what? Bowling? Axe throwing?" Jay asks.

"Goat yoga?" suggests Amory, one of the civil engineers.

We all give him a funny look.

"Okay, that's a no." Gaia laughs. "No way am I letting animals climb on me."

"Is Genie's a dive bar?" I ask, hopeful. "Honky-tonk?"

Griffin's attention cuts to me. "It's just a bar."

Gaia sighs. "Shouldn't Daphne decide where she wants to celebrate?"

"I don't know a lot of other places to go out around here. Genie's sounds fun." I flash Griffin a cheesy smile.

"Don't get too excited. It ain't fancy, just a bar," Gaia reminds me.

Even though she's echoing his words, Griffin's brows pinch together as he frowns before recovering. "Best wings and fried chicken in the area, and that's including the Pink Pony."

Jay's head jerks back. "We are not going to the strip club for another work function. I'm putting my foot down this time."

He and Gaia share a silent conversation with their eyes.

"Never again," she declares with a quick nod.

Observing the two of them, I'm reminded again that I'm the newbie here. This is my plight: always the new girl, a side effect of moving around every few months as I accepted seasonal ranger jobs.

Only, now I'm here permanently, though that isn't as permanent as it sounds. I think we all have our dream park of where we want to work. The golden ticket. The final frontier. The happiest place on earth.

For some, it's the big names. Yellowstone, Zion, Yosemite, the Grand Canyon, or an historical site that holds a personal connection. For others, it's the park close to where they grew up. Ranger Daniels falls into this group. So does Ranger Lee. Eastern Tennessee is nearest their family.

Some of us don't have roots near here. Gaia, me, Amory—most of us come from far away.

Even though I'm now a full-time, year-round employee in the Great Smoky Mountains National Park, I probably won't stay here forever. The world's a big place, and I want to see as much of it as I can.

After a little more back-and-forth discussion, the group settles on Thursday night for the celebration at Genie's.

If I'm supposed to play it cool, I don't. I'm excited to check out the bar. Yes, I've been here for months, but during the busiest season of the year. Now that things are slowing down a little with kids back in school, I'm ready to explore the area more. Maybe hot farmers like to hang out at Genie's, too. You never know.

CHAPTER SEVEN
DAPHNE

On Thursday, we split up into a couple of cars to head to Genie's. Gaia drives like someone's chasing her, taking corners so tight I have to hold on to the "oh shit" handle on my door.

"What's the rush?" I ask, nervous she will confirm someone dangerous is in pursuit. I've heard the rumors about biker gangs living outside of Green Valley.

"What? Nothing?" Her attention flits to my side of the car, noticing my fingers curled around the bar and what I'm certain is terror on my face. With a short sigh of exasperation, followed by a quick glance at the ceiling and a whispered expletive, she taps the brakes. "Sorry."

"It's fine." I release my grip and flex my hand, bringing blood back into my fingers.

She shakes her head. "No, it isn't. I obviously scared you with my driving."

"I wasn't afraid, more surprised and a little nauseated, but being uncomfortable is on me because evidently, I had certain expectations for how you would drive. Reality is different, and I need a minute to adjust."

Her warm eyes make contact with mine. "You're very logical."

"I like rules, like speed limits and which side of the road to drive on." I'm subtly referring to the fact she's drifted across the double yellow line while we've been talking.

She corrects our trajectory and gives me an embarrassed smile. "Okay, confession time. You should know I love to drive fast. Over the years, I've been pulled over by Officer James so many times he told me if I wanted to date him, I should just ask him out instead of driving these winding roads like a maniac."

"Wait, you like the deputy sheriff?" When I was hired, I met most of the local law enforcement staff during a joint training.

Gaia laughs. "No, and for the record, I wasn't speeding to flirt with him."

"Did you turn him down?"

She grins. "Nah, I went out with him once."

Jackson James is handsome but the two of them would make an odd couple. "Just the one time? Bad date?"

"It was fine . . . if you like boring, polite, perfectly nice men. I saw it as more of a gesture of peace and goodwill. Haven't been pulled over by him since." Her smile is wide and triumphant.

She's smart. "Devious."

With a shrug, she glances out her side window. "I let him down easy. We all have a type we're attracted to. Turns out the good deputy doesn't do it for me. Guess we can't help who we like. The heart wants what it wants."

Apparently, my type might be the Jolly Green Giant, only less green. It's been over a week and I'm still thinking about him.

The rest of the way to the bar, she drives at the speed limit, sometimes even braking when we take a tight curve.

Inside Genie's, most of the booths are filled, but we find our group seated at a large table near the back.

Gaia takes the seat next to Jay, and I slip in across from her by Griffin. Amory and several of the operations staff I don't really know round out our group of eight. We don't interact much given a lot of their time is spent repairing roads and doing construction; I suspect free food and beers might be the bigger draw for them being here as opposed to my promotion celebration. I get that. Still, it's nice of them to show up and I thank them all for coming like I'm the hostess.

A basket of wings sits in the center of the table, the bare bones in another basket next to a mostly empty pitcher of beer and two clean glasses.

"Thanks for waiting for us," Gaia jokes.

"Sorry. We were starving." Jay gives her a guilty smile. "Don't worry, we've already ordered more."

Griffin lifts one of the empties. "Beer?"

She shakes her head. "I'm driving."

I raise my hand.

"If you're riding with her, you should definitely have one," Griffin teases. "Maybe a shot or four."

I laugh, but Gaia doesn't. She's too busy throwing eye daggers at our coworker.

"Since my mom owns the place, wings and beer are on me," Griffin offers magnanimously.

"That's very generous of you." I give him a sincere smile.

"He probably eats for free." Gaia sniffs.

"Not free, but I do get the family discount."

"I'm not going to turn down free wings. Bring 'em on." I rub my hands together in excitement before lifting my arms over my head. "Extra ranch for all my friends!"

"You know, most people eat 'em with blue cheese dressing," Gaia explains.

"Shh," I tell her. "It's my party and I'll eat them however I want."

"Don't be a downer." Griffin wags his finger at her. "Let the lady have the sauce of her choice."

If Gaia were a plant right now, she'd be a cactus. I can feel her energy bristling from across the table.

Wanting—no, needing to change the subject, I scan the room for a distraction. The large dance floor is empty, but country music booms from several speakers.

"What time does the dancing start?" I point to the designated area.

"Some nights we have live music, but otherwise, it begins whenever someone is the first to take a twirl," Griffin answers.

"I'm not dancing," declares Jay, wiping his hands on his napkin.

"Still have PTSD?" Griffin laughs. "Man, you need to get over it."

I want to know what happened at the Pink Pony and also I don't, because I like my co-workers. Whatever went down was before my time, and imagining this crowd in a strip joint isn't something I want to do. Ever.

A waitress with a grin as wide as her hair is big drops off more baskets of wings. Glancing at the little plastic sauce containers, I know right away they're all blue cheese. I'm about to open my mouth when Griffin raises his hand.

"Can we get some ranch for the table?" He focuses on me. "How many? One? Two?"

"Three should be good, but bring four just in case." Go big or go home.

We settle into conversation as beer is poured from a fresh pitcher. Glasses clink in toasts to me, to us, to the national parks, and even to the Roosevelts, including Eleanor because she was fierce. I notice Jay barely sips his pint and Gaia drinks a coke. When asked, Jay tells me he's the designated driver.

"Ahh, responsible." I lift my glass and frown when I realize it's empty. "Should I get another pitcher? I should."

Before any of them can answer me, I'm out of the booth and weaving my way over to the bar. I'm not a big drinker, never have been, but tonight feels different. It's festive and celebratory, and safe.

"Barkeep," I call out to the lone bartender at the far end. To emphasize that I mean business, I slap my hand on the counter twice like I've seen done in old movies and lift my empty pitcher.

The bartender gives me a nod and holds up a finger, silently acknowledging me.

While I wait, I slowly spin the pitcher in lazy circles by its handle. Some country song plays on the speakers and I feel bad for the singer losing his truck, his dog, and his woman in the same weekend.

"Poor fella. At least he has his beer and whiskey, unlike some of us," I mutter to myself as the bartender takes his sweet time. He's chatting up waitresses and customers like he's the host of a late-night show.

"How you doin' today, Bubba? Catch any catfish lately?" I giggle at my terrible Southern accent. "Joanie Mae, did I hear you brought your baby in here last week? Startin' 'em young."

"Her name is Patty, and that other guy is named Mintor, but most folks call him Minty. Can't say I've ever heard him referred to as Bubba." The voice is familiar and a wall of shoulder blocks my view of the rest of the bar as a man slides between me and the random man in a trucker hat.

Sweet peas in a pod, it's the god of vegetables.

I lift my eyes and tilt my head back to confirm his identity. He's close, a little too close for polite company. *And if he doesn't smell like sweet earth and fresh grass, like a recently mowed field of alfalfa— well, bless my heart.*

I'm clearly taking this fake Southern thing too far.

He dips his head and meets my eyes. "Daphne, wasn't it? We met at the farmers' market not too long ago, didn't we?"

I still haven't spoken, afraid I'll drawl out a y'all or fiddle-sticks. Instead, I nod in confirmation.

His eyes narrow. "Cat got your tongue?"

Inhaling and reminding my brain we're from Idaho, I exhale through my nose, long and slow. "Nope."

Only one syllable. Nailed it.

"Sorry. I thought you looked familiar." He shifts, allowing air to swirl in the widened gap between us.

"No, I meant the part about a cat stealing my tongue." I pause, thinking about that visual. "Why is that even a saying? That's horrible."

His laugh is rich and deep. My stomach warms, and I swear my pulse quickens. He should laugh all the time, although, that might be weird and make it impossible to have a conversation with him, or go to a concert, or watch a documentary about the plight of polar bears in a melting Arctic.

Okay, he shouldn't laugh all the time. Only several times a day.

"You're right. It's something my granny would say. I'll have to ask her about it."

The bartender finally makes an appearance, but I want to ignore him until he goes away again. Staring at us, he waits for one of us to order.

My lips are parted and forming the word "refill" when he says, "Hey, Odin. Haven't seen you in ages. What can I get you tonight? Coke? Or you want a beer? Something stronger?"

Seriously? I've been standing here, waiting for how long? Does a woman have to flash her cleavage to get a drink? Not that that's an option in this crew neck T-shirt. I don't want to stretch the collar.

"Um . . ." I clear my throat as I lift the empty pitcher.

"Sorry. You were here first," Odin apologizes. "Joe, looks like we need a refill."

Joe the bartender's brown eyes meet mine. "What are you drinking?"

"Beer." *Duh.* He isn't very good at his job.

The two men chuckle.

"What kind?" Joe asks.

"Whatever's on tap." *Smooth.*

He points to the row of pulls. "You'll need to be more specific."

I feel Odin's stare on my profile. "I have no idea."

"You with Griffin?" Joe points behind me.

"I am!" Relief makes my voice sound overly enthusiastic.

"Gotcha." He takes the pitcher and begins filling it.

"You and Griffin Lee?" A small line appears between Odin's brows.

"Are coworkers," I explain.

"Oh, right. You're a ranger." Is that relief in his voice?

"Yes, sir. Here to serve and protect." I tip my imaginary hat.

He returns the gesture with a smile. "Good to know."

"How's Gracie doing?" Joe sets the large jug o' beer down without sloshing any. "Staying out of trouble?"

Who is Gracie? Girlfriend? Goddess of the harvest?

"As far as I know." Odin shrugs. "Has she been hustlin' again?"

Whoa. My eyes widen as I eavesdrop. I don't care what Griffin says—if this place is a hustlers' hangout, it one hundred percent falls into honky-tonk territory in my book.

"Not around here." Joe flips a bar towel over his shoulder and levels Odin with a serious gaze. "Haven't had any underage pool sharks since spring."

Ahh, that kind of hustling.

My attention swings to Odin. He's dating a teenage hustler? With a single comment, he's gone from wholesome farm boy to creeper. I totally misjudged him. Maybe he is a pig.

While I'm having an internal crisis, Joe continues like this is all normal conversation. "What is it with you Hills being teenage delinquents?"

Wait. Hills?

His younger sister is a child pool shark?

"Not all of us, and most outgrow that phase." Odin raps his knuckles on the smooth wood of the bar. "Speaking of drinks, I'll take a water if it's not too much trouble."

"Coming up," Joe tells him with a sheepish smile. "No hard feelings. I was just yanking your chain. Haven't seen you around here in a long time."

I feel like I'm not supposed to be hearing all of this, but since they're having this conversation right in front of me, it's kind of hard not to. I suppose I could go back to my table, but for some reason, I linger.

Odin's eyes cut to me but his head still faces Joe. "Don't spend too much time hanging around bars anymore. Not really my scene."

For some reason, I want to explain that I'm not a regular either, but I think that's obvious from my obvious lack of beer knowledge.

"Anything else I can get you?" Joe asks.

Odin slips his fingers into the front pockets of his jeans and rocks back on his heels. "Was hankering for some fried chicken, called in an order. Can you check to see if it's ready?"

"Sure thing." After Joe hands Odin a glass of water, he steps away to serve other customers, leaving the two of us to stand here in awkward silence.

I definitely have the feeling I've overheard something I shouldn't have about his family, unless Gracie and hustlin' are code for something else.

Unable to stop myself, I ask, "Who's Gracie?"

He blinks at my abrupt question like he's already forgotten his conversation with Joe and I've caught him off-guard. "One of my cousins, who happens to be sixteen."

Cousin. Ahh. The pendulum of my opinion swings back to the neutral middle. I've written an entire narrative about the man in the time it's taken him to ask for fried chicken and a water.

"Sixteen seems a little young to be hanging out in a bar, even in Appalachia." I keep my voice flat like I'm commenting on the weather.

He stares at a spot on the ceiling. "She's definitely too young, and also foolish enough to hustle pool around here."

"Was she any good at it?"

His lips curl with amusement. "Enough to win games and take people's money."

My sixteen-year-old self is both shocked and in awe. "Sounds pretty badass to me."

His eyes sweep over my face like he's confused by my admiration. "You approve of her breaking the law and skipping down the road to being a juvenile delinquent, Ranger?"

He's got me. I settle my face into a serious expression. "No, of course not."

"Just checking." The little curl of amusement spreads into a genuine smile.

"Something funny?"

"Nah." He sips his water. "Need help carrying your beer back to the table?"

"I think I can manage." To prove I'm right, I lift the container by the handle and support its weight with the other hand. "Put a stack of books on my head and watch me go."

Why do I say the weirdest things around him? I can have coherent, non-weird conversations with people of all ages and backgrounds. I'm actually paid to talk to people, yet every time I see him, my mouth-to-brain connection short-circuits.

No one walks around with books on their heads anymore. Not sure if they ever did or if it was something Hollywood made up. I really need to stop watching old movies.

Next thing I know I'll be calling someone yare like Katherine Hepburn in *The Philadelphia Story*. I'm still not sure of the exact meaning, but it's a compliment having something to do with yachts—another useless nugget I doubt I'll use in real life, like walking with books on my head for good posture.

Without waiting for his response, I say goodbye, turn, and march back to the group, careful not to spill the beer.

"Finally!" Griffin holds out his glass. "We're parched."

"I was about to send Jay out on a search and rescue mission." Laughing, Gaia elbows him, and he grunts. "What took you so long?"

61

"Bartender was swamped." Setting down the beer, I slip into my seat.

"Was that Odin Hill you were talking to?" Griffin asks, keeping his attention on the bar area.

Only now do I realize he has a direct sightline from our side of the table.

"Odin's here?" Gaia twists in her seat. "Seriously? I always assumed he was a hermit recluse."

"That's redundant." Griffin frowns. "Don't strain your neck trying to find him—he walked out after Daphne came back to the table."

Not subtly at all, Gaia rolls her eyes.

Jay states the obvious "He's a strange one. Did he have the pig with him?"

Guess everyone knows about Odin and Patsy.

"No swine allowed in here." Griffin crosses his arms in an X in front of his face.

"What's his story?" I ask the table.

No one replies.

I flick my gaze around the group.

"Best to keep your distance," Griffin warns.

"Why? He's seemed nice enough whenever we've spoken." I feel the urge to defend a man I've met twice and had two less-than-amicable conversations with.

"Are you and Odin hanging out?" Jay looks confused.

"No. Other than seeing him here, I met him at the farmers' market a couple of weeks ago. He had a booth and his pig."

"Weird." Jay cocks his head.

I don't know what part he means.

"Aside from his closest friend being a pig, he's . . ." Gaia frowns as she pauses.

"Bad news," Griffin interjects.

"I was going to say different." Gaia meets my eyes. "Keeps to himself. Seeing him in a social situation is not unlike a Big Foot sighting. You hear about them, but no one ever has proof."

"He ordered fried chicken to go. Not sure that counts as him socializing." I don't know which side I'm on, bad news or recluse.

Griffin dips a celery stick into one of my containers of ranch. "Mom said he showed up to rescue his cousin last spring. I think that's the last time he's been in here."

Giving him the stink eye, I confirm, "Gracie?"

"That's the one." He double-dips and flashes a quick grin at me as he slides the container closer to himself.

"Seems like an honorable thing to do." Again, I feel inexplicably compelled to defend Odin.

"Suppose so. Funny how Joe called him and not one of her sisters. Probably figured one bad apple would help out another. Guess the lifetime ban on coming in here got lifted."

"Or maybe his was the only phone number Joe had," Jay offers. "Not like you can look these things up in a phone book anymore."

"Surprised there isn't a phone tree behind the bar with all the gossips in this town." Griffin groans. "Hard to have secrets around here."

Maybe that's why he keeps to himself. The only way to keep a secret is to keep it to yourself.

I want to ask more about Odin, but the conversation moves on to things from our childhood that don't really exist anymore. Still, my mind lingers on the start of a bad joke.

A man walks into a bar with a pig . . .

CHAPTER EIGHT
ODIN

*I*n the early morning mist, Roman trots through the woods, his nose hovering a few inches above the ground the entire time. I don't bother to hold his leash now that we're off the official trail and away from potential foot traffic.

According to the federal statutes and park by-laws, dogs aren't allowed on the trails. Neither are pigs, but I prefer to ignore the posted signs.

I'm aware of the rules. I've even studied the official guidelines for visitors. For example, foraging within the boundaries of the park for personal consumption is allowed, but there are restrictions about how you go about harvesting and a whole list of plants that are off-limits. Picking a few morel mushrooms and springtime wild onions is okay if you only gather a small quantity. The codes put the burden on people to obey the law. Enforcement is up to the rangers.

Hence why I like to keep a friendly relationship with the staff. We have an unspoken agreement. I don't cause a fuss, and they don't pay us any attention.

The trick to getting away with semi-illegal activity out in the open is to act like everything is perfectly on the up and up. It also helps to be weird enough that people stop noticing every bit of odd behavior. In other words, my entire life has been building up to this. Also, knowing the precise GPS location of the invisible boundary between public land and private is key.

Our federal government might oversee the trees and rocks within park boundaries, but we've moved out of their jurisdiction.

An old grove of filbert trees surrounds us. Wild and overgrown, the orchard blends in with the surrounding forest. If you didn't know hazelnuts aren't native to the Smokies, you probably wouldn't realize this area had been deliberately cleared and planted at some point.

Hearing family lore about Granddaddy's failed hazelnut business back in the seventies, I did some research and discovered this narrow swath of land that isn't part of the national park. Technically, it still belongs to the Hills.

According to the documents I discovered in the local archives, my great-great-granddaddy, Samson Hill, was paid more than a fair value for the acreage he sold the government back in the 1930s. Around here, some folks are still perturbed about the Feds taking perfectly good farming land from the hardworking families and making a park. A hundred years later, their descendants still curse Samson and the others for selling out. Throw a rock around here and you'll easily find someone who ain't fond of big government and Washington, D.C.

Evidently, he was a wily bastard when it came to negotiating the boundaries of what was sold and what he kept. On the map, this narrow valley is like a middle finger giving the bird between federal property. Fifty or so yards to the north, east, and west, everything from the dirt and water on up is protected, belonging to the great American taxpayer.

Personally, I'm grateful the land is surrounded by the national park. Away from main roads and best accessed by an old logging path or on foot off the Cooper Road Trail, the majority of people will never know of its existence. Keeps them out of my business.

Many of the original trees in the grove have died and been

replaced with smaller, shrubby young ones, erasing the unnatural order of the rows. A commercial filbert, or hazelnut, tree is productive for about forty years, meaning the majority of these are past their prime. Good thing I'm not interested in nuts.

Hiding in plain sight, the grove provides the optimal growing conditions for Périgords, aka black truffles, aka fungi gold. I learned about the symbiotic relationship between the two during one of my trips to France years ago for the truffle harvest.

I whistle and Roman lifts his head from where he's found something good to sniff. Despite having had him over a year, he's still in the wild, puppy phase and we're only beginning his training. These days most truffle cultivators prefer to harvest using dogs. I agree that they are a good alternative, less damage to the dirt, and potentially to the truffles. However, I prefer to work with Patsy. For one thing, she's smarter than Roman. Patsy Swine is the best truffle hunter in all of eastern Tennessee, and I'll fight anyone who argues differently.

People are used to seeing us wandering around together. Unlike ordinary hogs, she'll indicate the location of a truffle, but rarely tries to eat them, mainly because she knows she'll be rewarded with her favorite food. Took us a couple of years of testing to figure out what she loves more than truffles.

Banana cake.

I wonder what Jennifer Winston would say if she knew I didn't buy her prize-winning cakes for myself. If Donner Bakery is closed, or they run out, Patsy also enjoys homemade banana bread and banana pudding

Truth be told, I can't stand bananas. The smell, the taste, the weird texture—I want nothing to do with them.

The things a man will do for his pig.

September is too early for truffles, but I like to come out here and check on things on a regular basis. Harvest season doesn't typically begin until November, sometimes later.

Mostly I'm looking for signs of other humans. The last thing I need is for someone else to discover my hidden treasure. If I take the trail, I always make sure I'm not followed. Call me paranoid, but when tens of thousands of dollars' worth of fungi are buried in the dirt, I need to take precautions.

Farther south from this grove is an even older apple orchard, probably planted by my great-granddaddy. Left fallow like the filberts, it still produces fruit. Not pretty enough for the farm stand, these are the wild, ugly cousins of the shiny red grocery store varieties.

While the truffles are by far my biggest cash crop, I'm curious about using these apples for hard ciders and vinegars. Still in the experimental phase, I'm excited to see what I can create. With its location closer to the logging road, I'll be able to drive my truck up here and pick enough bushels to make it worth my time.

Today is more of an exploratory mission and a chance to stretch our legs. We'll load up my backpack with fruit before we head out; then we'll circle back to the van via the park trail.

I find myself thinking about walking the loop through the campground and past the main ranger station to see if a certain brunette ranger is on duty. After running into Daphne twice in a month's time, I'm reluctantly willing to admit I'm intrigued by her—a first for me in a long time. Her pretty face isn't the only reason. Ranger Abbott is objectively beautiful, and while I respect the hell out of her, I don't feel compelled to get to know her.

When I had a hankering for fried chicken, my first thought was to make it myself. Then I remembered Genie Lee makes some of the best I've ever had. After picking up Gracie last spring and delivering her into Willa's waiting, albeit angry, arms, I haven't been back to the bar.

It isn't because of some supposed lifetime ban for a few broken pool cues back when I was one of those teenage Hill delinquents. I know Joe doesn't hold a grudge and Genie's practically kin.

Sure, I might still be a bastard, but I at least have the knowledge and the perspective I earned from all the screwing up and screwing over I did in my early twenties.

I stay away because of a feeling in my gut.

Every time I think about being around big crowds of people, the skin on the back of my neck gets tight and hot. I prefer being on my own and keeping my own company. Funny how I never feel lonely when I'm by myself.

My musings occupy my mind on the return trip to the van. The apples I picked weigh down my pack, creating an ache in my shoulders. Sunlight breaks through the low-hanging clouds, heating up the day and warming my skin, and my T-shirt is damp where the pack and straps press against it. I lift my old ball cap and wipe my brow, wishing I'd grabbed the hat I inherited from my granddaddy. Something about the wide brim makes me feel protected, shading my neck as well as my face and keeping my head cooler.

Despite being sweaty, I keep to my plan to extend my walk with a stroll along the loop road.

I find myself disappointed when I don't spot Daphne on my circuit. I'd been hoping to casually run into her outside. Pausing outside the main ranger station, I'm now faced with the realization that I might have to make an effort to see her. My social skills are rusty from neglect. However, I'm accompanied by an adorable dog, and I'm not averse to using him as bait.

I crouch down and adjust his collar, pulling a couple of twigs from his coat. Holding his head in my hands, I make eye contact. "Roman, I need you to be charming. Can you manage that?"

He barks and tries to lick my face.

"Good enough."

CHAPTER NINE
DAPHNE

I love my uniform.

Is it flattering? Probably not.

Comfortable? Not always.

But it identifies me as a ranger, and I'm proud of my job.

I love the hat, and don't even get me started on the badge and patches. They make me ridiculously happy. I never got to be a Girl Scout, but I would've rocked the badge sash.

Most of all, I love being able to wear pants every day.

For the first eighteen years of my life, I never wore pants.

Not in the sense of a "no pants" meme.

I mean I was only ever allowed to wear skirts or dresses and nightgowns. My thighs never experienced the joy of cloth-covered separation.

After I left home, one of the first things I bought with my own money was a pair of jeans. Apparently, they're the gateway to jeggings and leggings and the most sinful of all—shorts.

I can't fathom being a ranger without pants. Not a pantsless ranger —that I can imagine and whoa, no thank you. Hello, awkward.

I love finding historical black and white photos of women wearing trousers long before it became socially accepted. If clothes make the person, those rebellious women of the past centuries who wore trousers instead of skirts and petticoats are true heroines. There should be a patron saint of these trailblazers, a goddess of pants who smites thigh chafing and cold legs.

Clearly, I've given a lot of thought to cloth leg tubes. I've spent many quiet hours pondering the idea of modesty and body parts. If we're all created in God's image, why are men's legs less sinful than women's?

Being a park ranger allows for a lot of time to contemplate these types of questions, especially when I'm stuck manning the information desk at the visitor center on a slow Wednesday. There hasn't been a single person with a question in over an hour, and I've organized the maps and pamphlets twice already. I've even written several tweets and posts for our social media.

Staring out the front window, I think about how different my life is now.

Growing up, I wasn't allowed to do a lot of things.

Sleep in on Sunday mornings.

See movies. Watch TV. Use the internet.

Go to public school.

Wear pants.

My family belongs to a conservative church. I knew we were different than the random strangers we'd bump into at the store. Little girls with butterflies on their T-shirts and ruffles on their shorts would stare at us while we stared back. They probably thought we were strange in our modest, old-fashioned dresses and hair in identical braids.

In hindsight, we were definitely the weird ones.

A soft tone alerts me to someone entering the center. Standing, I slip on my friendly ranger expression, ready to welcome them to the park.

"Hello again." Odin's voice is warm and oozes charm like honey, not molasses. That metaphor is forever ruined by the beverage that shall not be called coffee.

"Hello," I reply, friendly but professionally reserved. We haven't seen each other since our brief encounter at Genie's, so I'm pretending I hardly remember him. I won't fall for his easy charm and those cheekbones he wields like weapons. "What can I do for you today?"

His warm brown eyes hold my gaze, a challenge or a concession in his expression. Perhaps both.

"I . . ." He starts and then stops before beginning again, "I'm . . ."

I wait for him to continue.

"I'm sorry, but didn't we meet at the community center last month and again at Genie's? Maybe I'm mistaking you for another Ranger Baum." He points at my name tag.

"Oh, right. You have the pig," I say with impressive casualness.

"You do remember me." His mouth widens into a genuine smile. "Or at least Patsy."

"She is memorable."

He flinches slightly, probably not used to women not swooning over him and his charms. He worries his bottom lip and dips his chin, angling his face in a way that makes him appear less intimidating and sweeter.

Must remain impartial.

Griffin's warning echoes through my head.

"Been hiking today?" I point to his backpack which appears to sag under its heavy weight. Maybe he's training for a longer trek? We're close to the Appalachian Trail and get a lot of long-distance hikers in the area, not that he seems the type. Whatever that means.

"Uh, yeah. Hit the Cooper trail area this morning before it got too warm out there. Guess I underestimated." He lifts his cap and swipes a hand through his hair. The shaggy blond curls are mostly contained in a low ponytail but a few have escaped and cling to the damp skin of his neck.

Rangers are trained in basic emergency medicine, and I scan him for signs of heat exhaustion. Because I'm a professional. *Not* because I'm ogling.

Overall, he appears flushed. Sweat has dampened spots on his faded navy T-shirt and he's wearing jeans, not shorts or hiking pants. A long-sleeved plaid shirt is tied around his waist.

He takes a hearty chug of water from the reusable bottle he slides out of a side pocket of the pack. His throat bobs as he swallows. Not all men have a well-defined Adam's apple, but Odin does. It's almost sculptural in its perfection of what an Adam's apple should be.

Is there nothing flawed about his physical form? Can't he have bunions or knobby knees? A third nipple? *Something* to prove he's a mere mortal like the rest of us.

Finished drinking, he wipes the back of his hand across his wide mouth and beard. My attention remains on his face, specifically his lips. I'm staring, and we both know it.

Needing a distraction to cut through the awkward silence between us, I glance behind his legs, half-expecting to see his pet pig. "No Patsy today?"

"No, I brought my dog with me. Want to meet him? I left him tied up outside next to the water bowl." He points at the door. Sure enough, there's a brown and white mop of a dog staring at us through the glass.

"Okay." I sound hesitant, probably because I'm still confused by Odin's appearance. I've worked here for months and have never seen him. Now he's randomly showing up and inviting me to meet his dog.

I've never gotten the feeling he particularly likes me, yet I find myself following him out the door. Who isn't a sucker for a cute puppy?

CHAPTER TEN

ODIN

"What kind of dog is he?" Daphne squats, stroking Roman's side where he's lying across her feet. Her fingers slip through the brown and white curls of his coat, and the jerk lifts his dark head and gives me a self-satisfied look.

Yeah, I might be jealous of my dog right now, and he knows it.

"He's an Italian water dog."

"I've never heard of that breed before." She lifts her eyebrows. "Sounds fancy."

"Not really. Roman's a working dog. Bonus that he doesn't shed. Think of him like an Italian poodle. In a way, he is."

"Like a noodle-doodle?" She laughs at her own joke.

I laugh despite not really getting the humor. "I guess?"

"You know . . . Goldendoodle, Labradoodle, Schnitzerdoodle—all the oodle mixes that are super popular right now? I can keep listing them if you'd find it helpful. You basically take a breed and add 'oodle' to the end." At least she's amusing herself.

"Got it. Think of him as the great-great-great-grandfather to the oodles of the world. He can trace his lineage back generations in Italy."

She sweeps her attention over me. "Didn't figure you for a fancy dog breed person. Not into the whole rescue-a-mutt-who-needs-love thing?"

"I'm not opposed. It was love at first sight with Roman." I'm not lying. Ours was supposed to be a working relationship, but when he arrived in his crate all the way from Italy and I saw him for the first time, we bonded instantly.

He lifts his head and blinks at me, his way of saying he feels the same—or so I tell myself. It's the same with Patsy. They could be playing me, but I don't even care. I'm a sucker for my animals.

"How romantic," she says drily. "It's just the three of you?"

Daphne's face and voice remain neutral, like she's simply asking out of polite conversation and not prying into details about my personal life.

"Yep. Me, Patsy, and Roman," I say with a nod. "We've got everything we need for a good life in the holler."

"In the holler." She mimics my deep Appalachian accent.

"Are you making fun of the hillbilly?" *How original.* "Hollow. Is that better?"

If I want, I can make my accent disappear entirely. I learned quickly that a lot of people equate a Southern drawl with lower intelligence and I enjoy manipulating them using their own ignorance.

Her eyes widen at being called out. "No, not at all. I just think holler is a funny word for a place. I imagine a lot of yelling and echoes."

"Actually, one of the reasons I like living in a holler is the quiet."

"Sounds like the ideal bucolic life."

"Beats the alternative of living in town with nosy neighbors. Or worse . . . in a city." I exaggerate a shudder.

"I feel the same way. Too much concrete and metal give me hives, not to mention the exhaust and fumes." She wraps her hands around her neck and coughs. "Suffocating. Can't breathe."

"Has anyone ever told you that you have a flair for the dramatic?"

"Me? Never." She addresses this statement to Roman by scrunching up his ears and wiggling his face close to hers, and he licks her nose. She focuses her attention on him, basically ignoring me.

I didn't have a plan other than to show up. Clearly, I didn't think this through. What am I going to do, loiter around her workplace all afternoon watching her play with my dog?

Giving Roman one more scratch behind the ears, she stands, still focused on him. "He's sweet."

"That's what all the ladies say." What am I saying? There are no ladies. Unlike my walks with Patsy, I don't parade through town with my dog. Someone would have to come to the house to see him and other than family, no one visits me.

Her eyes flash to mine. "I imagine they do."

I want to clarify, but if the past is an example, I'll only dig myself deeper into a hole with her.

"Well, I need to get back to work." She points to the building behind her.

Shifting my heavy pack, I slide it off my shoulder and set it down for a moment to put away my water bottle.

Eying it, she asks, "What do you have in there? Rocks?"

"Haha. No. Just apples." The statement is out of my mouth before I can take it back.

Her eyes turn into slits as she stares at the backpack and then up at me, her face full of suspicion. "You're hiking with apples?"

I don't want to explain about the orchard and family ties to the land, so I lie. "Easier to manage than soup cans."

It's nearly impossible to imagine that at one point in my life, I was considered a player. I've never been this awkward around a woman before. Time to cut my losses.

"I don't want to keep you from your rangerly duties." I lift the pack and reposition it on my back.

77

"Nice to see you again." Her voice has a professional polish to it that wasn't there a few minutes ago.

"Sure. Yeah. I'm sure we'll run into each other again." I walk backward away from her, gently tugging Roman with me. He normally follows me without any coercion but lingers near her feet. "Come on. Let's go home."

He lies down.

"Looks like you might have yourself a dog," I joke.

Thankfully, she laughs. "Not sure he's my type. Probably too fancy for me."

We're talking about Roman. At least I think we are.

Another pull on his leash gets him moving.

Finally figuring out it's better for me to remain silent, I flash her a smile followed by a wave as she heads back inside.

If I were an old Southern woman, I'd bless my own heart right now.

CHAPTER ELEVEN

DAPHNE

*A*t the end of the day, I'm still replaying my conversation with Odin.

Did I really say he's too fancy for me and not my type? I should've clarified I was joking about Roman being a fancy Italian water dog, not him, though maybe he is a little bit extra with his weird produce and Patsy. Are hipsters into pet pigs now? Floppy farmer hats are the new fedoras, so could be. Do people even refer to other people as hipsters anymore? I have no idea.

I don't have a ton of experience with men. I missed out on the typical awkward middle school social shenanigans and dating in high school. My sisters and I weren't allowed to date or hang out with members of the opposite sex without chaperones.

At the time, I didn't know what I was missing because I didn't know any different. Everyone I grew up around was like me. Their families were members of the same church. We were homeschooled or went to a small charter school populated only with kids like us. My world was tiny.

In college, Kacey introduced me to John Hughes movies and *High*

School Musical, Glee, and Taylor Swift. She used to joke I was an alien from another planet. In a way, she wasn't wrong.

We haven't talked much since the weekend she visited. I text her and tell her about my promotion.

Breaking the universal rule of responding to a text with a text, she immediately calls me. The ringer startles me.

"Congratulations!" I can hear other voices and music in the background.

"Where are you?" I ask her.

"What?"

I repeat my question, only louder.

"I'm at a bar with some coworkers." The noise decreases. "Okay, I stepped outside. They won't miss me."

I check the time on the screen. It's only seven but I'm already in my pajamas.

"Are you there?" she asks. "Hello?"

"I'm here."

"That's great about the official job. Glad you'll be staying in the area."

"For now. You know me. I like to move around."

"Someday you'll find a reason to stay put. Have you seen the hottie farmer again?"

"As a matter of fact, I have."

"Then why aren't you giving me all the dirt?" Her volume increases with her indignation.

"There isn't much to tell."

I proceed to spend the next ten minutes trying to recall every detail of seeing Odin at Genie's and today. I leave out the part about my body's involuntary warming and tingling whenever I'm near him.

"He so likes you." Her voice is a loud screech through the phone. "Sounds smitten."

"Let's not get carried away. He didn't ask for my number or ask me out."

I imagine her optimism deflating like a balloon.

"Maybe he's awkward like you. Or shy?"

"Men who look like him aren't shy." Although our goodbye today did feel clumsy.

"Fine. You're right. He's not interested. Random coincidences, that's all. So, tell me how you're doing. What's new that doesn't involve a Y chromosome?"

"Guess that leaves out my coworker suggesting I dress up in a salamander costume for school visits."

Her laugh is more of a cackle. "You should totally do it, especially if there's a headpiece. You can hide inside and avoid eye contact. Isn't that what you learned from ranger school about interacting with wild animals? Don't stare at them because they take it as a form of aggression?"

"I'm not dressing up as a weird amphibian."

"Think about it."

"No."

"Daphne." Her tone switches to serious. "Don't forget to have fun. Life isn't only about work."

She's said this to me countless times over the years. "I know, Pot. Enough about me. How are you?"

"Same as always, Kettle. Working, going out, not getting enough sleep. I swear my rebound ability has disappeared. Turned thirty-three and poof! Gone."

The background noise increases and I imagine her or someone else opening the door to the bar.

"Speaking of, I should get back. Lynne has been sucking up to our manager all night. If I don't watch out, she'll sweet-talk her way into my promotion."

"How dare she!" I exaggerate my outrage.

"I know! Let's talk soon. Text me if anything interesting happens or send pictures of the salamander suit. Love you!"

"Love you back."

She disconnects before I can protest the rest of her statement.

I really do love and adore her but our life paths are so different. She works in an office building downtown and lives in a condo with a balcony she barely uses. Even with the salary increase that comes with being promoted, I probably earn half of what she does.

After my student loan and car payments, I'm not left with much in my account for extras like fancy cheeses and charcuterie boards. I never eat out, although, I'll occasionally grab a muffin or sweet treat from the day-old selection at Donner Bakery.

Because I wear a uniform to work and rarely go out, I don't need a whole closet full of clothes.

Clicking on the worn keys of my ancient laptop, I scroll through Pinterest, pinning recipes of meals I'll probably never make for dinner parties I'll probably never host.

Creating imaginary menus both soothes and agitates me—a distraction from boredom and the meager contents of my fridge. Sometimes I'll pull up an online grocery app and load my cart with everything delicious, briefly living in a fantasy of not caring about the price and my budget.

A side effect of these imaginary menus is hunger. I've already eaten dinner, and there's nothing good to snack on.

I open my other fantasy board: travel.

Fifty states. Seven continents. Almost two hundred countries. There's a huge world out there, waiting to be experienced.

A quick glance over my shoulder at my map reminds me of all the states I've already visited. I have a pin stuck in every place I've been, and they're color-coded by the reason for the visit: college, work, and vacation.

Most of the pins are green for work.

I figure I'll be working my whole life to pay off my college loans, so the romanticized notion of retirement seems impossible even if I work as a ranger long enough to get a pension. My last boss encouraged me to open an IRA. With a very serious expression, he said he had two words that could change my life: compound interest.

Whatever little money I can save goes into a travel fund. Scanning the beautiful photos, I sigh at the impossibility of me ever having enough to spend a week or an off-season in Europe or New Zealand. Sometimes I scroll sites that give packing tips for visiting popular destinations during different times of the year. As if I'll ever need a fall wardrobe for Scotland or outfits for a summer on the coast of Italy.

Like my dinner party boards, I guess it's good to dream. Fantasies are free.

Speaking of fantasies, I open a new browser window and type in Odin. Sixty-two million results. I click on the first entry for the Norse god. Maybe his legendary namesake will give me more clues to the real man.

Things I know about him so far:

He has a booth at the farmers' market at the community center where he sells peculiar vegetables.

He lives in a holler.

He walks a pig on a leash.

He's kind of a weirdo.

He is not living with anyone.

Add to that comprehensive list: he also owns a fancy Italian dog.

Let's not forget the part about him resembling a younger, hotter version of the deity whose name he bears with the beard, the long hair, and the fierce expression that could probably conjure lightning from the sky if he so wished.

He also smells of the woods on a sunny day.

Yep. That's the extent of my knowledge.

So far.

I doubt he has a social media presence, but I still type in his last name out of curiosity. He might have a website for the farm.

The amended results fill the screen. My mouth hangs open.

In shock, I snap the laptop closed and set it aside.

I need to tell Kacey. Then I remember she's out tonight and who knows when she'll be home.

I can wait. I'll text her tomorrow. We can be on the phone while we sort through the pages of results.

I laugh—to think I first thought of him as a wholesome farm boy.

Eyeing my laptop like it's a snake coiled to attack, I stand up and pace my small living area. It's possible, although unlikely, that I mistyped his name. There could be an Owen Hill or an Odin Hall doppelgänger out there.

Without trying, I read a few of the headlines before I aborted the mission. One, in particular, stands out:

"Celebrity Chef Protégé Arrested on Drug Possession After Bar Brawl."

Beneath was a row of images of a younger Odin looking more scruffy bad-boy than mountain hermit. I briefly caught a mention of a Michelin Star, whatever that means.

This might explain the fancy dog.

Doesn't explain the pig, though.

Unless . . .

She's part of some act he's putting on while he hides out in his holler.

Kacey was right—why do all the handsome men have to be morally bankrupt? On the outside, he's a delicious-looking jelly donut. On the inside, he's filled with slime.

I've spent enough time thinking about Odin Hill. There are more productive things I could be doing—like sleeping.

Going to bed would be the smartest option right now.

Once I'm settled in, I toss and turn, readjusting my pillow and blanket a dozen times. Finally, I give up and turn on the lamp, looking to the stack of books on my nightstand. Picking the one on the top, I open it to a random chapter and begin reading about the early history of the Great Smoky Mountains National Park.

I'm dozing off when a car alarm starts screeching.

Freaking tourists. Who sets their alarm in the middle of the mountains? Jerks, that's who.

Cursing, I roll over and wrap my pillow around my head. On the rare occasion this happens, the owner will quickly silence the blaring.

Not tonight.

They must be the soundest sleeper ever. The entire valley can hear the honking.

Frustrated, I climb out of bed and pull a sweatshirt on over my pajamas on the way to the door. I grab my keys, planning to drive through the campground until I located the asshole.

A ranger's job is never done.

* * *

Apparently, I'm the asshole.

There is a bear. Inside my car.

The doors and windows are shut, just as I left them when I last drove my car. I think I would've noticed if there was a bear in the vehicle when I went to the Piggly Wiggly. I always lock the doors, or almost always.

The alarm continues to bleat. I'm surprised the entire campground isn't storming over here, an angry mob with flashlights. Anyone sleeping through this racket seems impossible.

My car rocks as the bear moves around, thrashing her body between the seats and against the glass. How she even fits in the passenger area is a mystery.

Mesmerized, I almost forget to freak out about a fully-grown black bear in my car. Almost.

From inside my Toyota Highlander, the bear stares at me through the window. She looks pissed and more than a little confused.

I know how she feels.

85

Gaia comes out of her cabin next door, pulling on her fleece and walking across the small porch in her socks.

"What is going on?" she asks from the top step. "Why was your alarm going off in the middle of the night? Did you hit the panic button by mistake?"

As both my neighbor and my boss, she sounds annoyed as if I'm up late, irresponsibly throwing a rager on a school night.

Light spills out from the open door of Griffin's cabin and then Amory's as they exit. Both are in pajama pants and their ranger jackets looking rumpled and sleepy.

"Um, Daphne? What's a bear doing in your front seat?" Griffin points to the partially steamed windshield and the ursine carjacker staring at us.

"Please tell me you didn't leave anything edible in an unlocked vehicle." Gaia groans and then gives me a pointed look. "First rule around here: bag it or can it. Don't create temptation."

"I know. I swear, I have zero food in there. Not even a mummified McDonald's fry under the seat. Nothing." As the most junior ranger here, I feel the need to defend myself.

"Appears you forgot to lock it. Bear got in and she has somehow triggered your alarm." Amory offers a summary of the events so far.

The four of us stare at the Highlander.

"Well, the bear can't stay in there all night. She's going to be one angry beast when she gets out," Griffin says, stating the obvious.

"Should we get the tranquilizer gun?" Gaia takes a step down, glances at her socks, and returns to her porch. "Someone can break the window, but if we do that, we better be prepared for a freaked-out bear."

I can't afford to fix a broken window. In reality, the interior of my beloved Toyota is probably toast anyway.

"What's the range on your key fob?" Amory asks, standing in the space between the cabins and my parking spot.

Pressing the button, I finally silence the panicked screeching, and the blissful silence of the night returns. I think we all sigh with relief, including the bear. The alarm is the least of our problems, though.

"Can you pop the back hatch?" Amory asks.

I nod.

"Okay, here's what we're going to do." He's remarkably calm about this whole situation. Then again, he's generally low-key and unflappable. "Everyone is going to return to our cabins, including you, Daphne. Once we're inside, you'll push the release, and we'll wait. Hopefully, our furry friend will be so relieved to be free, she'll exit and be on her merry way."

"Sounds like a solid plan." Gaia backs up through her door. "We can examine the damage once the coast is clear."

"Or in the morning," Griffin says with a yawn. "Unless you have a pot of honey in there that will attract more bears."

"I swear, there's no food." I do a mental inventory and know I haven't left any food in the car. I never eat snacks in there.

They all give me looks that say they don't believe me.

"We'll see," Gaia says, closing her door.

The bear rocks the Highlander, which groans on its shocks. She lets out a growl of frustration mixed with fear.

"Hold on, we're going to set you free," I tell her, not that she understands. Even so, when our eyes connect, a sense of under-standing passes between us.

Once safely inside, I click the button on the fob, and the rear door softly opens.

"Turn around." I gesture through the window. "Freedom is behind you."

Holding my breath, I wait for her to sense the fresh air and make her escape.

"Come on, come on. You've got this." I quietly encourage the bear despite being fully aware she can't hear me.

"Go, be free," I shout through the glass.

The car shifts as the bear moves from front to back. With a quick hop off the tailgate, she scampers away and into the woods.

With a long exhalation, I silently give thanks she was able to run off on her own.

Relieved, I open the cabin's door and spot my colleagues on their porches.

Gaia is now wearing boots and has added her jacket. "Well, let's see if we can figure out what lured her into your SUV."

"I swear I locked the doors. How did she get inside to begin with?" My voice trembles with emotions.

"Where there's a will, there's an entrance," Griffin muses.

"There's a way," Amory corrects him.

"You say to-may-to, I say to-mah-to." Griffin waves him off with the beam of his flashlight.

"Yikes," she says as we peer through the open hatch. Padding and upholstery from the seats and ceiling are strewn everywhere. Claw marks gouge the dashboard and center console.

"Wow," Griffin whispers. "This should be photographed as a cautionary tale for visitors."

"Griff, now might not be the time," Gaia warns him.

"I don't see any crumbs or wrappers." Amory's moved to the driver's door and peers into the front.

"There's a shredded paper bag in the backseat," she declares from the other side, holding up a scrap of white and what appears to be wax paper.

My stomach sinks as tears burn my eyes. "Oh no."

"Do you remember what food you had?" Gaia asks, sounding remarkably nonjudgmental.

I sigh. "I keep telling you, I may have forgotten to lock it, but I wasn't stupid enough to leave food inside the car."

"Then what was it?" Amory shifts through the rubble of my backseat.

"Soap," I say, the word barely audible. "I bought soap at the farmers' market last month and completely forgot about it."

"What kind of soap?" Even Griffin sounds serious for once.

"Oatmeal with vanilla . . . and honey." I cover my face with my hands.

"That'll do it." He clicks off his flashlight. "You'll always attract more bears with honey than vinegar."

"I can't believe I forgot it." I don't mention my soap addiction or the possibility that I deliberately left it in the car to hide it from myself. This is definitely proof, very expensive proof, that I have a problem.

Amory collects the bits of paper mixed with the deliciously scented flakes. "Let's lock the vehicle for tonight. We can assess the full damage in the morning."

Gaia touches my shoulder. "It will be okay."

Tears spill from my eyes and I turn away. I don't want to cry in front of my boss and coworkers. I manage to choke out, "Thank you."

She gives my arm a squeeze. "Don't beat yourself up. Things will be better in the light of day."

CHAPTER TWELVE
DAPHNE

*T*hings are not better in the light of day.

No, most definitely not.

Even in the soft, diffused light of a foggy morning, the damage is shocking.

The metal shell of what was once my pride and joy encloses a disaster zone. The shredded ceiling and seats could possibly be replaced. The floor carpet could be steam-cleaned.

"It can be fixed," I tell myself.

Then I see the electrical wires hanging from below the steering wheel.

The truth hits me.

My car is totaled. Because of soap and shame and forgetfulness and being distracted by beautiful men and their extra-long root vegetables. Yes, I'm throwing Odin into the blame mix, too.

I'm not completely sure about my insurance deductible, but I vaguely remember it being more than I have in savings. After my student loan payment, it's the only option I could afford. How much can a ten-year-old car with over a hundred thousand miles be worth? Especially one redecorated by a bear?

Silently, I chant *I won't cry. I won't cry. I won't cry.*

Rebellious tears pool and spill down my cheeks.

After sobbing myself to sleep last night, I promised myself I wouldn't cry in front of my coworkers. Even if we're not technically at work, it's still the same. Crying equals being too emotional.

And emotions are weakness, especially in professional environments.

My first boss taught me that lesson. Buck up. Straighten your spine. Bite your tongue if you have to, but never show others your soft underbelly. No one likes a crybaby.

Did the bears cry when Goldilocks ate their food, trashed their furniture, and drooled all over their pillows?

My answer to that is the baby bear probably did.

Which only proves my old boss's point about crybabies.

These reminders don't stop the tears from continuing to run down my cheeks. Angrily swiping them away with the back of my hand, I remind myself that crying won't fix my car.

I snap a couple of photos with my phone.

Gaia walks over to me, holding two mugs, and hands me one. "I brought you coffee. Thought it might help."

Similar to me, she's wearing leggings and an oversized sweatshirt. Her face is clear while my eyes are so puffy it hurts to blink. My hair would make an ideal home for squirrels with its tangled mess that was a bun when I fell asleep last night.

Sniffling, I try to pretend I'm okay. "Thanks."

She gives me a sympathetic smile. "It's okay to be devastated. I'm upset for you."

I nod, worried about opening my mouth and a sob falling out.

"You should probably call your insurance company this morning. Take some pictures for the claim. The sooner you file, the sooner they'll process it."

"It's totaled. I'm not sure there will be any money after my deductible."

She nods in support, but I see the pity in her eyes. "You can always use one of the NPS rigs. I mean, don't take it on a road trip to Florida for spring break or decide to drive to California for tacos or anything, but it will get you around town."

"Really?"

"Sure. One of the perks of the job. Probably best to avoid any joyrides and drag races—Deputy James might not approve."

Still feeling on the verge of a good cry, I manage a weak smile. "Darn it. I already challenged a bunch of local high school kids to a street race."

She laughs. "That I'd like to see."

"Stupid soap," I mutter.

"Yeah. You might want to lay off the oatmeal honey for a while."

"I can't believe I left it in the car. I know better. I'm the one in charge of lecturing the visitors on bear safety. How could I be so stupid?"

"We all make mistakes. It's just a car. No one was hurt or killed."

If only she were right. This car is more than a vehicle. It's a symbol of my independence and success, as modest as it may be.

A big, fat tear escapes down my cheek. I hide the evidence by lifting my mug and taking a long chug of hot liquid. The coffee burns more than usual, and I sputter and cough.

"Sorry. I should've warned you I added some Bailey's. Figured you could use more than caffeine on a morning like this." Gaia lifts her own cup and sips.

"Little early for drinking, don't you think?"

She shrugs. "No comment."

Now that I'm prepared, I drink more slowly, savoring the sweet burn from the alcohol.

Griffin joins us, his hair still messy from sleep. "Mornin."

"Hi." I give him a small wave.

Without glancing at him, Gaia mumbles hello with no enthusiasm.

"Car's totaled, huh?" He drinks from his own steaming mug.

"Yep." I rock back on my heels and then up on my toes. "Spectacularly eviscerated."

He nods. "We should definitely take pictures and share them as a warning. I don't think people understand how destructive bears can be. They're not all cuteness and cuddles like we've been led to believe."

"Good idea," Gaia praises. "Someone could post it on social media as an example."

As the someone she means, I groan. "Can we at least leave my identity out of it?"

"Of course." His warm smile is full of empathy. "You should call Cletus."

"I think even this might be too much for the Winstons to fix."

"His brother Beau loves a challenge, but you're right. I was thinking they could help you find a replacement." Griffin's eyes hold hope.

"Unless they know of a car that's cheaper than free, I'll have to stick with Gaia's offer to use one of the park vehicles—not that I have to go anywhere more exciting than the Piggly Wiggly. I'll make do until I can save up."

"No insurance?" he asks.

With a sigh, I finish off my coffee. "High deductible. What's the point in paying premiums if I can't afford to make a claim?"

"I hear that." He lifts his mug. "Welcome to America."

I don't know whether to thank him for his empathy or remind him I'm American too. Instead, I heave another sigh and hand my empty cup to Gaia. "I should see if there's anything salvageable and then call for a tow truck."

"Or we could see if it starts and park it by the campground." Griffin steps closer to the car.

"Not sure that's an option. Wires were pulled from the dashboard." I open the door and point at the tangled mess.

"Keys?" He holds out his hand.

I give them to him.

After unlocking the doors, he slides the seat back and slips inside. "One for the money, two for the show. Three to get ready and four to go."

When he turns the key, nothing happens.

"That's disappointing. We need someone who can hotwire a car. Don't suppose either of you has experience?"

Gaia and I both shake our heads.

"Shame." He frowns and stares down the drive. "Ah, here's someone who can probably help us."

Griffin stands and greets Odin who walks out of the mist accompanied by his pig.

"What are you doing here?" My shame and embarrassment cause my voice to sound overly harsh and unwelcoming.

"Mornin to you too. Patsy and I decided to take a walk around the loop today. She was craving acorns." Odin lifts his baseball cap by the brim to adjust it before replacing it back on his head. Patsy tips her head back, her nose wiggling as she sniffs.

Griffin gives her a scratch on the top of her head, and she snuffles his palm.

"What's going on here?" Odin asks, leaning down to peer through the window.

"Bear," Griffin tells him.

"Ahh." Odin walks a circuit around the trash heap formerly known as my car. "Someone leave food inside?"

"Soap, actually," Gaia explains.

"Honey oatmeal," I add.

Odin's warm brown eyes meet my gaze. "Yours?"

"Was."

"Ouch."

Blinking back yet more tears, I twist my head away from the wreckage and his judgment.

"Pity." Odin worries his bottom lip. His concern appears genuine, but as I learned last night, appearances can be deceiving. The soap incident has distracted me from my internet search, but it all comes back now that I'm face to face with him.

"We're going to use it as a lesson for visitors," Griffin explains. "Silver lining."

"Insurance?"

Shaking my head, I don't elaborate. I can't have this conversation again. "I need to get ready for my shift."

"Right. We all have a busy day ahead. Odin, you think you can splice the wires to get the engine to start? We want to move the vehicle over to the campground."

"Why would you think I know how to do that?" Odin asks.

Griffin snorts. "Seriously?"

Odin removes his baseball cap and runs his hand through his hair. "It's been almost twenty years, but I can give it a shot—if that's okay with Daphne."

I barely meet his eyes before shrugging. "You can't make it any worse."

"Actually, if it caught fire, that would be worse. We'd have to get the fire crew over to put it out."

"Griffin." Gaia chastises him with a single look.

"Oh, right. Sorry, Daphne."

"Let's get more coffee. I still have half a pot left." Gaia touches my elbow. "We have time before your shift."

Once we're inside her cabin, I turn to Gaia, finally able to ask the questions bubbling inside me since Odin's appearance.

"Do they come to the park often? Isn't that weird? Are pigs even allowed? Dogs can't be on trails, but what are the rules about other pets?"

"So many questions." She gives me a quizzical look.

"He walks a pig on a leash—how could I not be curious?"

"They avoid the official trails and crowds. Otherwise, they're not causing trouble."

Neither of those sentences provides answers. It's unlike Gaia.

"A pet pig is less of an issue than the wild boars in the park, less dangerous, and Patsy doesn't cause damage. We should be more worried about bears who might develop a taste for honey and oatmeal. We'll need to file a report with Dr. Runous about the bear destroying your car. Can you handle printing and distributing flyers about the incident? We'll need to be extra vigilant about bear cans and bags. If the bear comes back, we might need to take steps to relocate or euthanize." She finishes her lecture as she refills our cups with coffee then holds up the bottle of Bailey's.

"Thanks."

Pointing to her couch, she settles into an armchair. "Why are you so concerned about Patsy?"

"Besides the fact he's flouting the park rules?" My dander is up and I'm not willing to put it back down just yet.

"I don't believe pigs are specifically mentioned in the bylaws. Oscar the donkey escapes and roams around on occasion. I've never heard you complain about him."

Her point is valid.

"Because he's an animal that doesn't know better."

"Could it be more about Odin?" Peering over her mug, she sips her coffee.

Dear Lord in Heaven, I really do not want to discuss my feelings with her. "Why would you ask?"

"You act differently around him. Your face gets pinched like you've eaten something sour. And you touch your hair a lot, which tells me he makes you nervous. Or . . ."

I drop my hand into my lap. "Habit."

". . . you're flirting with him."

"Pfft," I scoff.

"Yeah. I didn't think so." Her eyes are knowing and wise.

A knock sounds on her door.

"Come in," she shouts, without moving from her chair.

Odin's head appears around the jamb and his eyes seek me out in the room. "Hey. Sorry to interrupt. We got the car started and Griffin drove it to the station for now. Wanted to let you know."

My fingers tug on the ends of my hair near my shoulder before I realize what I'm doing. I sit on my hand and refuse to look at Gaia.

"Uh, thanks," I mumble.

He doesn't leave, nor does he enter the room.

"Thanks for your help this morning," Gaia tells him. She sounds genuinely grateful, particularly compared to my reluctant tone.

"Sure. Happy to help. Let me know if I can do anything else." He meets my eyes. "I guess I'll see you around."

"Don't be a stranger." She's all warm friendliness.

Through the screen door, I watch him walk away with Patsy beside him. Gaia sips her coffee, her eyes on me.

"What?" I ask.

"Nothing really. I've seen Odin around for years, and I think this morning is the most I've ever heard him talk."

"What do you mean? He was chatting up customers at the farmers' market a couple of weeks ago. A genuine Mr. Chuckles."

"He was working the booth?" She sits up and places her empty cup on the table next to her chair.

I bob my chin.

"Interesting."

"That a farmer would be hawking his own vegetables?"

"Are you sure it was him?"

"Patsy was there too."

"Interesting."

"How so?"

"Usually it's a cousin or two, never Odin. He told me himself he avoids the 'weekly circus'—his words, not mine—at all costs."

"He seemed to be having a grand time."

She picks up her cup and stares at the empty interior like she forgot she finished it. "Guess we should get ourselves ready. Unless you need the day off, which you're welcome to do. Jay can cover the talks."

"I should probably figure out how to file the report on the car. Otherwise, I'm fine." Standing, I finish my lukewarm coffee. "Thanks for the caffeine."

"You're welcome. Go ahead and take a couple of hours this morning. I'll clear it with your boss."

She chuckles, as do I.

I should be too dehydrated for more tears, but I feel gratitude for Gaia welling up within me. I say goodbye before I do something weird like hug her.

* * *

I spend an hour on hold with my insurance company before an agent eventually tells me to fill out the form online. Well, that was a waste of time.

After showering and putting on my uniform, I call Kacey while I walk to the station.

"Hi." Her voice is gravelly and sounds half-asleep.

"Long night?"

"Karaoke. You know I always overdo it. What's up?"

"A bear ate my car." A wave of sadness hits me, and when I go to laugh off the absurdity of that statement, I choke.

"Are you kidding? How is that even possible?"

"Soap."

"That doesn't make sense. Were you in the car? Are you hurt? Are you in shock? Is anyone with you?" Her voice rises in panic.

For the hundredth time today, I swipe away tears. "I'm fine. The car was parked outside my cabin. I was in bed asleep."

"Oh, thank God you're okay." She exhales audibly. "Hold on, what did you say about soap?"

"I left the consolation bars you bought me at the farmers' market in the back seat. Apparently, bears like honey."

"This is crazy. Your life is so different than mine."

She's not wrong.

"Is it salvageable?"

"No, the bear ate all of it. At least it was organic and made from goat's milk so it shouldn't be toxic."

She laughs. "Not the soap. Your car."

"Totaled."

"Oh, Daphne. What are you going to do?"

I share Gaia's offer and tell her about the guys helping this morning. "And then Odin showed up."

By now I've reached the station and enter the building to make my way to my cubicle. I pass Amory on his way out and wave at him. Like Griffin, he's always got a smile on his face and a happy pep about him.

Kacey's frustrated voice brings my attention back to my phone. "Stop burying the lede. Wasn't he there yesterday too?"

"He was."

"He likes you." She's giddy.

"He was walking his pig."

"Wasn't the dog with him yesterday? What was the breed? I want to look it up. Unless you have pictures."

Exasperated by her excitement, I mutter, "I did not take a photo of Odin's dog. It's something Italian."

"I'll just have to come up one weekend and meet him."

"The dog?" I'm confused.

She laughs. "The man. Oops, I'm late for a meeting. Gotta go. Love you!"

I end my call with Kacey and feel Griffin staring at me.

"Uh, Daphne?" His voice holds confused amusement.

"Yes, Ranger Lee?"

"I won't pretend I wasn't overhearing your conversation."

"Okay." I try to replay my words to see if I said anything embarrassing.

"I'm not sure what kind of dogs you had out west, but here in the Smokies, we call that animal a pig, or a hog. Not to be confused with the wild boar."

My eyes seek the sky through the layers of commercial ceiling tiles, insulation, plywood, and roofing shingles. "I know the difference between a pig and a dog."

"No need to be curt. Seeing as how both can be seen being walked on a leash, there could be some confusion." He gives a flippant shrug of his right shoulder.

"Really? People around here confuse canines and swine on a regular basis? Do they not teach the Old MacDonald song in preschool? That's a shame. However, it explains how you might assume someone could be confused." My tone is snarkier than he deserves. I'm just in no mood to be teased today. *Read the room, Griffin.*

He levels me with a flat stare. "I grew up here."

"And?" He's not my boss, but he does have seniority over me. I probably shouldn't keep poking the bear when it takes a swipe at me.

His nearly permanent smile fades. "May I give you a piece of advice?"

"Can I say no to this unsolicited tip?"

"If you want to make friends around here, I wouldn't be mocking our education. If you haven't noticed, we're a touch sensitive about Appalachia's reputation for being full of backwoods hillbillies and toothless yokels."

First, I want to tell him, I'm not here to make friends. I have no interest in popularity. Second, it isn't like I'm turning down social engagements due to my calendar being full. Third, everyone's been nice to me and honestly, I could use more kindness in my life.

With a deep exhalation, I release some of the pent-up frustration I shouldn't be taking out on my coworker.

"I'm sorry. It's been a rough morning. For the record, I'm not the one who accused someone of not knowing the difference between a pig and a dog."

"Point made."

"Also, Odin Hill has both a pig and a dog."

"Good to know." He turns his back to me.

Since we're already on the subject, I might as well ask him.

"Griffin?"

He slowly spins in my direction. "Yes?"

"If I suspect someone of breaking park regulations, but not necessarily any criminal laws, how should I proceed if I don't have proof? Is there a procedure for an investigation that wouldn't necessarily be official?"

He blinks a few times as he processes my convoluted question.

"Did you see something specific?"

"No, but a couple of things don't add up."

"You're saying this wasn't an isolated incident? Local or a visitor?"

"I'm not sure if there was an incident, but to answer your second question, yes, he's a local."

"Anyone I know?"

"He was walking his pig this morning and apparently knows how to hotwire a car."

He nods with understanding, not surprise. "Ahh. Care to elaborate?"

"He was here yesterday with his dog, said they'd been hiking. Ignoring the dog on the trail issue, he had a heavy-looking backpack. When I asked him about it, he told me it was full of apples."

"The fruit?" Griffin asks.

"I doubt it was miscellaneous iPhones and iPads." Though I guess anything is possible. I'm not sure which would be weirder.

"That's definitely odd." His dark brows pull together.

"I thought maybe since you know him, you could follow up?"

"Sure thing." Lost in thought, he focuses on the wall behind me.

"And Griffin?"

His eyes snap back to my face.

"Thanks for your help this morning."

"You're welcome."

"I appreciate Odin's assistance, too, and I don't want him to get in trouble, but . . ." I'm not sure where I'm going with this. Do I tell him my theory about Patsy and the one random article I saw online but haven't read?

He waves off my unfinished sentence. "Say no more. I'll follow up."

CHAPTER THIRTEEN
DAPHNE

*T*he next week, Gaia and Dr. Runous hold an all-staff meeting about the bear incident. I feel guilty about being the reason everyone has to take time out of their day to gather in the conference room. I can hardly look the game warden in the eye while he reminds us to be on alert for a repeat offender. Once a bear gets a taste for people food, it's likely to seek out more, and as we head into the cooler fall months, the bears will be looking for extra food before their winter hibernation begins.

On top of the guilt and embarrassment, all day I've ignored the unwelcome tickle at the back of my throat and my runny nose. Even now that it's more like a faucet with a drip, I keep reaffirming to myself that I'm fine.

The power of positive thinking compels whatever allergens are afoot to listen to my command.

I refuse to give in to this nonsense. It's Friday and I have big plans this weekend to do nothing after my shifts.

I sneeze three times into my elbow.

"You sound like you're sick," Griffin comments from the other side of our shared wall.

"The air must be dry in the office today."

"It's been raining all week—can't imagine the humidity in here is all that much lower than outside given we don't have the AC running and the heat isn't cranked." His explanation is so logical and not at all what I want to hear. "Also, dry air won't explain away your congestion."

"I'm fine." My rough voice says otherwise.

"Who's sick?" Gaia walks out of her office.

"Daphne," Griffin declares as he stands.

"It's nothing. Just allergies. Dust. Or mold, from all the rain." I play off of Griffin's comment.

My boss narrows her eyes at me. "You should go home."

"I'm—" My nose twitches as I resist the urge to sneeze. I lose the fight and cover my mouth with my arm.

"You sound the opposite of healthy." Protecting her face with her ranger hat, Gaia takes several steps away. "Home. Now."

"It's allergies. Not contagious."

"Right," Griffin murmurs, dragging out the *i* in exaggerated doubt.

"Why don't you believe me?" My nose is stuffy and drippy.

All I need is some tissues and a Benadryl. Normally I don't take it while working because it can make me loopy or sleepy, or loopy then sleepy. I only use it if I know I have the capacity to nap.

"It isn't that we don't trust you," he replies, "but your voice sounds like you've been smoking menthols for five decades."

Gaia lowers her hat to say, "He's right. Pack up and go to bed."

"For allergies?" I sniffle.

"Didn't you have a school visit this week? You know kids—probably caught a cold from one of them." Over the brim, Gaia's eyes bore into mine. She doesn't bother to move her hat when she says, "Go home."

"Fine," I mumble. "I'm going. I'm going."

I sound pitiful even to myself.

"I'll drop off tea and soup later," Gaia offers. "Do you have any cold or flu medications?"

Opening my desk drawer, I sift through pens and paperclips until I find my emergency supply of pink pills. Showing it to my colleagues, I declare, "I'll be okay. No need to buy out the drugstore."

To prove I'm being responsible, I pop two of the packets open and swallow the capsules dry. I immediately regret this and take a long drink of water from the stainless bottle I keep on my desk.

Both annoyed and congested, I tug on my jacket and place my own hat on my head. I could stay and argue with them, but a cup of tea and curling up under a blanket does sound good. Before I leave, I stuff some extra tissues in my pockets.

"Off you go." Gaia shoos me away with her hat.

After promising to take care of myself, I head out the door for the short walk to my cabin.

The rain has finally stopped, leaving behind wide puddles and squishy mud along the path. I avoid the deeper water by walking along the edge of the road that loops from the ranger station into the campground. This route takes me closer to the forest and will add a few minutes to my trip, but that's better than slipping and getting soaked.

Grumbling to myself, I keep my focus mostly on my footsteps. That's probably why I don't notice I've passed the turnout for the ranger cabins until I'm at the Cooper Road trailhead.

"Seriously?" I stomp my foot in frustration, splashing my pants with water. "So much for auto-pilot working."

Turning to switch directions, I spot a large white van parked on the other side of the lot. It's the only vehicle here. Given the rain and promise of thick mud, there haven't been too many people on the trails this week.

"I know that van," I declare to the trees. No one else is around to hear me.

The *Be the Light* logo is faded and mostly peeled away; only the faint outline of the words still lingers enough to be legible. A cross still decorates the door panel but has been painted over to resemble two carrots.

There's only one person I know who drives an old church van like this.

I glance around to see if there are signs of him or anyone else nearby. The area is empty. "What's Odin Hill doing out here in the mud?"

There's only one way to find out.

The last thing I want to be doing is clomping through the woods, but my instincts tell me he's up to no good. Catching him in the act is the only way to prove I'm right.

A set of prints indicates someone has recently used the trail, and next to the human tracks are the tidy marks from cloven hooves. They only go in one direction, which means he's still out there and Patsy's with him.

Hiking with a pig is weird, but I suspect it's the least of my worries when it comes to Mr. Hill.

My feet sink and slip in the mud, which quickly covers my boots and splashes the lower half of my pants. Wonderful. Now I have to do laundry. *Thanks, Odin.*

Past the small ranger cabin, the official trail winds off to the right to continue up the hill, but there's a gap in the trees and the footprints I'm following cut to the left, going down the slope.

"Of course, he doesn't follow the rules to stay on the marked path. Why would he? He's vegetable Thor," I mutter to myself, sniffling as my nose runs. Reaching into my jacket pocket, I extract my pack of tissues. A silver foil packet of allergy meds falls to the ground by my feet.

I think the Benadryl was expired and not potent anymore. I'm definitely not feeling better, so I swallow both of these pills in hopes of drying out my sinuses.

After blowing my nose, I ask, "Where are you and what are you doing?"

Not expecting a reply, I continue on. There is a faint trail through the underbrush, indicating this path has been used enough to prevent regrowth. I'm not as familiar with this area of the park because my work is concentrated around the visitor center. From memory, I know the official trails, but obviously not all the offshoots and spurs.

Water plops from the branches and birdsong filters through the air, but there's no sign of Odin or Patsy. From my estimate, I've been walking for at least ten minutes. I should've checked the time before I set out. I also should've let someone know I was coming out here. If something happens to me, no one will know where to look.

Great, now I'm imagining getting lost in my own park. Happens all the time to visitors. Easy to get disoriented and think you're hiking in one direction when you're actually going in the opposite. Up and down aren't straight shots with the boulders and streams crisscrossing these mountains.

Stay on the trail is the number one rule, and I've broken it.

The path I'm following leaves the trees and takes me to a meadow that's more of a field. Glancing down, I realize there aren't any footprints in the mud ahead of me or behind me, only mine.

Uneasy in the fading light, I decide to turn back. Honestly, what am I going to do if I find Odin? Confront him? Arrest him? Put him in handcuffs and . . .

My mind takes the image and begins conjuring all sorts of scenarios. Odin on his knees. Odin handcuffed to a bed—specifically, my bed. *Whoa.* Apparently, I have a vivid imagination when it comes to the farmer.

Laughing at how quickly my thoughts escalated, I end up coughing.

"You sound sick," a familiar voice says from a few yards behind me.

It makes me jump and clutch my chest, even though I'm out here looking for him.

"How'd you get over there?" I ask as I whirl around. Odin is standing between me and the way home.

He's wearing a felt hat with a wide brim like he's a young wizard on an epic quest, a younger, hotter version of Gandalf. He's friggin' Gandalf the Blond.

His posture is nonchalant like he doesn't have a care in the world. It's completely infuriating. Patsy lifts her head and her pink snout twitches as she sniffs the air. The two of them are a pair of . . . something. I can't think of the right word right now, but they're something.

With a lazy smile, he responds, "Walked."

"What are you doing out here?" Sniffling, I cross my arms and wish my nose would stop running.

A big splat of water falls on his floppy hat, darkening the dull green felt. One drop turns into dozens and then hundreds as the clouds decide this is the perfect moment to release more rain.

Because of course what this day needs is for me to get soaked.

He tips his head back to stare at the sky before letting his gaze land on me. "I was going to ask you the same thing. Are you lost?"

Affronted by his question, I scoff. "Are you?"

Too late, I realize I basically sound like one of the middle school kids I encounter so often. At least I didn't say *I know you are, but what am I?*

Thank God for small mercies.

"Not sure about you, but I'm going to get out of this weather." He clicks his tongue, and Patsy lifts her head from where she was sniffing the ground. "Care to walk back to the lot with us?"

"Why are you being nice?" I ask, not moving.

"Is there a reason I shouldn't be?" He cocks his head and peers at me from under his hat brim.

"What are you doing here?" I repeat my earlier question.

"Enjoying the great outdoors before the rain came back." He points to the sky. "Or I was."

His hat is even darker than it was a few minutes ago. Streaks and spots of water cover his gray jacket.

A crack of thunder makes both Patsy and me jump.

"Probably smart for us not to be standing in this field." He turns to go, not waiting to see if I follow.

Of course I do, because there's only one way to get back to the main trail.

Back in the woods, the rain softly drips from the branches onto us, the moss, and soft earth. It's quieter here too. Patsy's snorts and my congested breaths are the only sounds other than the occasional snap of a twig or boot scraping over stone. It's almost peaceful—or would be—if I could forget the reason I'm out here.

The walk back seems to take longer than I remember, and the going is mostly uphill. Unable to keep up, I slowly fall behind the two of them. Normally I have no issues with inclines. I'm fit as a fiddle, whatever that means.

Realizing I'm parched, I wish I'd thought to bring my water bottle. If only I'd known I would spontaneously decide to go on a long hike. I'm also exhausted. Resting for a minute sounds like the best possible idea, so I find a log and take a seat.

My butt lands on the rough bark, and I groan like an old lady. *"Oof."*

Stuffing my hands in my pockets, I search for a fresh tissue as my nose begins to tingle with an impending sneeze. When it arrives, I swear it comes from my toes.

"Gesundheit." Odin steps closer and hands me a tissue.

"Thanks," I mutter and accept his gift without tilting my head back to look at him. "I'm fine." After I answer, I realize he didn't ask me if I was getting sick. "I have allergies."

"All this rain brings out the mold spores." He sways back on his feet.

"Um, sure." I have no idea what I'm allergic to. Never been tested.

"Should probably get you home."

"Or I could sit here until some dwarves find me and take me to their cottage."

He dips his chin but remains quiet.

"You know, like Snow White?" I explain.

"I'm familiar with the fairy tale," he says flatly.

Every word from him is slow, measured, like the effort of speaking to me is taxing on him in some way.

Since he's not pulling his weight on his side of this sparkling conversation, I continue down the path of my previous thoughts. "Then again, I'm not very good at domestic duties and the dwarves would probably kick me to the curb when I burned their supper."

He chuckles. "You should really get out of the rain."

I press the toe of my boot into the mud. "Thanks for the suggestion."

"Are you going to stay here all day?" He squats down so our eyes finally meet.

"Maybe."

"Stubborn much?" He laughs.

"I was tired. I sat down to rest." Feeling a pout coming on, I cross my arms.

With a small but earnest smile, he says, "I can see that."

Patsy lets out a louder harrumph and nuzzles the ground near the fallen log. She paws at the soft earth and then digs her nose into the mud.

"What is she doing?" I lean to one side, trying to see what has caught her interest.

"Hold still." Odin's voice has switched from amused concern to direct and a bit bossy.

Still crouching, he leans forward, closer and closer until I can feel his breath gently brush across my skin.

Oh, my dear sweet Lord.

He's going to kiss me.

Odin Hill is making a move. Here in the woods during a rainstorm, unexpected and out of nowhere, and I am not ready. Not at all.

And yet, I've dreamed of this moment happening. In fact, it's actually happened in my dreams more than once.

Fantasy is about to become reality.

Do I want this? How could I not want this?

Odin Hill. The man. The demigod.

My mind flips out and short-circuits into white noise.

My body takes over as I close my eyes and lick my lips on instinct, anticipating the press of his mouth against mine.

CHAPTER FOURTEEN

ODIN

*P*atsy's still sniffing and pawing the ground like she's found a treasure, but I'm too distracted by Daphne and the faint aroma of skunk spray lingering in the air.

Daphne's closed her eyes and tipped her head back as if she's waiting to be kissed.

By me.

Stranger things have happened in my life, but this moment definitely hits somewhere in the top twenty.

Patsy gives up her quest with a disappointed huff and tugs on her leash to get going.

Neither Daphne nor I have moved.

I take in the tiny freckles across her nose and cheekbones and the way the fine hairs along her forehead curl slightly, how her dark brows fade into points near her temples. Her skin is bright and clear without a trace of makeup, but her lips are a soft rose. Natural color or lipstick? My guess is the former.

A short, exasperated exhalation startles me from my musings.

She opens one eye while scrunching the other tight. "If you're going to kiss me, quit taking so long."

Patsy gives another tug and I lose my balance, landing on my ass. The fabric of my pants quickly turns damp from mud or water, or both.

"What? No, I wasn't going to kiss you." I bounce up and brush off the wet seat of my jeans.

First, she's interrogating me, and then I find her almost asleep on a log. Now she thinks I'm making a move on her?

Her expression falls. "No, of course not."

She can't possibly be interested, not with the way she acts all suspicious and awkward around me. I recognize her behavior, been experiencing it my whole life—Odin, the hillbilly.

Given her hot-and-cold and downright odd behavior, I think Daphne might be drunk, possibly high. She's been sneezing and blowing her nose, so she might be sick.

I also suspect the log she's sitting on has recently been marked by a skunk, which I don't think she realizes given her congestion.

"Come on, we need to get you home." I hold out my hand but notice my palm is covered with mud. Rubbing both hands on my jeans, I attempt to clean away the dirt. The action is pointless and only serves to smear soil deeper into both skin and fabric.

Reluctantly, she stands, unsteady. "Well? Let's go."

She steps around Patsy and me and continues up the slope.

I swear the rain falls harder the closer we get back to the trailhead. After her initial quick pace, Daphne's dragging her feet again. A wild look has settled in her eyes, and I'm not sure she's even aware of where she is or who she's with.

"What's my name?" Holding out my slightly cleaner hand, I offer support over an uneven scramble of rocks.

"Vegetable Thor," she mumbles with slumped shoulders.

I laugh. "Close enough."

She refuses my gesture of goodwill and stomps past me. "Whatever. I know you're committing nefarious deeds on federal land. You're a bad man, Odin Hill."

116

"Is that so?" I follow after her and grab her elbow when her boot slips in deep mud.

"I'm on to you, bub." Jabbing her finger into my arm, she frowns. "Stupid vegetables."

This woman makes no sense. One minute she's accusing me of being a criminal, and the next she's petting my bicep like a baby animal.

"Let's get you inside and warmed up. You're going to wind up sick if you stay out here any longer." Reluctantly, I remove her hand from my bicep and use it to pull her along.

"Not sick," she mumble-whispers.

"What?"

"I have allergies. That's why I'm outside."

Now I'm completely confused. "Some strange cure you read about online?"

"No, I sneezed and Gaia sent me home."

"Did you get lost?"

She stares up at the heavy dark clouds. "We already covered this. No."

"Then how did you end up in the woods?" She's not making sense, but I get the feeling I should keep her talking if I want to make sure she makes it back to her place safely. If she can talk, she can walk. I really don't want to have to carry her and hold Patsy's leash.

"I saw your van at the trailhead and came looking for you."

"Why?"

"To catch you."

"Doing?"

She rolls her eyes. "Nefarious deeds on park property."

"Can you give me a hint about what laws I'm breaking out here?"

She points at Patsy, who isn't paying any attention to us as she meanders ahead, like she knows this whole situation is ridiculous and doesn't want to get involved. Smart girl.

"Walking your pig, for one thing. Pets aren't allowed on trails."

117

"Busted." I hold up my hands.

"You're awfully cocky for someone who could be facing serious charges."

"Do you have one of those citation pads? Are you going to write out a ticket? What's my penance? Jail time or can I pay a fine? Will you take a check?" Searching for an imaginary checkbook, I pat my pockets.

"Don't think you can talk your way out of this one. I'm immune to your charms and your bone structure. Your muscles won't save you."

From her fierce stare, I don't think she realizes how hysterical she sounds. She lifts her arm and sneezes five times into her elbow.

I'm beginning to believe Daphne might be delirious.

Risking further finger jabs, I remove my glove and place my hand on her forehead beneath the rim of her official hat. The skin there is warm but not hot. I don't think she has a fever.

"I'm fine. How many times do I need to tell people? Fine, fine, fine." She sneezes again.

"We're almost back to the campground. I'll put Patsy in the van and escort you home."

As she rolls her eyes again, her entire body sways with the movement.

"Humor me," I tell her, more stern than I intend. The van is about five yards ahead. "Can you make it, or do you want me to drive you?"

She mumbles something about kidnappers but waits while I load Patsy into her crate and secure the door.

"Walk or ride?" I point to the passenger door.

"Getting into a white panel van with a stranger? Thanks, but no thanks."

I'm tempted to point out that I'm not really a stranger. She knows my first and last name, knows about my farm stand business, and could easily track down my home address if she asked Griffin.

"Suit yourself. Which one is your cabin?"

Waving behind her and then turning in that direction, she wanders away.

"Driving would've been the drier option, you know." My stride lengthens to keep up with her.

"You didn't even offer me candy or ice cream to get inside your van. You're a terrible kidnapper. Better stick with your other criminal activities." She sounds serious despite the silliness of her accusations.

"Thanks for the advice. I'll make a note to buy some candy for next time." With some effort, I suppress my chuckle.

The ranger cabins are situated off of the main road opposite the campground, tucked together in neat rows. I follow her to the steps of one of the single-story log buildings.

"This you?" I watch her pat her pockets and then pull out a collection of keys. When she unlocks the door, I add, "Guess so."

"What are you doing?" She spins when the boards of the stairs to her little porch squeak.

"Following you inside." Okay, maybe not the best thing to say to a woman I barely know.

"Why?" She's right to be wary.

"Because no matter how many times you declare yourself to be fine, you're obviously unwell. I'm already here and can make you something warm while you get out of your wet clothes."

Her eyes bug out and her pupils dilate and maybe narrow then dilate again. "I'm not having sex with you just because you followed me home."

"Whoa." Holding up my hands, I give her space, which isn't easy on the narrow landing. "I was thinking tea or soup. As far as I know, that isn't code for sex, or anything else. Just trying to help."

I'm out of my comfort zone and should probably leave. Patsy's not going to be happy with me for leaving her in the van.

I expect Daphne to protest, but she says "Okay."

Removing her hat and shaking off the rainwater, she opens the door and enters, leaving me standing awkwardly on her porch.

I stomp my boots and try to brush off as much water as I can from my jacket and hat before entering. If I were a dog, I'd give myself a head-to-toe shake.

The interior of her cabin is simple, if not generic. Other than a bookshelf clogged with paperbacks and a map full of pins, there aren't a lot of personal touches. No girly pillows on the blue couch or framed sayings like *You've got this!* or *Live, Laugh, Love* on the walls. Honestly, I'm not sure what I expected because until I walked through the door, I hadn't given her home much thought.

Prior to a few weeks ago, I hadn't given Daphne much thought either. Yet here I stand.

"Feel free to snoop in my cupboards for tea and or soup. Not sure if you'll find anything. I'm going to go change." She points at the open kitchen on the wall opposite the door and then disappears down a short hallway to the right.

Having been granted access, I decide I should follow through on my offer and make her something warm. Not a fan of canned soup, I'm hoping she at least has tea. Maybe some honey and lemon too.

The first cupboard I open contains oil, jarred marinara, elbow macaroni, peanut butter, canned beans, and an opened bag of rice. On the lowest shelf are a couple of bowls stacked on two plates and an assortment of mismatched glasses and mugs. The other cupboard contains a box of generic cocoa, instant coffee, and a single black teabag. A few spices and cupcake liners along with oatmeal and flour occupy the upper shelf.

That's the entirety of her pantry contents. I've seen better supplies at questionable short-term rental properties.

Moving on to the fridge, I'm greeted with condiments, a loaf of white bread, cheese slices, apple butter, and a bowl full of the little half-and half-pods, the kind diners put on the tables for customers.

Did she steal a bowl of creamers from Daisy's Nut House?

Where is the rest of her food?

Not feeling hopeful, I open the freezer to find ice cream, a few frozen dinners, and a single-serving pizza.

Examining one of the boxes, I mutter, "That's it?"

"If you're looking for a kettle, it won't be in the freezer. Also, I don't have one. I heat water in the microwave." Dressed in sweats and a Grand Canyon fleece zipped all the way up, she opens the cupboard, and takes out a dark green mug with Smoky Mountains scrawled on the side and pauses. "Why are you glaring at that pizza?"

"You only have one teabag."

Not meeting my stare, she turns to the sink. "Hmm, that's not surprising."

"No soup, either." The lack of food is bothering me. "What are you going to eat?"

"I have options." She points at the box still in my hand.

"You need something healthy, not freezer-burned plastic."

After pressing the buttons on her microwave, she faces me. "Why are you so concerned?"

"You're unwell." The idea cements itself in my brain before I have time to consider my motive. "I'll take Patsy home and stop at the store for supplies. Meanwhile, you should nap. I'll only be gone an hour or so."

Our eyes lock for a moment in a silent challenge. Her cheeks are flushed and her eyes are still glassy, but she's not backing down. Rather than stick around and argue with her, I decide to go.

"I like the noodle soup in the box." Her chin juts up. "If I get a say in what you're buying."

"Okay then. You rest. I'll be back."

I'm halfway to the door when she calls my name. "Odin?"

Squaring my shoulders, I face her.

"Why are you being so nice to me?"

"Because I suspect you need someone to be kind to you." I don't wait for her to reply.

CHAPTER FIFTEEN
ODIN

*O*nce I get Patsy and Roman fed and settled, I unload the contents of my backpack into a bushel basket and place it inside the fridge.

After taking care of business, I pull out a wooden crate and load it with food from my pantry and fridge while making a mental list of recipes.

"Honey, lemon, broth, ginger, cayenne, cinnamon, apple cider vinegar," I say to myself as I double-check my supplies. I'll swing by the Piggly Wiggly for the things I don't have, including her powdered soup mix.

Her question about my motives keeps echoing through my head.

Her bare cupboards remind me of the empty shelves in my parents' kitchen. Things were often tight and too often, the gap between paychecks meant we made do without extras. Hunting, veggies from the garden, and whatever my grandmother could forage kept us going through the lean days. When I was real young, anything store-bought was a rare treat.

Maybe she's just been busy with work and hasn't had time to stock up.

Or maybe it's none of my damn business and I should stop speculating.

My crate packed, I scour my bathroom for anything that might help with allergies. I didn't have the chance to inspect Daphne's medicine cabinet, but I doubt she has much. I rarely get sick, so my stores are similarly lacking.

Not sure she'll take it, but I add one of the mushroom extracts to my supplies. Nannie Ida swears by them, and she's almost a century old. Must be some truth to her old tinctures and remedies.

After successfully avoiding anyone I know at the Piggly Wiggly, I drive back up to Cades Cove. I've been gone well over an hour and hope Daphne's taken my advice to nap.

After a soft knock on her door, I wait a moment and then turn the handle.

Daphne is asleep on her couch beneath a blanket. One arm dangles off the side, her hand almost brushing the floor. The other hand is resting on the pillow behind her head. She reminds me of a cartoon princess or an old black and white film star in mid-swoon.

"Hello?" I say, softly because I don't want to startle her.

She doesn't stir.

Torn between knocking louder to wake her and letting her sleep, I choose the latter. With care, I cross her small living room to the kitchen and set my crate down without making too much noise. I unpack anything perishable into the fridge and put away a few things in her cupboards.

Deciding to make Nannie Ida's remedy, I search for a decent pot and a paring knife. I quickly realize I should've brought my own knives with me. Her one chef's knife is so dull I wonder what's she's been using it on—is she opening cans with it? Cutting cardboard? With no sharpening steel in sight, I'll have to make do.

God, I sound like a snob.

Probably because I am one when it comes to cooking and using the proper equipment for the job.

At least all my clanging around in the kitchen hasn't awoken Sleeping Beauty.

Once everything is chopped and added to the pot of simmering water, I glance around the compact living space. These old cabins were built with local timber during the early years of the park, and from the looks of it, the kitchen was last updated in the nineties. The electric range is too clean to be used on a regular basis. When I open the oven door, I expect to discover it being used as pantry storage.

Not wanting to give in to the urge to snoop, I take a seat in the lumpy old armchair adjacent to the couch where Daphne quietly snores.

A small wooden bookcase in the corner draws my attention. Paperbacks and hardcovers fill two shelves. Upon closer examination, I realize all of the books relate to world religions. Her collection includes everything from *The Tao of Pooh* to various editions of the Bible, a couple of Deepak Chopra titles, and an Eckhart Tolle book I also own.

Glancing around the room, I notice the absence of family photos or framed pictures of Daphne with friends. The map and its pins hint at some travel. There isn't much that feels personal to her, nothing to give insight into who she is and what she loves other than books on religion and spirituality.

The memory of our first meeting comes back to me, how easily she quoted the Bible. She's obviously into religion, maybe even a religious fanatic. Could explain her over-zealous appreciation for rules and regulations.

Her reading list hints at someone who's seeking answers. *Maybe she hasn't found what she's looking for.*

With nothing to do but wait, I select a random book off the shelf and bring it over to the chair to read. *Women Who Run with the Wolves: Myths and Stories of the Wild Woman Archetype.*

Hmm. Daphne wants to be a wild woman?

When I open to the beginning, a photo slips out. A younger

Daphne stands with her arms spread wide in a vertical starfish with the Golden Gate bridge behind her. Her hair is cut short, almost boyish. I recognize her eyes and smile, joy illuminating her face. Flipping it over, I don't see a date, but I'm guessing she was in college when the picture was taken.

Daphne who runs with wolves.

The woman in question softly moans and rolls to her side. One of the blankets shifts, its weight dragging it to the floor where it pools on the rug. Sensing the lack of warmth even in her sleep, she curls her body into a tighter ball.

Without thought, I'm up and out of the chair to readjust the blankets to keep her covered.

As I'm standing over her, a knock on the door startles me. I jerk back, bumping my calf against her coffee table's sharp corner.

"Shit," I curse. The expletive hangs in the air, not loud enough to wake the dead, but definitely loud enough to wake a sleeping Daphne.

She sits up, stares at me, and screams.

"Whoa. It's me, Odin." I wave at her while backing up. "Just your friend Odin who brought you soup. In a packet, like you asked for."

My words come out stilted and exaggerated like I'm speaking to someone who doesn't understand English.

Hand to heart, her chest rapidly rises and falls as she tries to regain her composure.

Continued knocking on her door startles us both.

"Daphne? Everything okay?" a female voice asks from the other side. "I thought I heard screaming."

"I'm fine," she replies, so quietly I can barely hear her from a few feet away.

Whoever is outside turns the knob, barely opening the door before repeating, "Daphne?"

Given I'm standing between the visitor and Daphne, I turn to face the door.

"Odin?" Ranger Abbott asks, stepping across the threshold. "What are you doing here?"

"Good question." Daphne's voice sounds like she's trying out for lead frog at the pond.

"I brought groceries." I point at the counter, where my empty crate sits.

Gaia lifts her chin, inhaling deeply. "What's cooking?"

"I can't smell anything." Daphne's now sitting with her feet on the floor and the blankets wrapped around her shoulders.

"Probably for the best." Gaia frowns.

"My great-grandmother's remedy," I explain.

"I didn't ask him to make it," Daphne tells Gaia. "He was here when I woke up."

Way to throw me under the bus.

"Oh really? You sensed someone was sick and came over with a pot full of vinegar and groceries?" Gaia's expression is questioning and more than a little confused.

"The recipe only calls for a quarter cup of apple cider vinegar." That's my defense and I stand by it.

Both women stare at me, waiting for a better explanation.

"I was walking with Patsy in the woods and ran into Daphne, who was clearly unwell. I escorted her home, and when I saw the sad state of her cupboards, I went to get groceries while she napped. We discussed this. Don't you remember?" I direct my question to Daphne.

Her mouth pops open and her forehead wrinkles as she visibly struggles to recall our encounter.

"You and Patsy weren't on the trails again, were you?" Gaia asks. "We've talked about this."

Now is not the time for official reprimands.

"You snooped through my kitchen?" Daphne says in disbelief.

I've admitted as much, so there's no point in denying it. "Guilty."

"And you came back when I was asleep and started cooking? Then . . . what? Watched me sleep?"

When she puts it that way, I sound like a creeper.

Gaia crosses her arms and widens her stance in a posture that tells me she's ready and willing to take control of this situation if I can't explain my way out of it.

"Again, I told you all of this before your nap. How would I know you like noodle soup from a box unless you asked me to get you some?"

"Okay, I vaguely remember, but . . . was that today? I feel like I've been asleep for a hundred years." Daphne scoots to the edge of the cushion and slowly stands, bringing her blanket cape with her as she shuffles over to the kitchen.

Gaia still watches me with a guarded expression.

"Will you tell your boss to stand down, please?"

From her spot near the stove, Daphne lifts the lid on the pot and inhales. "This isn't soup."

"How long has she been acting like this?" Gaia relaxes her stance.

"Since I found her. She seems really spaced out." I don't want to tell her boss I first suspected Daphne was drunk or high.

"I sent her home earlier this afternoon, and I saw her take a couple of Benadryl. Why was she in the woods?"

"No idea," I say, leaving out the details of my conversation with Daphne.

Either she's ignoring us or she's not paying attention, because Daphne doesn't answer for herself. Instead, she stirs the liquid in the pot while inhaling the fragrant steam.

"Daphne?" Gaia walks over and taps her shoulder. "Maybe you should lie down."

"Odin mentioned soup," she mumbles.

"We'll get you some in a minute," I tell her.

Reluctantly, she obeys and returns to the couch.

"It's probably a good thing you're here. I'm not sure she should be left on her own." Gaia's tone switches from suspicious to relieved. "I can come back later if you need to get home."

"Either way. I've got nowhere to be. Happy to stay and keep watch." I force a shrug, hoping she buys my couldn't-care-less-either-way attitude. Without a doubt, Daphne would be fine under Gaia's care, but I'm reluctant to walk away.

What can I do, other than watch her while she sleeps?

I might be a weirdo, but I'm not a creep.

The two women whisper to each other near the couch. Daphne's eyes cut to me, and then she nods. Whatever their discussion, I'm certain I'm the topic.

"Yeah, I can go. Let me set a timer and after an hour, strain what's in the pot into a jar. Add half a cup to the same amount of hot water. Sip as often as needed."

"I want you to stay." Daphne's voice is determined.

"If you're sure. I don't . . ." I leave my sentence unfinished.

We stare at each other. Her hair is disheveled and she's paler than normal, but her eyes are clear. Something passes between us.

"Well, then . . . I'll text later." Gaia stands and shifts her attention between the two of us.

I don't realize she's left until I hear the soft snick of the door closing.

"Soup?" I ask, because I don't know what else to say.

Daphne nods and drags her blanket over her legs.

"One mug o' chicken noodle coming up."

I busy myself with heating water, unwilling to think too hard about what I'm doing here and why it's important I stay.

The microwave dings at the same time someone knocks on the door, startling Daphne. It's busier than a church on Sunday around here.

Cursing as I open it, I growl, "What is this? The state fucking fair?"

Ranger Daniels stands on the narrow porch, holding two glass jars of liquid.

"Oh." He falters and takes a step back when he sees me. "Hey there, Odin."

"Jay." I lean my shoulder against the jamb like I'm security and I'm not allowing him into the club. "What's in the jars?"

He holds up one and stares at it with curiosity. "Olive heard Daphne's sick so she sent over some of my mom's recipe for ramen."

"Interesting. Homemade broth?" Would it be wrong to eat some myself? Daphne asked for rehydrated soup, so she might not even want ramen. She'd probably put saltines in it.

Handing over both containers, he tells me, "She swears it cures everything."

Daphne sneezing behind me declares her presence. I step aside and she stands next to me, taking the jars from my hands.

"Thanks, Jay. And thank Olive for me, too."

His eyes widen. "You look terrible."

"Jeez, thanks. So many compliments from men today. My ego won't know what to do with itself." Hands full, she shuffles back inside the cabin.

"Has she been to the doctor?" Jay asks me.

"I have seasonal allergies and I can hear you," she replies from somewhere near the open kitchen. "Why is everyone worried about me? I'm capable of sneezing without supervision."

"Given I found you in the woods, wandering around in the rain, soaked to the bone, I'm not so sure about that."

Jay's brow furrows and his mouth opens like he's going to ask a follow-up question.

I cut him off with a shake of my head. "Long story. Point is, she's here, dry, and warm now."

She declares, "I'm a grown-ass woman who is perfectly capable of taking care of herself."

Quickly twisting around, I'm met with a dirty look. Facing Jay, I ask, "Did she flip me off behind my back?"

"Yep." He grins. "Good luck with the caregiving. You'd probably have an easier time with a sick skunk."

His mention of skunks reminds me of Daphne's brush with the spray. Her uniform needs to be washed with baking soda, which she doesn't have. Soaking in vinegar might work.

"I'm going to ignore that comparison because you brought me soup, Jay."

"And I'm going to leave before I ruin my good deed. Let us know if you need anything." With a quick wave, he bounds off the steps and jogs over to his vehicle.

"That was nice of him." Daphne struggles to open the Ball jar's metal lid.

"Step away from the ramen and go lie down." I point at the couch and her abandoned nest of blankets.

Other than holding up her hands, she doesn't move.

"Why are you so stubborn?" Exasperated, I cross the room, stopping when I'm on the far side of the kitchen island.

"Why are you so bossy? I appreciate you making sure I got home safely and bringing me groceries, which I will be paying for, but you're under no obligation to play caregiver."

She's exasperating but if she thinks she's going to get rid of me, she's sorely mistaken. Her stubbornness is adorable. Mine is reinforced with steel.

"You're alone and unwell. Since you don't have kin nearby, I'm volunteering. You could be nicer about it."

Using the blanket around her shoulders, she spreads her arms like bat wings. "As you can see, my coworkers are capable of checking in on me. They're close by."

Her point is fair, but I choose to ignore it.

"I've got nothing better to do," I mumble. "Indulge me."

As my confession lingers in an imaginary cartoon bubble above my head, I stare at her, willing her to accept my act of kindness without making it more awkward.

"Fine. Stay," she whispers and then she adds, "My soup is probably cold."

Distracted by Jay's visit, I forgot about the mug in the microwave. After reheating it, I wrap a paper towel around the hot surface and carefully carry it to the coffee table.

"Anything else?"

Eyeing me over her cup, she doesn't respond to my question.

"Okay. I'll be in the kitchen, cooking. Mind if I play music?" I ask, opening the app on my phone.

"Go ahead. Bluetooth speaker is over there. I think I'm going to nap." After taking a few sips, she wipes her mouth with the paper towel and sets the mostly full mug on the table.

"Okay, I'll skip the death metal." I flash a smile.

"Why? I love sleeping to thrashing guitars and screaming. So soothing." Tucking herself in, she snuggles down into the cushions.

Selecting a playlist, I keep the volume low enough to not disturb her.

Cooking brings me peace, distracts me from my own burdens. Once I'm in the flow of prep, I lose track of time until everything is simmering on the stove or baking in the oven. Casting a glance between the stack of dirty dishes and Daphne softly snoring in the living area, I decide to wait until she's awake to clean up.

Now what?

I could leave a note and go.

My good deed is done.

There's really no reason for me to stay.

CHAPTER SIXTEEN
DAPHNE

*M*y alarm didn't go off this morning, and I'm late for a test. In a panic, I run out the door and don't even change out of my pajamas.

Now I'm wandering around a building on campus I've never been inside, desperately trying to find the right classroom. Other students give me weird looks and move out of my way as I run down the halls.

"Crap, crap, crap," I mutter to myself, feeling sweat break out on my forehead and skid down my back, my body shifting between hot and cold. I might even throw up.

I've never missed a final before. My breathing goes shallow and I struggle to inhale deeply. Slowing my pace, I attempt to calm my anxiety.

"Okay, okay. Think. Remember. What class is this for?" I'm speaking aloud to myself in public, but these are desperate times. People stare at me like I've lost my mind.

"Are you all right?" someone asks in a soothing voice.

"It's okay. I'm late for my final in . . ." As I'm talking, one of my front teeth falls out and skitters across the floor.

A hand rests on my arm. "Daphne?"

"Oh, thit," I lisp. My hand flies up to my mouth as my tongue probes the gap.

"Shh. It's okay." The kind man rubs circles on my shoulder. He called me by my name, but I don't think I know him.

"I have to go. I'm late." While I'm attempting to extract myself from this conversation, I realize I no longer know what I'm doing here.

"You're dreaming. Wake up." Rough fingers soothe my forehead.

"Stop hugging me." I don't even know this guy, so I try to push him away. He's heavy and slippery like he's oiled up. Maybe he's a bodybuilder or really sweaty.

"Open your eyes for me, darlin'," a familiar male voice whispers from nearby.

Of course, Odin Hill has to show up while I'm wrestling a human eel.

Hold on a hot minute.

If I am dreaming of Odin calling me darlin', I definitely don't want to ruin it by waking myself up right now. "Shh, sleeping."

"I know," he murmurs, close.

Unwilling to let the fantasy go, I still haven't opened my eyes. I reach for the spot where I think his wrist should be and only grab air.

"Come back, Odin," I whisper, deciding I must be having crazy dreams from too many antihistamines.

Loud clattering noises snap me out of my haze. Sitting up too quickly, I pry my lids open into slits as the room rights itself. I feel like I've been drugged, which I guess I have.

There's no one else in my living area or kitchen. A pile of pots, pans, and dishes covers my counter, though I don't remember cooking anything. The room smells weird, a mix of citrus and vinegar along with rotisserie chicken, which I don't remember buying. *When did I go to the store?*

How much Benadryl did I take?

Standing, I immediately regret listening to whichever part of my mind thought it would be a good idea to be more vertical. As I'm trying to get my bearings, a tall form lumbers down the dark hallway.

"Hey, you're awake," a male voice drawls like it's no big deal he's broken into my home and is robbing me.

I do the one logical thing I can think of: I scream.

Odin steps into the light.

I scream again.

The garbage bag he's holding drops to the floor when he lifts his hands, palms forward. "Shh. You'll wake the whole park."

"What are you doing here?" Shocked, I press my hand to my chest, gripping my sweatshirt in an attempt to shove my heart back through my ribcage. If it were a horse, she'd win the Kentucky Derby with how fast she's galloping.

"I've been here the entire time."

"You have?" Now that he mentions it, I do have a vague memory of him showing up with groceries.

"I said I'd stay, and I kept my word."

Odin Hill being a man of integrity is almost as surprising as him standing in my hallway. It's too much to handle, so I focus on the bag at his feet.

"What's that?"

"Your uniform."

"Why are you stealing my clothes?"

He balks. "I'm not. You got skunk spray on it when you sat on the log."

I wrinkle my nose. "Ew."

"I was going to put them in the wash, but then you woke up."

"How long was I out? What time is it?" All I know is it's dark outside. Could be six, could be midnight.

Without checking the time on his phone, he answers, "Around eight. You've been asleep on and off for four hours."

"I took a double dose of antihistamines. I think I'm okay now . . . maybe. Unless this is a hallucination."

He stares at me a beat and then at the floor. "You were talking in your sleep."

I cringe. "Please tell me I didn't say anything embarrassing. Lie if you have to."

"No, not while you were sleeping." A glimpse of a smile tugs at his mouth. "Earlier you were kind of rambling and disoriented. I thought you were feverish."

"I don't want to know."

"You were funny." He chuckles.

"That's not reassuring." I close my eyes and try to remember anything from this afternoon. I come up blank. "Haven't you ever taken antihistamines? They really knock you out."

"I'm not really familiar with medications."

"Lucky you. Never get a headache?"

"Sure, but I grew up using the old remedies."

Now I remember the steaming pot on my stove and the cup of tart liquid. "Like the potion you made earlier?"

"Potion?" He laughs. "No magic, just some plant-based medicine."

I eye him before turning to retreat to the kitchen. "I had a brief Wiccan phase, and that sure sounds like herbal magic to me."

He follows behind. "Really? Did you dance around in your nightgown under a full moon?"

"No. Those are pagans. Easy to confuse the two," I tell him dryly.

"Right, of course." He cuts around me to get to the stove.

"Is it ready?" I ask as he removes the lid from the pot.

"Needs to cool a little, and then I'll fill a mug for you."

"What's in it?" Inhaling, I sniff the air as best I can with a stuffed nose. "I promise to not steal the recipe."

"Lots of good stuff."

"Smells like Cletus's coffee. I'm guessing there's some molasses and apple cider vinegar."

"What's he doing drinking the bowel blaster?"

I snort and try to cover it with a cough. "That's a terrible name."

"Terrible, yet accurate. I didn't invent it, and neither did he. The old-timers have been drinking similar brews for generations, long before we had over-the-counter relief. A lot of folks can't afford health insurance or don't trust modern medicine, so they still use the old ways."

"How do you know all this stuff?" The adrenaline shock of finding Odin in my house is wearing off, and I'm tired down into my bones.

I shuffle over to my couch and rearrange the blankets over my lap, pulling them up to my chin as I slump down into the pillows. I don't remember bringing either out to the living room and wonder how much snooping he's done under the guise of being helpful.

"I learned from my mother, who learned from hers and so on back a few generations. My great-grandmother is still alive, and I've been able to study with her. Still perfecting the recipe."

"Won't she give it to you?"

"Nannie Ida doesn't write anything down. It's all in her head with adjustments made on the fly as she's cooking."

"What if she forgets?" Great-grandmother? The woman has to be old.

"Then we're all screwed and the knowledge is gone forever. Hence why I'm working with her to collect all of her secrets. She learned from her mother, who was one of the original granny-women in these mountains. They knew how to do everything."

"I've never heard of granny women. Isn't that kind of . . ."

"Redundant?" He smirks. "Yes, I know, but that's what folks called 'em. Some might say they're healers who practiced herbal magic mixed with pragmatic Southern stubbornness. Throw in poverty and the fear of God, and you've got yourself a real Appalachian granny."

I'm intrigued. "She kind of sounds like a witch."

"Nannie Ida wouldn't approve of that label. No matter how cool it might be to younger women, in her day, it was a slur. She'd tell you she's only using what the mountains provide."

"Fascinating." Now I'm even more curious about the brew simmering away on my rarely used stove.

"Ready to try some?"

Enthusiastically, I nod.

He fixes me a cup and watches while I take my first sip. At first taste, it's both bitter and sweet, sour enough to pucker my cheeks. A heat from the spices lingers in my mouth and burns going down my throat. As soon as it appears, some other ingredient numbs away the discomfort.

"I wouldn't call it delicious, but it is good. I can feel my sinuses clearing up already." To prove my point, I inhale through my nose.

An expression I haven't seen before flashes across his face: pride.

"Are you hungry? Jay dropped off his mom's ramen, or I can make you another cup of noodles?"

"I'm good for now." I continue drinking the magical liquid while trying not to stare at Odin. It is strongly possible that I am still asleep.

"You seem better now." He stands behind the unoccupied armchair. "I'll get going."

There's no reason for him to stay. He's been here for hours and hours. I can't ask him to hang around.

"You probably need to get home and take care of your pets."

Even so, I don't want him to leave. As odd as it is to have him here, I feel comfortable with him in my house.

"Eh, they'll be all right." He lingers behind the chair.

"Thanks for cooking for me. What do I owe you for the groceries?"

Dismissing my question with a wave of his hand, he smiles. "Nothing. I enjoyed helping."

I may still be dreaming.

CHAPTER SEVENTEEN
ODIN

I'm on my own today and decide to switch up my routine, and take a trail that heads north from the loop road. This route leads me past the historic buildings clustered together in the open spaces of the park. None of them are original to this site; each has been relocated for optimum historic charm—a lie formed from pieces of truth.

This false narrative has always bugged me, turning a community into a zoo for tourists to come enjoy as a slice of real Appalachian charm.

Hundreds of families—thousands of people—were displaced from this area when the park was formed. Structures deemed unworthy were torn down, dismantled, and erased. Sure, there are plenty of period buildings still scattered around the mountains, some still in the same families that homesteaded the land where they sit. Like my place, these homes remain closed to the public.

Despite a successful foraging experience, I find myself crankier than when I set out on my hike. The whole reason I came out here was to gather more mushrooms for Ida and Lena to make a new batch of tinctures. Nannie asked and I wasn't about to turn her down.

The leaves are beginning to turn so the foliage peepers cram the trails and jam the single-lane road. I don't know how they stand the crowds. Enjoying nature isn't possible if you're surrounded by people and cars. Misses the entire point of losing oneself in the wilderness.

I'm not fit for other humans today. Deciding to take the shortest route back to my truck, I leave the trail and walk alongside the road.

My foul mood has nothing to do with the fact that it has been almost a week since I hung out with Daphne. I assume she's well and recovered.

A white NPS SUV passes me, slows, and pulls to the shoulder a few yards ahead. After the bear destroyed her car, Daphne said she'd be driving an official vehicle until she could get something else, and I quicken my pace, hopeful she's behind the wheel. The passenger side window is down when I approach and I lean in, expecting to see her face.

"Afternoon, Odin. Mind if we have a talk?" Griffin flashes a friendly smile.

I don't mask my disappointment as my mood sours further. "Guess not."

"Hop in."

Griffin Lee is probably a nice person, but the last I knew of him, he was a class clown who never took anything seriously. Now he's a ranger and law enforcement within park boundaries. Someone even decided it was a good idea to let him carry a gun—not that I'm saying he would be irresponsible with a firearm. I'm sure he passed all of the tests with flying colors.

Life is strange. If I'm proof that people can change, I guess nothing should surprise me about anybody else.

"How's the farming?" he asks.

"Fine. Harvest is almost over and most of the field is getting prepared for winter." I scratch behind my ear. "How's the ranger business?"

"Good. Busy now, but come November things will really quiet

down." He glances out the window and back at me. "Must be nice to have some more free time on your hands."

I nod, confused as to the point of this chat.

"I know we grew up together and share kin in common, Odin." Bringing up family doesn't comfort me. "It was important for me to be the one to question you."

"Does your aunt marrying my uncle even make us kin? Being cousins through marriage won't change anything, will it?"

"Depends on you."

"Care to elaborate?" I refuse to give him a confession when I'm not certain of my crime.

"Want to tell me what's in the backpack?" He points to the floor by my feet.

"What do you think I have in there?" Yes, I'm being an asshole, but I'm also curious. I'm guessing he has no idea.

"Come on, cut me a break and open it." He rests his elbow on the steering wheel as he twists to give me his full attention. "The sooner we can be honest, the quicker this can be resolved."

If Griffin were a different man, a Hill instead of a Lee, I'd think he might be open to a bribe. Everyone has a price, and I wonder what it would take for him to look the other way.

"Are you going to arrest me?"

"Hopefully not." He doesn't sound optimistic.

"Issue me a citation?" Definitely a possibility. "Fine me?"

"Open the bag."

Lifting the pack, I rest it on the console between us and challenge him with my eyes. "Go ahead. See for yourself."

"Stubborn as always." Muttering, he reaches for the zippers at the top. "Nothing in here is going to bite me, is it?"

"Really? You're bringing up the kitten? How old was I? Four? Five?" He's being too dramatic about this whole ridiculous situation, so I unzip the bag for him. "Look."

"Please don't let it be pot," he whispers before peering inside.

I have to admit, I am still shocked to be sitting in Griffin's official NPS vehicle, being questioned about illegal activities on federal land. Seriously never saw this moment coming.

"What the fuck?" I jerk back, pulling the pack with me. "Why would I be out here with a bag filled with drugs?"

"Are you growing or dealing marijuana within park boundaries?" His voice is so ridiculously serious, I laugh.

"Jesus, Griffin." Dipping a hand inside, I gently pull out a handful of the bag's contents and show him. "They're mushrooms. Fungi. They're not even the psychotropic kind."

"I know what a turkey tail looks like." He widens the opening and sniffs.

"Why the hell would you think I had drugs?" I carefully return the cream and brown striped, fan-shaped mushrooms to the backpack.

"We've had reports." He doesn't make eye contact. Instead, he twists his head to stare out the driver's side window. "People don't all come to the park to commune with nature in the ways you'd think. We have our own microcosm of crimes. Unfortunately, being a national park doesn't mean we exist in an enchanted land of happiness."

"Are you telling me the animals don't talk and help clean tiny houses for vertically challenged miners?" I scoff.

"For the record, I didn't think you were walking around with a bag o' weed."

I laugh at his phrasing. "You could've asked me directly instead of acting out this law enforcement shakedown."

"Better family than a stranger."

"We're not blood kin." Changing my mind, I shake my head. "Never mind. I guess I owe you a debt of gratitude."

"Nah. We're good. I'll clear the report."

"Want to weigh the mushrooms? Make sure I'm within my personal limits?"

"Why? Are you planning on selling those?" He eyes me with suspicion.

I have a quick, internal debate about lying to my "cousin" and decide to tell the truth.

"Maybe I'm hoarding them all for myself."

"What are you going to do with so many mushrooms?"

"Honestly?"

"Sure, let's go with that for a change."

I don't miss his sarcasm. "I'm freeze-drying them for medicinal purposes."

"Seriously?" His eyes hold doubt.

"One hundred percent. Mushroom extracts can heal whatever ails you."

He purses his lips. "Not sure about that."

"Suit yourself." I pat the bag. "Appalachian grannies have been using fungi to address health issues for generations."

"You know there are laws about foraging on federal land for commercial purposes."

"Is there any regulation about gathering mushrooms that aren't on park property?"

"Not that I know of. My jurisdiction doesn't extend past the boundaries."

"Good to know."

"You collect these on private property?"

"Pretty confident I did."

"Well, that's between you and the owners."

I give him a blunt nod. "Then let's say that's where I found them. Has anyone thought about buying some orange spray paint and creating a clear boundary line between what's federal land and what is private?"

"That sounds like something I'd come up with." He chuckles.

"You're welcome for the tip."

"I'm sorry I thought you were the Pablo Escobar of the Smokies."

"In a weird way, I'm flattered you believed me capable."

"You've never given yourself enough credit for everything you've done. Some folks would give their front teeth to be a fancy chef in the big city. Fame, money, traveling the world—"

"All meaningless if you're miserable."

"Guess we have different definitions of the word. I'd rather be unhappy in first class than in a middle seat that doesn't recline at the back of the plane next to the bathroom."

"That's pretty specific, but you make a good point." I finish zipping the bag closed. "We all good here?"

"Yep, as long as everyone is observing the rules and regulations of the park."

"Deal."

"Want a lift back to the cabin? Or wherever you're going?"

"I'll take a ride to pick up my truck."

After a few moments of comfortable silence, I ask, "Can you tell me who filed the report on me? Visitor? Park staff? I'd like to know who's spreading these rumors."

"There wasn't an official report. More of a concern about suspicious activity."

"And my accuser came to you directly?" I'm making a list in my head like a less generous Santa.

"I'm not going to tell you. No point since they were under the wrong impression."

Pretending he answered my question, I continue my inquiry. "Was this in an official capacity or as a friend?"

"Can we let it go?" He gives me a sidelong glance.

"Am I sitting in an official government vehicle, subject to search of my personal belongings?"

I swear he pales.

"Don't put it like that. We're having a friendly conversation. Better me than one of the other rangers. Not everyone would give you the benefit of the doubt."

He's basically admitting another one of the rangers has a gripe with me . . . interesting. Wonder who it could be.

"Meaning guns and drug dogs in a raid at dawn? Jeez, thanks for saving me the embarrassment of being dragged out of bed naked."

Cringing, he gazes out the window. "Thanks for the visual."

"You brought that on yourself with your own imagination."

"I'm just doing my job." He shifts his attention back to me. "Maybe if you weren't such a weirdo, people might hold you in better regard."

"What people think about me is their own damn business, not mine."

"Suit yourself." He offers a shrug. "We're here."

My truck sits alone in the lot at the trailhead.

"Can't say it's been enjoyable, but it's been memorable."

He grabs my arm before I hop out of the vehicle. "Hey, don't hold a grudge. We're all overlooking your walks with Patsy."

"Very magnanimous of you. We stay off the official trails the majority of the time, even though there's nothing specific about pigs in the park. The wild hogs are wreaking more destruction around here than she ever could."

"Agree. There are also guys out here with their guns, all jacked up on chew and Dew, excited about shooting a boar. They may not verify Patsy's pedigree before firing."

His words unsettle me. "Okay, okay. You made your point."

"Good." He flashes his classic smug grin.

My own smile is less enthusiastic and less toothy. "Yeah, thanks."

"Any time. Don't be a stranger."

"Right," I say, distracted.

The phrase reminds me of Gaia's words the morning of Daphne's bear incident, the day after she asked me about my backpack.

I have a very good idea who's likely behind Griffin's interrogation. Might be time to have a conversation with Ranger Baum and set her straight.

As far as she knows, I run a small farm on some family land where I grow weird vegetables. All of that is true, but it's not the entire truth.

Does Green Valley need another orange carrot or red radish at the farmers' market? No. A green bean is a green bean, unless it's purple when raw and magically switches to verdant green when cooked. Magic. Fucking. Beans.

That's why I farm as well as forage. Why have a plain radish with a red skin and a white interior when you can have one swirled with both colors throughout? Purple carrots with bright orange middles. Japanese turnips that go from spicy to sweet as the seasons change. Daikon radishes that will make both your mouth and your eyes water. Tiny Thai chilis red as a stop sign and scalding with concentrated heat. Life is too short for boring, uninspired food when nature is more creative than we could ever imagine.

Foraging is more interesting. An adventure.

Back to the land in the most primitive way.

Generations before white settlers claimed land in these mountains, Cherokee lived among the hills and valleys, foraging and hunting, living off the land while respecting Mother Earth. They understood the cycles of life and death, fertile and fallow, when to plant and when to harvest.

There is wisdom in waiting and reward in trusting the timing.

CHAPTER EIGHTEEN
DAPHNE

I'm out of sorts, living in a constant state of frustration. Everything makes me bristle.

Could be PMS, but I think it's deeper than hormones.

At the end of work yesterday, Griffin told me he spoke to Odin and confirmed he wasn't doing anything illegal. The turkey tail mushrooms in his possession were well under the daily limit.

Why anyone would want an entire backpack full of fungus is beyond me. No less strange than apples.

Nothing about that man makes sense.

He took care of me when I took too many antihistamines and also smelled like a disgruntled skunk.

I'm bothered I was wrong about him being up to no good, and that bothers me.

I need to change the channel in my brain. Some people might meditate or practice yoga or go for a run to work out the bad energy. I am not among those people.

Tired of being in my own head, I set my alarm extra early Friday night so I can have some time before my Saturday shift. After I make tea in my travel mug, I head out on foot from my cabin, following a familiar route into the woods. As the white steeple appears between the trees, I exhale some of the tightness in my chest. Whenever I'm struggling, I return to the chapel to clear my mind.

This time I triple-check that the door is closed behind me before slipping into a pew.

Inside, time pauses as a quiet peace settles over me. I bow my head and breathe.

Unbidden, the words of the Lord's Prayer flow through my mind. Like a mantra, I repeat the lines from memory. When I get to the part about forgiving others and ourselves for our trespasses, I pause.

Our debts. Our sins. Our mistakes. Our ignorance. I often substitute another word for trespass because I've always imagined the most straightforward definition of unlawfully being on private property and felt it didn't apply to me.

Until today.

"Haha. Thanks for being obvious."

Me sitting in this church, using it as my personal sanctuary isn't quite the same as breaking the law, but it could be considered against the rules. I'm not doing any harm by sitting here.

Neither are Odin and Patsy, no more so than the donkey, and less than many tourists who clomp along the trails.

Beyond the obvious interpretation, I shouldn't let some random, unsubstantiated information on the internet change my opinion of Odin. We all have a past and actions we'd prefer to forget.

"Okay, I get it. Message received. Thanks."

As much as he's the town weirdo, I doubt Odin thinks he has conversations with the divine in an empty old chapel.

Feeling better, I fold my hands in prayer and say, "Amen."

This time there's no echo, no open door when I look up.

I pick up my mug and take a moment to listen to the stillness, confirming to myself that I imagined the second amen last time.

* * *

After work on Sunday, I find Odin Hill sitting on my porch steps looking like he could throw thunderbolts with his eyes.

I put the SUV's engine in park while we lock stares through the windshield. My heart does its trout-out-of-water impression and my pulse kicks into fight-or-flight mode. He looks angry and intense, slightly dangerous . . . which only makes him sexier.

His messy hair is loose, not contained by a cap or ponytail holder. That, combined with his untamed beard, gives him a wild appearance, and I think I'm more nervous about him than I was about the bear.

He doesn't move to stand. Simply sits there, waiting for me with his broad shoulders hunched and his hands clasped between his knees.

After a few moments of staring at each other, me feeling more and more like I'm trapped in this vehicle, he lifts up a paper bag from beside him. "I brought a peace offering."

If either of us should be apologizing, it's probably me. I'm the one who ratted on him to my colleague. I'm the one with the suspicious mind.

"You can't stay in there forever, Daphne." He bends his finger toward himself. "Come on out."

Alarm bells go off in my body as I contemplate fleeing. Instead, I find myself unbuckling my seatbelt and opening the door. Once out the car, I hesitate near the hood. "How are you?"

"Good. You?" He doesn't smile.

"All's well. Allergies are better. Happy it stopped raining. Work's been busy. Doing more school programs. New bear attacks remain at zero." My words crowd together as I try to fill the space of his silence. "Everything is A-OK."

"That's . . ." He doesn't finish his sentence.

"Good?"

His head bobs. "Can we talk?"

"Okay." I remain where I am.

"Maybe inside?" He stands, rising to his full height. "If you don't mind."

Do I? I check in with myself. If we're going to have a come-to-Jesus conversation, I'd prefer it not be out in the open with a potential audience of witnesses.

Silently, I pass him on the stairs, and he waits for me to open the door. I turn the key in the lock and motion for him to go ahead.

"Odin?" I touch his arm.

He stares down at where my hand rests on his forearm.

I wait until he lifts his gaze to mine before speaking. "I owe you an apology. I'm sorry I asked Griffin to investigate you. It was before we met in the woods and you took care of me. I don't want you to think I was ungrateful for your kindness."

The fire in his eyes dims. "Thank you for being honest."

CHAPTER NINETEEN
ODIN

I wasn't anticipating her apologizing and owning up to what she did, nor was I prepared for her gentle touch on my arm. Hesitant yet firm, I believe it's the first time she's touched me, not counting the finger jabs when she was hopped up on Benadryl. If I'm being fair, I know I shouldn't hold her actions that day against her.

Once we're inside, she stands in the middle of the room like a doe in a field. Alert and uneasy, she's watching me, waiting for me to say or do something.

"Do you want to sit?" She points at her chair.

"Sure." I place the bag down on the table first. "Are you going to stand?"

"No." Shaking her head, she takes a seat on the far corner of the couch.

"We need to clear up a few misconceptions."

"I apologized."

"I know, and I appreciate it." I give her a small smile. My earlier anger is already fading. "How much do you remember about our interaction on the trail?"

She grimaces. "Not a lot. Sorry."

"Do you recall any conversation, or the accusations you made?"

Her fingers play with the end of her ponytail while she stares out her window. "I'm guessing I asked you what you were doing off-trail with a pig in the rain."

"All of the above. You also said you knew I was committing, and I quote, 'nefarious deeds' within the park."

Folding her legs beneath her, she faces me. "Sounds like me."

"Do you want to know the truth?"

"Griffin says you were foraging for mushrooms. Nothing illegal if you keep within the limits."

"Do you believe him?"

"Yes, but I still have questions." She lifts her shoulders.

"So do I. Given the circumstances, I think I get to go first."

With a sheepish smile, she says, "That's fair."

"Did you tell Ranger Lee you suspected I had drugs in my possession?"

"No."

"Hinted at it?"

"He may have interpreted my words to infer I meant illegal substances, but I never said those words directly." Glancing out the window, she worries her bottom lip with her teeth.

I untangle her sentence in my head. "I'm not a drug dealer, nor do I use drugs. The last thing I need is folks around here gossiping about me being either of the above. There are people who want to see me fail because they expect the worst."

"Okay." Her voice is barely a whisper. "I get that."

Her meek reaction causes me to catch my tone. I sound stern, cold. "I'm not angry."

"Are you sure?" A dry laugh follows her question.

"I am. I swear." I change the subject before we get into a full-blown discussion of my past and this conversation becomes an NA meeting. "Back to the foraging. Believe it or not, I've studied the

Code of Federal Regulations. I'm fully aware of the rules and statutes."

"Impressive." I can tell she's being honest and not sarcastic by the light in her eyes. Ranger Baum is a type-A rule-lover.

"I knew you'd like it. Within the document, near about page seven, there is a specific line about not foraging near motorways or nature trails. See the contradiction? I'm allowed to forage, but not within 200 feet of a trail, and I'm supposed to stay on the trail."

Her brow furrows. "That isn't very clear."

"Not at all."

"Leaves room for interpretation." She leans forward.

"It does. Now, in my mind, I place wild cultivation underneath the umbrella of foraging. Am I plowing and planting seeds? No. Am I introducing invasive species like kudzu that will choke out the native plants? Nope. Am I clear-cutting forests to turn into lumber at the local mill? No."

"You lost me."

"If we're going to move forward as friends, or whatever, I think I need to explain a few things."

"Like why you went hiking with a pack full of apples?"

"I didn't bring them with me."

She unfolds her legs and plants them on the floor.

"There's a wild apple orchard not too far from the Cooper Road ranger station. Planted before the park existed."

"No there isn't. I'd know if there were." Her chin lifts with her certainty.

"We can make a bet if you like losin'."

"I think I know the park where I'm a ranger."

"And I know there's an old, fallow orchard that's still producing fruit near the Cooper trail. I've been picking them all season to make cider."

"You know I can't support illegally obtained apples." She digs in, arms crossed.

There's something wrong with me because I find her obstinance a turn on. "Not illegal."

"According to section 2.6 of the code, those apples are protected from commercial usage."

"Actually, they're not, because they're not mentioned."

"You have no right to use them for commercial gain."

"Didn't say I was."

"The federal—"

I cut her off. "The federal government is comprised of the people for the people, yes? Acting on behalf of citizen taxpayers, correct? Feel free to nod in agreement."

She glares instead.

"I'm a citizen. I also pay my taxes—local, state, and federal. I'm not stealing rocks or plants or archeological treasures. The apples aren't a native species, nor are they technically on national park land."

"They could be feeding the bears, deer, squirrels, or birds. Even the wild boar."

"All true, and I leave enough behind for all of them to enjoy. Anything on the ground belongs to them."

She squints at me in judgment. "You must've been on the debate team in high school."

A bark of a laugh escapes my mouth. "Not even close."

Keeping her eyes narrowed, she twists her mouth. "What's that supposed to mean?"

"I wasn't exactly studious in school. Not a real joiner or team player."

"Hmm. Your talents were wasted. You should've been a lawyer."

I snort. "Maybe I only like arguing for argument's sake."

"I've never heard of anything more pointless." Her ire colors her cheeks a nice shade of pink.

"Like fighting about apples?" I chuckle.

She flops back into the cushions on the couch. "You win."

"Want to see what's in the bag?"

She sits up as I remove the two green, glass bottles from the brown paper.

"It's a hard cider I've been brewing. I think this batch has the perfect combination of tart, sweet, and alcohol level."

"Home-brewed alcohol? Like moonshine?" she asks, her fascination clear on her face.

"Sorry to disappoint you, but there's no still involved."

With a shy smile, she accepts the bottle I hold out to her.

"Not going to try my cider?" I focus on unscrewing the cap on my own bottle instead of her face. "I promise it's not poisoned."

Hesitantly, she takes a sip.

As I watch her lips press against the opening, I feel a familiar stirring in my body. My dick thickens.

After swallowing, she smacks her lips. "It's both crisp and refreshing."

Her tongue licks the corners of her mouth, which doesn't help the intensifying situation in my jeans.

She waves her hand in front of my face. "What are you staring at?"

"Nothing." I shrug and take a sip of the cider.

"Tomorrow you can show me the location of this supposed orchard."

"I can?" I lift my eyebrows in doubt. When I came over here to talk to her, my plan was to use the apples and the cider to deter her from further snooping and thus protect the filbert grove. I didn't anticipate her wanting to see the orchard for herself.

"You will."

"Will I? I think my schedule is packed, mostly with semi-legal and wicked activities. Not sure I can fit in another appointment."

Her stern look returns. I like it more than I'll ever admit.

"Okay. Quit plotting my death." Turning my palms toward her in surrender, I laugh. "I'm kidding. What day do you want to lose the bet?"

"Tomorrow morning work for you? We can meet at the trailhead."

I nod, allowing a slow, satisfied grin to spread across my face. "I'll be there by 7:30."

"Why are you smiling?"

"Because when you lose, I know what I'm asking for."

"I never agreed to your bet. I don't gamble." Her jaw locks tight. Stubborn.

Instead of infuriated, I'm charmed.

I give her a grin. "Technicalities."

My smile fails to disarm her. "Are you always this infuriating?"

If she only knew. "That's a matter of opinion."

"What's the general consensus?"

"I'm a charming asshole. Some people even agree I'm good-looking."

The bright pink on her cheeks deepens. If she were a cartoon character, I'd expect flames to burst from her head.

"Insufferable," she mutters.

"Heard that one too. I prefer inscrutable, if I get a vote." My mouth slides into a smile.

"For the record, we don't have a bet. This is an ongoing investigation."

"Acting as law enforcement now? I thought you ran the educational programs." I tease. "I thought we came to an agreement. I'm not your enemy."

"Never said you were."

"Not in words, but the way you acted says otherwise."

"I take my job seriously. I have a duty to protect the park from damage." Her eyes challenge me.

I almost expect her to suggest pistols at dawn. "And I respect the hell out of that."

We sit in silence for a minute or two, each of us lost in our thoughts. I make up my mind to be straight with her.

"Daphne?" I lean forward in the chair and rest my elbows on my knees.

"Yes?"

"While I enjoy sparring with you, I'd like to call a truce." What I mean is more of a capitulation. "I don't like most folks and try to avoid having to spend time around them. Normally, I don't give a fuck what people think or say about me. I can't control whatever stories they make up to fit their own agendas or world views. You're different. For some reason, it would bother me if you thought poorly of me." My sincerity makes me feel vulnerable, something I try to avoid.

She places her bottle on the floor near her feet. "I don't. I promise."

I want to believe her.

Our eyes lock, and I see nothing but genuine truth in her expression.

Not used to this new openness, I stand to leave. "7:30 then?"

"I'm looking forward to it." She rises from the couch at the same time I reach for her bottle on the floor.

The action brings us within a foot of each other, and we both freeze. I don't think either of us is breathing.

I've already laid my cards on the table. *What am I waiting for?* Cupping her face with one hand, my fingers thread through her thick, dark hair near her ear. I pause for a moment, drinking in the softness of her skin and the freckles across her cheeks.

"You thought I was going to kiss you in the woods," I whisper.

Eyes on mine, she nods, lips parted, waiting.

"I didn't think you were serious." I wait a beat for her to respond, to tell me she didn't mean it.

She swallows but doesn't speak.

As I used the hand still tangled in her hair to tip her head back, my mouth brushes against hers.

The lightest touch flips a switch inside me and I pull her closer, wanting more contact.

A soft moan escapes her lips and she melts against me, her hands gripping my jacket before slipping underneath to my T-shirt.

I didn't know how much I craved her touch until this moment.

I didn't know how much she could affect me with a single kiss.

CHAPTER TWENTY
DAPHNE

*I*f you'd told me this morning when I woke up that I'd be kissing Odin Hill, demigod farmer before the sun set, I'd have laughed right in your face.

I might've even called you crazy.

Now I'd say you're an oracle.

The way his large hands grip and pull me close, how he moans when our tongues slide against each other—it all combines to make me feel like an irresistible siren.

I want him to crash his ship on my shore and never leave.

Who needs a job, or food, or even air when Odin's mouth is sending sparks of lightning through my body?

Unfortunately, my lungs disagree, and I find myself breathless. He must feel the same because his chest rises and falls rapidly against my breasts. Breaking away from my mouth, his lips trail along my jaw and down my neck. His beard tickles as he traces kisses along my skin. Lifting his head, he brings his gaze to meet mine.

"Daphne . . ." He whispers my name like a prayer, sweeping his thumb against my cheek.

His ability to form an actual word is impressive. All my brain can come up with is a long *wow* with a bunch of extra syllables and vowels. Thankfully, I don't make this sound out loud.

I feel cherished, honored by his touch. It takes some restraint to resist yanking his mouth back to mine and devouring him.

With a groan, he releases me and drags a hand through his hair. His long exhalation is slow and controlled, as if he's trying to regain his composure.

That's a terrible idea; all I want is for him to continue ravishing me.

Someone knocks on my door, breaking us out of our lust-filled bubble.

"Go away," I yell. Whoever is out there is dead to me. "I'm not home."

Odin chuckles before leaning down to give me a chaste peck. "I think you've given yourself away. Should've kept quiet and maybe they'd have believed you."

Dammit.

"Daphne? It's Gaia. Are you okay?"

This is not the moment for a friendly chat with my boss. I stare at the unlocked door and wait for her to open it.

"I'm fine. Just out of the shower. Can I come find you in a couple minutes?"

"Sure. Nothing urgent. Wanted to see if you'd like to grab dinner."

I don't know if I do. Staring at Odin, I silently hope he'll shake his head no or give me some sign I'll be busy for the rest of the evening.

He gives me nothing, standing stock-still.

"Okay. I'll be ready soon," I tell Gaia through the closed door.

Odin's shoulders slump a tiny fraction, and I immediately feel like I've made the wrong choice.

"I could tell her no," I tell him quietly at the same time he murmurs, "Or you could have dinner with me."

We both chuckle.

His hand tugs through his waves. "Sounds like a plan."

I like Gaia, but I'm going to have to cancel. "I'll text her."

"Okay. Do you want my address? You'll need to use the maps app on your phone because the road is hard to find. I've driven by it in the dark and it's my own house."

"Um . . . you mean dinner at your house?"

"Changed your mind?"

"No. I just don't have a car anymore, remember?" I form my hands into claws and growl in a bad impression of a bear.

He laughs. "Right, of course. You can ride with me, then I'll bring you home after."

Or I could stay the night. Should I sneak my toothbrush into my purse? Wait, I don't even have a purse. I could put it in my pocket. No, too visible. My bra might work, but what if we're making out and he goes for my breasts and discovers my toothbrush? That would be weird.

This is why women carry purses. Bringing a backpack to dinner is strange.

"Daphne?" His voice breaks through my inner panic.

"Sorry." I glance down and see the olive green of my work pants. "I'd like to change first."

"Sure. I can wait outside again." He steps through the door before I say anything more.

I want to tell him to stay out of sight, but I realize I don't know how long he sat on my porch earlier or who saw him. My instinct is to hide him from my coworkers, though why would it matter if they know I'm hanging out with him? Am I embarrassed to be seen with Odin? I should probably examine that impulse another time.

Wondering if I have time for a quick shower, I quickly jog to my bedroom. Deciding I do, I gather a pair of jeans and a black turtleneck out of my dresser. Nothing says *let's make out again* like a well-covered neck. I replace the sweater with a V-neck white tee. Clean underwear and the one lacy bralette I own go on top of the pile of clothes in my arms. If this were a movie, I'd have a matching set of lingerie to slip into. However, this is real life. If I squint, the pink lace matches the floral pattern on my underwear, and does it really matter anyway? Do men care? Also, am I being presumptuous in imagining Odin seeing my undergarments?

I can't believe we went from opposite sides of a fight to betting on the existence of an orchard to kissing in less than an hour. I've never wanted to rip a man's clothes off from a single kiss. Most of my previous experiences have been . . . *nice* with a certain warm-up period of getting to know each other, almost methodical in their predictability. Not Odin's kiss. He's a match and my body is kindling. *Whoosh! Engulfed in lust in less than a minute.*

With my head still spinning, I have no idea what to anticipate. We could be married in a week or not speaking by Thanksgiving.

Marriage. *Ha!*

Reminds me I need to return Isaac's text to congratulate him. With school visits, bear attacks, allergies, and playing amateur detective, I haven't had time to reply.

My shower is speedy. I don't have time to wash my hair or shave any bits—good thing I took care of all the important grooming yesterday.

I'm done and dressed in record time. With a sigh, I leave my toothbrush in its cup on the bathroom counter.

When we were teenagers, Isaac used to tell me the best way to be happy was to have low or zero expectations. At the time, I thought he was being dramatic and kind of depressing. Dreams and goals were what I clung to as we navigated our way into adulthood.

Again and again, over the years, I've learned the truth of his advice.

Outside, I find Odin sitting on the steps, chatting with Gaia.

When he hears the door snick shut, he stands and faces me, turning his back to her.

With wide eyes and lips pressed tight together, she silently yet clearly communicates her thoughts on this tableau.

"Odin said you have other plans tonight." She grins before he can turn his head and catch her smug expression. "We can totally reschedule for another time. In fact, we should have a girls' night soon. Watch a movie or something."

In spite of her friendly tone, I'm suspicious. We've never hung out just the two of us. *Girls' night?* She sounds like Kacey, which is hysterical because Gaia's about as girly as I am.

"Uh, sure."

"Sounds good. Nice to see you." She addresses Odin. "Have fun!"

None of us move to leave. We can't descend the stairs because she's blocking them.

"Shall we go?" I step down off the porch.

Gaia catches on and moves out of the way.

I glance around. "Where's the van?"

He points to a very nice black truck at the end of the road. "I didn't need it today."

"It's kind of fancy," I joke.

"Like my dog?" He opens my door for me.

"Exactly."

"Beats the van. When you see Patsy, don't tell her it kind of smells like a pigsty in there."

It hits me: I'm going to his house. Goin' to the holler. I feel like I'm being invited to a secret lair.

The reality is he lives down a dirt road in a log cabin surrounded by fields, gardens, and greenhouses. Unless he has a secret bunker, he really is a farmer and not a supervillain.

CHAPTER TWENTY-ONE
ODIN

*A*fter a brief tour of the gardens and greenhouses, I lead Daphne up to the porch. The reality of what I've done hits me. Not only did I kiss her, I casually invited her over to dinner like it's something I do all the time. The opposite is true. I can't think of the last time I had someone over for a meal. I don't even feed the cousins who load the produce for the farmers' markets and food pantries.

Something happened in her cabin. One minute we were arguing about the location of my orchard and the next, I was kissing her like a desperate man, starved for human contact. In some ways, I guess that's the case, but I'd never before pined for a woman's touch. Now I can't stop thinking about kissing Daphne. The drive back here was one long torturous exercise in keeping my hands to myself and my eyes on the road.

She's standing near the porch railing, giving me a funny look, and I realize I haven't said anything in the last minute or so. Could have been longer.

"You okay?" Her teeth worry her bottom lip. "If you've changed your mind . . ."

I rest my hand on the back of my neck and give her a slow, shy smile. "I'm out of practice. I should invite you inside and offer you something to drink."

"I'd like that." Crossing the short distance between us, she rises on her toes and tentatively touches her lips to mine. It's a balm to my nerves and an invitation.

Kissing her is easy, effortless. If I quiet my brain and let my body's instincts take over, I'm fine. She twines her arms around my shoulders, and I rest my hands at the dip of her lower back. We have a few moments of awkwardness. Our teeth bump and we're not quite sure where our noses should go, but we laugh our way through until the clumsiness passes.

Once again breathless, we break apart, our chests heaving, and my heartbeat throbbing.

"Right. Okay. Dinner." With my thumb, I trace the rosy swell of her bottom lip.

I wasn't thinking when I asked her to come here for dinner. If I had been, I probably would've considered taking her out. It never occurred to me to go somewhere else. Where would I have taken her, anyway? Genie's for fried chicken? I don't go to any of the other restaurants in the area, mostly because I'm a better chef than all of those hacks. Now, if we were going for pie, Daisy's Nut House has me beat. Pastry is not my strength.

I leave Daphne to hang out with Roman in the living area while I figure out what the hell I'm going to make us for dinner. Pulling open the fridge door, I inventory the contents and come up with a plan. Nothing fancy, but it will be good. Better than boxed soup or a frozen meal.

Daphne sits on the floor and lets Roman crawl on her. Patsy's outside enjoying the mud in her pen; she'll need a bath before she's allowed back in the house.

I get lost in the prep and production of cooking, occasionally glancing over at the beautiful woman across the room. It's strange but not unwelcome to have her in my house. Other than family, she's my first visitor in a long time. Memories of her mouth and her body pressed against mine flash through my mind in a welcome highlight reel.

"What's for dinner?" Not tall enough to look over my shoulder, Daphne peers around my upper arm, inhaling deeply. "Smells delicious."

Fresh, not floral or cloying, the scent of her shampoo—or maybe her perfume—teases my nose.

Shifting to the left, I block her view into the pot I'm stirring. "I'm not telling until we sit down."

"What if I have a deadly food allergy?" Undeterred, she stands on her toes, her hand pressing against my shoulder blade. She's close enough for me to feel the warmth of her body close to mine.

"I imagine you would've told me when I asked if you had any food sensitivities on the drive over here. If my memory is correct, you said as long as snails, squid and sea urchin weren't on the menu, you'd probably be fine."

"You've only listed a few of the S foods. I have more."

"Yes, I know—turnips remind you of feet." I bump her out of my way with my hip.

"You remember me saying that?" Her eyes widen with surprise. "That was over a month ago."

"You made an impression." I steal a kiss. "How could I forget your love of iceberg and the Bible quote?"

"I like what I like."

"Why doesn't it surprise me that you're a picky eater?" I reply dryly. "I have a feeling you like what you know."

"Also true." Her smile doesn't reach her eyes.

"You might like a lot more things if you're open to trying them."

Her nose wrinkles as she scrunches up her face in disgust. "If you're making sea urchin and snails, I can tell you right now, I'm only going to eat bread."

To placate her, I lift the lid from the cast iron Dutch oven. "Give it a sniff."

She leans closer and inhales deeply. "Smells like chicken soup."

I don't miss the slight flatness in her voice. "Chicken and dumplins to be accurate. Disappointed?"

Stepping to my left, she leans a hip against the counter next to the range. "A little."

"What if I told you it was squirrel?" I bite the inside of my cheek and focus on stirring the stew.

"It isn't!" She jumps away. "You wouldn't!"

"Your face." The laugh I've been suppressing breaks free. "Calm down. It's chicken."

"Promise?" Genuine worry creases her forehead.

"I'll swear on something, if you'd like. My life? If I had a Bible, we could use it."

"No, no. No need for anything so drastic." She holds up her hands.

"You should try squirrel sometime, though. It's especially delicious in Brunswick stew."

She fake-gags. "I'll pass."

"You might like it. Tony Beard was a fan."

"Then Tony and his beard can have my share."

"Do you know who he was?"

"A fan of eating rodents?"

"And snails. Beyond those two dishes, he was one of the greatest chefs in the world."

She observes me as if seeing something new.

"What?" The familiar heat of discomfort crawls up my neck.

With a shake of her head, she dismisses my question. "Nothing. I've never heard of him."

"Tony was one of the chefs I admired most when I was working my way up in restaurant kitchens."

"You haven't always been a farmer?"

"No. This is fairly new." I remove the quick dough from the fridge where it's been resting. "Want to help make the dumplins?"

"Say it again."

Confused, I repeat the question. "Want to help make the dumplins?"

"I love your accent." She sighs, her eyes all dreamy, like I'm her favorite boy band member.

"Okay." I never know what to say when someone tells me that. Half the time it's a backhanded compliment, but coming from Daphne, I think it's genuine.

I set the bowl on the counter and peel away the flour sack towel I covered it with. "Have you ever made dumplins, darlin?"

"Now you're using your voice as a weapon. Completely unfair."

I laugh at her pouting. "I thought you loved it."

"I do, but it distracts me. If you want me to help, you need to cool it with the drawls." Her exaggerated glare only makes me laugh harder.

"Okay. Here's what you need to do." I hand her a spoon. "Scoop some up and drop it in the pot. Think you can manage that?"

"Yes, Chef." She salutes me.

"No one has called me that in a long time." I chuckle. "And no one salutes in a kitchen. We're all too damn busy for that sort of nonsense."

She tentatively drops her first spoonful into the gently boiling liquid.

I kiss the top of her head, surprising myself and her. I recover and say, "Well done."

Pride in her eyes, she beams up at me.

I never imagined enjoying having someone in my kitchen but I'm loving having Daphne here. Her laughter is quickly becoming one of my favorite sounds.

CHAPTER TWENTY-TWO
DAPHNE

I successfully complete my task of scooping and plopping the sticky dough into the pot, and wash a few dishes we've used so far while Odin works on the rest of the meal. I suspect he's making a salad, but I'm too afraid to examine the ingredients closely. I highly doubt he has a bottle of ranch dressing hiding in his refrigerator.

While Odin continues cooking dinner in the kitchen, I hang out with Roman, playing keep-away with one of his toys. Sitting on the floor with the dog gives me an opportunity to check out the house. The old beam and log interior must be a hundred years old, if not older. His furniture is simple but has an expensive quality and I suspect some pieces are real antiques. Nothing he owns is from Ikea or the home section of Target.

Like me, he doesn't have a bunch of family photos or sentimental knickknacks cluttering flat surfaces. The most personal touch I can spy is what decorates his refrigerator.

"You said you don't get out much, but you have all these post-cards from around the world. Do you ask people to send them to you when they travel?" I point at a picture of the Colosseum in Rome held on the door with a magnet.

He glances over his shoulder. "No, those are all mine."

"All of them?" I try to quell my rising jealousy. His postcards are my Pinterest boards come to life. "You've been to Italy?"

"Yep." He doesn't expand or explain.

"Care to elaborate?"

"I've traveled around some." He pours oil into his bowl.

"All these places?" I point at a rocky coast. "Where's this?"

"Australia."

"Wow." There are landmarks I recognize like the Eiffel Tour and the Brandenburg Gate in Berlin, but most of the images are only vaguely familiar. He's so nonchalant about visiting destinations that are castle in the sky dreams for me. How can a farmer living in a holler afford to travel the world? I want to ask him all the questions. Instead, I point to a brightly lit cityscape. "Is that Tokyo?"

He glances over his shoulder at the night scene. "Yes."

If he's not going to share more than one-word sentences, I guess it's up to me to keep the conversation going.

"I remember the first time I flew on an airplane at night. Dark, inky expanses of nothing broken up by small galaxies of lights from towns and cities of varying sizes. Glowing street and porch lights, sprinkled like stars, creating unfamiliar constellations. The disappointment that my first flight wasn't during the day quickly faded as I pressed my forehead against the window and pretended to be zooming through space."

"Where did you go?"

"Nowhere exotic like Australia. My best friend Isaac and I went to Arizona so I could see the Grand Canyon on my nineteenth birthday. That's the trip where I fell in love with national parks." It was also part of my first adventure away from home.

"I never flew anywhere either until I turned twenty. Guess we were late bloomers." His smile brightens his whole face. "Look at us having something in common."

"We also enjoy walking in the woods."

"We're practically the same person." His grin widens before he kisses me again.

I discover it is nearly impossible to kiss someone while laughing. In so many ways we couldn't be more different.

"What's so funny?" He pulls away but holds on to my hips, slowly walking me backward until I'm up against the counter and can't escape.

"Nothing."

He drags his beard along my cheek, causing me to shiver at the sensation. "Are you sure? If I'm a terrible kisser, you can tell me. Be gentle, though—I'm not sure my tender male ego can handle it."

His statement makes me giggle. *He has to be kidding, right?* Demigod or mortal, he's the best I've ever had.

"That bad, huh?" He closes one eye and ducks his chin.

"Horrible." I nod, silly-grinning.

"I should probably keep practicing." His lips brush mine in the gentlest caress.

My exhalations are all trembly. My pulse beats a loud rhythm in my ears.

He doesn't deepen his kiss and the teasing drives me mad.

More. I need more.

Tangling my fingers in the messy curls at the nape of his neck, I urge him closer. Surprising myself, I take the lead, swiping my tongue into his mouth, exploring him.

I'm not sure if it's possible to overcook dumplings, but I think we should forget about dinner for the foreseeable future.

His kisses embolden me. I wonder what his bedroom looks like. *Forget that*, I decide. We have a perfectly good kitchen island right here.

I've never been the instigator when it comes to being physical with a man. Odin makes me want to change that.

More than half my life was spent trying to be a "good girl" and all that idea entails. Chaste, prim, perfect—whatever that means. Turns out, I don't want to fit into that box, or any box. I'm not a cat.

Good girl. Bad girl. Virgin. Slut. They're all just labels slapped on us like rogue bumper stickers. We can't see them ourselves, but other people can.

I press my body against his, feeling the planes and angles of his torso. When our hips meet, the thick length of him presses against my abdomen.

He slows the stroke of his tongue against mine.

I don't want slow. I want more. Everything. Now.

As if reading my mind, he whispers, "There's no rush. We have time."

I'm a bomb with a minute left until detonation. Sweet lord, I don't want to die of pent-up sexual tension right here in his kitchen.

"Darlin'?" He tips my chin up with the tip of his thumb. "I want to savor whatever is happening between us. Let me enjoy you. Don't skip ahead to the dessert."

I think that's chef for *Slow your roll.*

Breathless and flushed, I tell the party in my jeans to chill.

"Wouldn't sex be the main course?"

"I prefer to think of the meal as a whole event. Kissing is the amuse bouche to entice our palate." He proves his point with a nip to my bottom lip.

"And what's dessert?"

"The sweetness that follows everything else, made more enjoyable by the delicious satisfaction of the previous dishes."

Odin is offering me a multi-course gourmet feast when everyone else was fast food. I'm not going to turn down the best meal of my life for mediocre fries.

With a nod, I agree to slow down. My breath shakes as I inhale, trying to return to a state of normal functioning. I feel like I'm at the top of a rollercoaster when there's an announcement the ride is broken. If I'm stuck waiting for a while, I can at least enjoy the view.

Intensely studying my face, he tucks my hair behind my left ear. "I don't know if I remembered to tell you this before, but I like you a whole lot, Daphne. I can't remember the last time I wanted to spend time getting to know someone new. Be patient with me. I'm a little rusty at all of this."

My cheeks heat as my heart races. "I like you, too," I manage to whisper while a thousand thoughts swirl like snow in my head. My brain is a snow globe of feelings and words I want to share, and absent among them are embarrassment or shame. Tapping the brakes is the right thing to do. For now.

Stepping away from me, he announces, "Let's eat."

When Odin places our bowls on the table, the scent of butter and herbs creates a delicious cloud around us. I take a moment to examine the meal he's prepared. Definitely doesn't look like any simple home cooking I've ever seen. Tiny flakes of parsley garnish the top of the dumplings, and the bowl of "salad" is a riot of colors and textures I've never seen in the bagged lettuces down at the Piggly Wiggly.

"This looks incredible. Thank you for making me dinner."

"Bon appétit," he says softly.

Without thinking, I interlace my fingers like I did a thousand times growing up. I haven't said grace before a meal in years but my brain sometimes defaults to its deep-seated training.

"Amen." The word escapes my mouth before I realize I'm saying it out loud.

A chuckle rumbles in his chest. "Amen."

My head jerks up and I gape at him. "Say that again."

"I think once was enough. I don't want to get struck by lightning." He digs into a dumpling with the side of his spoon.

Meanwhile, I've seen, or more accurately, heard a ghost. "It was you that day."

His brows pull together in confusion.

"In the church."

He laughs. "Darlin', I haven't attended church services since my grandfather died when I was eleven."

"I meant in the chapel in the woods."

His eyes go wide before a slow grin spreads across his face. "That was you?"

I nod. "I thought I'd imagined an echo, or the voice of God."

A full-blown guffaw bursts out of his mouth, the force of it pushing him back in his chair.

"What's so funny?"

"I've been compared to the devil himself, but never in my life has someone mistaken me for the good Lord." He wipes genuine tears from his eyes.

Waiting for him to compose himself, I poke at something pink in my salad. Could be a slice of red grape or watermelon radish. Instead of biting into something and having to spit it out, I taste the chicken. It's delicious. Next is the dumpling, which is like a savory cloud.

"Good?" He bites into a carrot.

"Amazing." I give him an enthusiastic thumbs-up.

"In case you were wondering, the salad has pink apples in it." He spears one on his fork and holds it closer to my mouth. "You like apples, don't you?"

I eye him and the sliver with trepidation. "I've never heard of them being anything but white on the inside."

"This is an heirloom variety. Trust me?"

I part my lips and bite into the blush-tinted fruit.

Relieved at the familiar taste, I hum. "Mmm."

"Amazing, right? It's from the fallow orchard."

I throw a sidelong look at his smug satisfaction. "Nicely played."

With a casual lift of his shoulder, he goes back to eating his food.

I do the same. Every bite is incredible. "Where did you learn to cook like this?"

"My formal training is from the CIA. Not the spy group, The Culinary Institute of America. And before you say it, yes, it's fancy."

I pretend to button my lip. "I wouldn't."

"Sorry. I'm a little sensitive about my former career. When I returned home, my family gave me a hard time. Even after I explained cooking was similar to any other trade, like being a mechanic, the men asked why I wanted to waste money learning to do what the women folk figured out from their mommas and grannies. Unless grilling or smoking are involved, cooking is considered women's work."

"Sounds a little like my family. They're big on clearly defined gender roles, too." I give him a sympathetic smile before I change the subject back to safer territory. "Why did you come back here if you were traveling the world as a chef?"

"Most of the travel came after I walked away, a farewell tour to a life I no longer wanted to live."

"You quit to be a farmer? Isn't that going in reverse? Table to farm?" I may be the opposite of a foodie, but even I'm aware of the farm-to-table movement.

He rests his spoon on the edge of his bowl, his expression growing serious. "I didn't have a choice. If I wanted to save my life, I needed to stop living the one I had."

Whoa. "Sounds drastic."

"Desperate times call for desperate measures." He shrugs, and I stop pressing him.

The headline about his drug arrest flashes into my mind. If I ask him about it, he'll think I was stalking him online. Which I wasn't. Not really.

Some struggle flickers in his eyes. "My mentor and one of my best friends died."

"I'm so sorry."

"Thank you. In hindsight, I think I always had a sense he'd check out early. Tony was a sober heroin addict. Not recovered, not former, just wiser in that he figured out a way to not use and still wake up every day and get shit done in his life . . . until one day he made a stupid decision and it all ended. I'm sure you could find all the gory details on the internet if you wanted to."

I feel my eyes bug out. Does he know I know? Or think he knows I know when really I know nothing?

"I try to avoid the celebrity gossip sites and social media."

"Then we have that in common too." His smile is dimmer than it was a few moments ago. "Nothing puts a damper on a great evening like bringing up the dead." He wipes his mouth on his napkin. "It's getting late. I should probably get you home since we're meeting at 7:30."

"No dessert?" I ask. Realizing the double-meaning, I clarify, "I meant the food."

"Sorry, I wasn't prepared."

For sex? For company? Who doesn't have a pint of ice cream in their freezer? His statement could mean several things.

"That's okay."

"Another time?" He pushes himself away from the table.

"I can do the rest of the dishes." I stand as well.

"Nah, I'm happy to do them later."

If we weren't in the middle of nowhere, I'd offer to request a rideshare to pick me up and save him the hour of driving. Somehow, I don't think he'd allow it.

CHAPTER TWENTY-THREE
ODIN

*O*nce we're in the truck, Daphne apologizes again for making me drive her home. I tell her for the third time I don't mind. Our interlaced fingers rest on the console between us.

"Where'd you grow up?" A casual, innocent get-to-know-you kind of question. I might be out of practice, but I'm pretty sure I can manage to still make polite conversation.

"I'm not from around here." Her response is oddly curt.

"That part I already know. For one thing, you don't have the local accent. Second, never heard of any Baums, and I pretty much know every family in Green Valley. Third, I'd remember if you grew up around here." The last statement is both a compliment and my attempt at flirting. I tell my heart rate to settle.

I'm trying out being a gentleman and I'm not sure if I'm succeeding. Took all my effort not to lift her onto the counter and have sex. She wanted it. I sure as hell wanted it. Yet . . . we didn't, because I stopped us. Clearly, I'm an idiot. That line about dessert? Pulled it out of nowhere when I saw rejection creeping into her eyes. I meant the part about savoring her, but I sounded like a pompous chef.

After a long moment of silence, I clear my throat before speaking again. "You didn't answer my question. I'm excellent at evasion, so I'm an expert at knowing when someone is avoiding talking about something."

"Does it matter? We moved around a lot, mostly in the northwest before my parents settled in Idaho. I left as soon as I turned eighteen."

"For college?"

"Sure." Her voice is flat and she doesn't add any more to her response.

That's a strangely vague answer, but I don't say anything. Sometimes the best way to encourage others to talk is by remaining quiet.

"I guess you could say I ran away. Although, technically an adult can't be a runaway, can they?"

This information surprises me. As a rule-loving, law-abiding ranger, she doesn't seem the rebel type.

"You never went back?" My voice lifts with disbelief. "Did your family ever look for you?"

"If I ever left, I would be dead to them. That's what my father told me."

"What about your mom?"

"My mother cried, begged me to believe him. She always took his side, never mine."

"Harsh." Sounds like an abusive situation. I'm torn between wanting to know more and not wanting to have to drive to Idaho to kick her father's ass and end up in jail.

"I haven't seen or spoken to them since."

"You were on your own at eighteen?"

"Pretty much."

I didn't expect to have this in common with the strait-laced ranger. In my head, I'd created a whole narrative about her perfect family life growing up, full of love and support. I should know better. Both assumption and bias have "ass" in them.

"Were you homeless?" I hate the idea of Daphne alone in the world. As much as my family annoys the ever-loving shit out of me ninety percent of the time, I know at least a couple of them would show up if I needed them.

"In a way. I stayed with a friend. We grew up together and he always said I would have a place with him if I needed one." Her eyes close for a beat or two before she shakes her head as if clearing away an old memory.

He.

"Are you still close?"

"Yes, but we rarely see each other. After I started traveling for seasonal NPS jobs, he moved to San Francisco, and then New York. He loves cities. I'm happier away from concrete. Did you know people can have an allergy to concrete? I think I'm one of them."

He.

I assumed the friend had been a girl. Maybe even the woman who was with her at the farmers' market.

"Boyfriend?" I blurt before I get a hold of my thoughts.

She laughs. "Depends on who you ask."

Next time someone accuses me of being cryptic, I'm going to introduce them to Daphne. "I guess I'm asking you."

A small line appears between her eyebrows before she gives me a bland smile. "It was a long time ago. Isaac is off living his life and I'm living mine."

Daphne's ability to avoid giving details about herself is impressive—and really annoying. Why do I care if she had a boyfriend in high school or college? She's right about it being in the past. If I open up this topic, do I really want to talk about my past "relationships"? *Hell and no.* What's done is done and better left to fade away into memory, or be forgotten altogether.

"Why does it matter?" She raises a good point.

"I'm curious what teenage Daphne was like. I'm trying to imagine a younger version of you. Were you always this self-assured and determined?"

With a shake of her head, she dismisses my words. "No, not at all. I don't think I'm either of those things even now."

"No? Funny how we rarely see ourselves as others do."

"What was it like growing up in the Smokies? Are you happy to be back?"

The answers to those questions are complicated.

"Have you heard of someone being dirt poor?"

"Of course."

"Growing up, I used to think the expression was invented for my family. The only thing we owned of value was our land, handed down eight generations over three centuries. Turns out, the expression has something to do with dirt floors in old England. Since some of the older Hill homesteads have dirt floors in their cellars, I think it still applies."

Soft understanding in her eyes, she squeezes my hand. "We didn't have much either. I never realized how poor we were until I left home and saw how other people lived. Is your current house from your family?"

"Sure is. Samson Hill used to own property all around these mountains. Most of it wasn't worth much—too steep or inaccessible for farming—except a few parcels, one of which is where I'm living now."

"During dinner, you mentioned moving back to save yourself. Why not keep traveling?"

"Even with leaving after high school, moving to Atlanta and then New York, traveling the world, I could never fully escape Green Valley. I was sitting on a piazza in a small town in Tuscany, enjoying the cool hours of a summer morning with a cappuccino and a flaky cornetto pastry when Duane and Jessica Winston sat down at the next table."

"Small world."

"Has it ever happened to you? Seeing someone from home far away from Idaho?"

She thinks for a moment. "Once or twice."

"It's the strangest sensation to have your past show up in your present. I took it as a sign. I'd been traveling for a while when I ran into them. I think they'd just moved there, and we recognized each other the way folks do when they see someone from their hometown in an unfamiliar context. Like identifies like. Seeing their faces and hearing their accents sparked a yearning for the Smokies I hadn't felt in years. Guess I can partially blame Duane and Jessica for why I moved back."

"I know there are half a dozen or more of the Winston siblings, but I can't keep them straight. The sister is married to Dr. Runous, the game warden. Beau's the one who owns the garage with Cletus, right?"

"He does. You should talk to him about the Highlander. If anyone could bring a vehicle back from a bear attack, it would be them."

"In my head, I've put it on a Viking funerary raft and pushed it out to sea. The park is going to use it as a warning to campers." She rolls her eyes. "Can we not talk about it? I'm still in mourning. Back to Duane and Jessica—were you friends growing up?"

"Not really. As kids, we didn't socialize together. The twins, Beau and Duane, were a few grades ahead of me, and their younger brother Roscoe was a couple years behind. The farm kids didn't hang around the sons and daughters of the Iron Wraiths.

"In fact, my mother forbid it. There's poor, and then there are the bikers. Never the two should mix. She made it seem like we were too good for those kids. Ironically, the Hills are considered lower than the bikers on whatever social scale exists in people's minds. Probably because we keep to ourselves and live on old farms and homesteads tucked into hollers. I think she worried we'd join one of the local gangs, tempted by the glamorous lifestyle of motorcycles and leather jackets."

"She was right to be worried. I'd be tempted to join a club for the patches alone."

"You should probably avoid temptation."

"I'll keep that in mind. No biker bars for me."

The thought of Daphne at any of the club hangouts makes my blood run cold. It would be like sending a kitten into a den of vipers. Sexism flows through my family's veins along with the genes for attached earlobes and the ability to roll our tongues. Despite my genetic predisposition, I try to refrain from being a jerk to and about women. Working in kitchens right out of high school and putting myself through culinary school taught me it wasn't just my family who had issues with women and anyone who wasn't exactly like us.

"Seriously, please avoid them. They're all bad news. If you thought I had questionable ethical standards because I was foraging mushrooms, your head would explode if you knew a tenth of the kind of shit the Iron Wraiths have pulled over the years."

She watches me. "Okay, I promise. The only bikers I'll interact with are retirees on Harleys in the park. Deal?"

Somehow, we've arrived back at the ranger station. I barely remember the drive over here.

"I have an idea." I release her hand to put the truck in park. "How about I pick you up in the morning? Save you some time getting from your cabin to the trailhead."

"Or you could spend the night." She whispers so softly I'm not sure if I'm meant to hear the words.

"What was that?"

"Nothing."

"I'd love to spend the night with you, but I have Patsy and Roman back at the farm. If Patsy doesn't get her coffee right when she wakes up, watch out." I give an exaggerated shake of my head. "Woo-e. Total diva."

"You give her coffee?"

"No, of course not." I dismiss her wild suggestion by making a funny face.

"You're weird, Odin Hill."

"Tell me something I don't know." Before she can speak, I lean forward and capture her mouth with mine. It's been too long since I kissed her and I need to tide myself over until morning.

CHAPTER TWENTY-FOUR
DAPHNE

*L*ast night I slept like a rock. How I managed to fall asleep after making out with Odin in his truck is a mystery bigger than . . . Big Foot. Apparently, pent up sexual frustration knocks me out. I'm guessing this isn't typical.

I'm up early and waiting for him at the end of the road to the ranger cabins. When I see his truck, my pulse quickens at the memory of our semi-bridled session in the cab. I'm grateful I didn't try to smuggle my toothbrush in my bra.

I'm definitely not standing out on the main road to avoid encountering a coworker. That's my story and I'm sticking to it. Imagine trying to date someone local while you're at sleepaway summer camp. Not as a camper, obviously, but a counselor. We deserve a shred of privacy in our lives.

Somehow, he's even more handsome than my brain can retain. Freshly showered, his hair is pulled away from his face, exposing his high cheekbones. I never understood how some cheekbones could be higher than others until I met Odin Hill. His are on a whole other plane.

"Morning. I bought you coffee. Creamer and sugar on the side because I don't know how you take yours." He holds a familiar bag between his fingers.

"You brought me breakfast from Donner Bakery?"

"Presumptuous of me, but I've seen your fridge and cupboards."

In my excitement, I practically stuff my head into the bag to reveal my edible present. "How did you know these are my favorite?"

"I asked."

"They remember my order?" I'm both shocked and pleased.

"The joys of living in a small town." He makes a U-turn.

"Aren't we going the other direction?" I point behind us.

"We could, but I know a shortcut, which will mean a quicker hike to the grove."

The scent of cinnamon and sugar intensifies as I peel back the paper from the Ring of Fire muffin. It's still warm from the oven.

"Are you going to eat that or just cuddle it in your hand while licking your lips?" Odin teases, but his look is intense as he watches me break off a piece and slip it into my mouth.

After slowly savoring the sweet spiciness, I swallow and reluctantly hold out the paper cup. "Want some?"

"And deprive you of something you're obviously enjoying?"

"I'm offering to share, not give you the rest." I separate a tiny morsel.

He chuckles, and the lines around his eyes deepen. "Very generous."

"Sharing is caring."

"You only care about me one tiny morsel?" He parts his lips and waits.

"Fine, if you're going to be ungrateful." I pop the crumbs into my mouth.

"Hey," he complains. "I'm the one who bought that muffin with my own money."

"What's the saying? Beggars can't be choosers?" I smile, smug.

Before I can anticipate his actions, he's lifted my arm toward his face and stolen a giant bite.

As he chews and then swallows, I gawk at him in shock.

"You're right—delicious. I like the heat along with the sugar. Gives it a nice edge." He eyes the small remaining portion in my hand.

"Don't even think about it." I cup my hand over the rest. "You owe me half a muffin."

"Okay." He shrugs. "I'll buy you a dozen muffins to make up for it."

"That's excessive. I don't need twelve muffins. I could never eat that many in one sitting."

"If you say so. I'll buy them for myself and give you half of one."

Too late, I realize I've bargained myself into a corner. I should've accepted his offer and frozen them for later. How can I retract my statement?

"By the way, that's a horrible expression." He licks sugar from his fingers.

"Which one?" I ask, hopeful he means the part about denying my ability to inhale small cakes disguised as breakfast foods.

"The part about beggars not deserving a choice." His brows pull together. "If they're poor and asking for help, it means they should take whatever is offered to them without question? Say thank you and shut up?"

He makes a good point. "I never thought about it that way. On one hand, shouldn't we always be grateful for kindness and generosity?"

"Have you ever been on the other end of charity?" His voice has lost the teasing tone from when we were talking about muffins. Softer around the edges, it hints at a vulnerability I haven't seen in him before.

Hesitating about how much I want to share, I pause before answering him.

"That's what I thought. Easy to be magnanimous if you're the one doing acts of goodwill, patting yourself on the back for being so generous."

"I know what it's like to have nothing."

He grimaces. "Sorry. I wasn't thinking. Being on your own at eighteen had to have been difficult. I bounced around from grunt job to grunt job until I got my shit together and earned a decent paycheck."

"Park rangers don't make a lot of money, especially seasonal employees who might work six months at a time with long periods of downtime. Pile on student loan debt and car payments and there isn't much left over at the end of every month."

"No, I imagine there isn't."

"Farming can't pay as much as a chef."

"Barely covers my expenses." He nods. "What's that Bible saying about something's price being above rubies?"

I suck in a breath and hold it. *Why is he asking me about this verse?*

"Do you know it?"

Closing my eyes, I recite from memory. "'Who can find a virtuous woman? Her price is far above rubies.' From Proverbs."

He drums his fingers on the steering wheel. "Maybe I'm thinking of something else."

"There's another version, also in Proverbs, which I've always preferred. 'For wisdom *is* better than rubies; and all the things that may be desired are not to be compared to it.'"

"Yes!" His hand slaps the center of the wheel. "Wisdom. I think one of my grannies told me that one. The other quote sounds like some predator selling virgins."

I choke out a guffaw. "I don't think that's exactly how the writers intended their words to be interpreted."

"How do you know the Bible so well?"

"Oh, you know." I keep my tone as casual as I can. "Sunday school."

He gives me side-eye. "I saw your bookshelves while you were napping."

"Oh, those. Some are from a world religions class in college. Others are more recent." .

"You've moved them around the country?"

"I have. I find myself reading them over and over again. They all fit in one box. Wisdom over things."

He presses his lips together as he bobs his head. "Why not download the ebook version?"

"I like to write notes in the margins, and seeing the collection all together brings me comfort. I can remember where I was when I bought each one."

"Kind of like my postcards. I kept a journal of sorts by writing them to myself."

"I love that idea." I wonder what past Odin wrote to himself while he traveled. "I've never kept a diary or journaled."

"Rereading them can be cringe-inducing, but they're a good reminder of who I was then compared to now."

Introspective Odin wasn't on my bingo card.

CHAPTER TWENTY-FIVE
ODIN

I've said more to Daphne about myself than I have to anyone else. Ever.

There's something about her that allows me to open up, though not because she's an open book herself. On the drive home last night, I realized we spent most of the evening talking about me and she shared very little about her own history. I suspect she has more secrets than I do. Like seeks like. If only I could get her to trust me enough to be real. I'm hoping showing her the orchard today will be a good first step.

I want to know her, the real Daphne, and I want to be known by her.

We pass through the entrance to Cades Cove and I turn left onto the main road.

"Remind me where we're going? Cooper Road is back thataway."

"We're sneaking in through the back door."

With narrowed eyes, she worries her bottom lip with her teeth before pulling out her phone and opening an app. She holds it up, so I can see the screen and swirls her finger in the general area of the trail. "According to this map, there is no other entrance by car. No roads."

"No paved roads," I correct her.

Glancing in my rear-view window for the twentieth time to make sure we aren't being followed, I slow at the familiar curve. Up ahead, I spot the pale-green, plastic tie I left around a poplar tree to mark the road. I've thought about putting up *No Trespassing* signs but changed my mind when I realized they'd only draw attention.

I haven't driven on the logging path in a long time. It occurs to me that with all the rain we've been having, we might have an issue with mud, but the truck should do okay even if there's standing water. I hope.

Daphne lifts my favorite knife from the tray on the console. "What's this for?"

"Mostly mushroom foraging, but a good blade can serve many purposes. With a knife, string, and duct tape, you can get yourself out of a lot of binds."

"Or kidnap and murder someone." She leans forward so she can see my eyes.

I can't really take them off the road as I navigate the ruts and dips of the old path, avoiding thicker tree branches and underbrush, but I cast a quick glance at her. "You're kind of fixated on the kidnapping."

"Am I? That sounds like a weird thing to say to someone." Her brows pull together.

"You mentioned it after I found you in the woods, advised me to use candy or ice cream to lure you inside."

"Is that why you brought me a muffin?" She cringes.

"Could be." I find myself smiling at the memory of that afternoon.

Her voice softens. "Ahh. The things you remember and I don't. A part of me wishes there was a video I could watch to help me recall all the details . . . a very, small, tiny part that's immune to embarrassment."

"No reason to be ashamed. For the most part, you were funny and charming."

"It's the hedging in your statement that worries me."

"You were fine."

We successfully arrive at the edge of the glen without getting stuck in the muck. I feel like we survived the Oregon Trail game.

Daphne taps her phone's screen and waits for the map to update. When it doesn't, she sighs in disappointment. "No service."

"I know where we're at. Come on." I step out of the cab before she's unbuckled her seatbelt.

Taller grass indicates the end of the road where a chain or barricade would normally be. There aren't any other obvious tire tracks in either direction, so I'm fairly certain no one else has been here since my last visit.

"Where's the trail?" She hesitates near the hood.

"We have to forge our own for a few yards." I take the lead and she follows.

Single file, we march through grass and underbrush until we head down a slope and into the orchard.

Small red and green swirled apples decorate the sinewy trees, their branches covered in lichen and tangled together from neglect.

"It's a real orchard." Daphne steps around me and heads down one of the rows, touching leaves and fruit as she passes by each tree. "I feel like I've stepped into a fairy tale. This place is definitely haunted by a headless horseman or the ghost of a little girl who drowned in a well."

I follow behind her, because what else am I going to do? "I can't verify either of those things."

"How come I didn't know about this place? I've studied everything about the GSM to be qualified to teach classes about it to visitors. There was a test. I only missed two questions. No one told me about secret orchards." She sounds insulted.

"This land belongs to my family, not the federal government. A long time ago, long before the concept of the national parks, Hills settled here. They built cabins and planted crops. One of them created this orchard." I snap an apple off its branch, polish it on my shirt and then take a bite.

Listening intently, she nods along with my story. "You said belongs, present tense. According to the maps, all of this is under the protection of the Department of the Interior."

"Not all of it. This valley, extending northeast from the pavement toward the Cooper trail, is private property."

"I don't believe you."

"Thought that might be the case." I reach into my pocket and extract the map I printed at home this morning. "Here."

She accepts it from me and studies it, occasionally glancing up and around the orchard to get her bearings. "You're right."

"I know."

"Your apples . . ."

"Technically, they're wild, but the land is mine. Or more accurately, it belongs to my great-grandmother."

"Nannie Ida?"

"The one and only."

"And she knows about the orchard?"

"She's the one who pointed me to this area, said I might find it of interest. Also made me promise to keep quiet about whatever I found."

"Why is that?"

"Why do I have the feeling you've switched over to official business, Ranger Baum?"

"Sorry. Too many questions?" She flashes an apologetic smile. "My curiosity gets the better of me sometimes."

"If I had to guess, she has memories of this place when the trees were young. Over her lifetime, she's witnessed her family's history get erased and rewritten to fit the tidy narrative you share on your tours." My tone is harsh, unflinching.

Her fingers flutter over the ends of her hair. "I didn't know."

Rolling my shoulders back, I ease some of the gathered tension from my body. "Might be good to spend more time with the locals and learn more than the official history."

"You're right. I've been here less than half a year. A problem with moving around every six months or so is I don't have time to do much research. If I have questions, I tend to ask the other rangers with more seniority or the volunteers. Maybe you can introduce me to a few more of the old-timers?"

Her lack of deflection tames my frustration. She could've denied or defended her actions. I respect someone who can own knowing what they don't know. "I can help. Have you met Lena Walker at the farm museum?"

"I don't think so. I haven't had much time off to explore other areas of the park. Typically, I work my ass off for six months and then travel in between gigs."

I didn't realize she'd be leaving after the fall season. Griffin, Gaia, and Jay have been here for years. I assumed she'd be the same. If I'd known, I wouldn't have wasted weeks being a grumpy codger instead of asking her out. We've barely gotten to know each other.

A month won't be enough time with her.

"Where are you going next?" I manage to ask without sounding petulant.

Blinking, she tilts her head. "Today?"

"I meant after your contract here is over."

"Too soon to know."

"You don't line up the next job before the current one ends?"

"In the past, yes, but I don't have any plans for after here."

Maybe I can convince her to stay. We could spend the winter together holed up in my cabin. A whole fantasy unfolds of her wearing nothing but one of my shirts, curled up in my bed next to me while snow falls outside, closing us off from the rest of the world.

"Feels weird to be planning my next move when I've only had a permanent position for a month or so." Her eyes meet mine, confusion in them. She probably sees the same in mine.

"Like Ranger Lee?"

"Yes."

"Good." I hug her and then kiss her luscious mouth, relieved to know she'll be around for a while.

She takes a beat before she responds. Once she does, a switch flips and we're all hands touching, grabbing, seeking skin while we explore each other with our lips and tongues. Stumbling across the uneven ground, I finally press her against the trunk of an apple tree. The added support allows me to lean into her, feeling her soft curves pressing against my body. I ache to strip her naked, taste her, and be inside her. I curse our current location and my lack of foresight. I don't have a condom. I doubt Daphne has one in her pocket.

We come up for air a few minutes later.

Pressing my forehead against hers, I attempt to calm my frantic pulse.

"This might be my favorite Monday ever." She giggles.

"Call in sick," I whisper against the tender spot behind her ear. She shivers in response and the sense of power to create a reaction in her body with only my breath goes straight to my head. "Spend the day with me."

"I can't." She shakes her head.

"Sure you can." I'm not above begging.

"No, I can't call in because I have the day off." She gives me a little shove in the middle of my chest. "Look, I'm not wearing my uniform."

While her jacket is typical NPS standard issue, she's wearing black jeans and a T-shirt underneath.

"My powers of observation suck." I dip my head for another kiss. "Good thing I have other skills."

CHAPTER TWENTY-SIX
DAPHNE

*W*hen Odin pinned me against the tree and kissed me until we were both breathless, I thought I might implode. If I'd known up-against-an-apple-tree sex was a potential option, I would've been better prepared. *Frickin' hindsight with its perfect vision.*

Why did we have to be in the middle of actual nowhere when he mentioned his skills?

Why didn't I bring a condom? I have a supply in my bathroom. Not much use when they're miles away from the location of the action.

Why must I hate skirts and dresses? The ones with pockets are perfect—for carrying the aforementioned condom—and, they're more convenient than pants for spontaneous outdoor romps, which is ironic given their reputation for being more prim and proper.

If this man doesn't take me directly home and do wicked things to me while I do the same to him, I can't be held responsible for my actions.

Inhaling for three, exhaling for five, I resort to yoga breath to contain the raging lust that's about to overwhelm me.

Freaking demigod, lord of the vegetables.

Is this how Zeus could disguise himself as all those weird things and still seduce mortal women? Swan? Ant? Golden shower? Come on, Danae. Seriously? How? Stop. No woman in her right mind is going to look at a swan and think, *I must have you now. Get in my pants.*

Only she was probably wearing a dress. Or a toga. *Argh!*

My namesake turned herself into a tree to avoid Apollo's unwanted advances. Girlfriend wasn't playing when he refused to accept she wasn't interested.

Reaching across the truck's console, Odin squeezes my thigh. "Are you okay?"

"All good. Why?" Realizing I'm clenching my jaw, I smooth my face into a pleasant expression.

"You were breathing kind of strange."

"Hmm. Was I?" I cock my head.

"What should we do with our wide-open day?" He stops at the end of the overgrown logging road and gives me his full attention. "Breakfast at Daisy's?"

Silently, we stare at each other for a few seconds. The air crackles with sexual tension.

"How long does it take to get to the farm?" I lean over and kiss him.

I think my cabin is closer but it's also closer to neighbors, who happen to all be my coworkers. I am not okay with anyone inter-rupting us by knocking on my door.

He smiles against my lips. "Daphne?"

"Mmm," I hum.

"Might be easier to drive if we're not making out." He chuckles.

"Right." I continue what I was doing.

He indulges me, sweeping his tongue against mine as his hand comes up to kiss my face.

The kissing doesn't help relieve the ache; it merely fans the flames. With an exasperated sigh, I pull myself away from him.

With a quick bob of his head, he says, "Right. Let's go back to my place."

* * *

Patsy's in her pen and Roman stands on the porch when we arrive at the farm.

"Don't you have work to do?" I ask Odin as we exit the truck.

"Already finished up most of today's projects." He slips his arm around my shoulder.

"You were at my place by 7:30." I gape at him. "What time do you get up?"

"Early." He guides us in the direction of the house.

Roman stretches into a perfect downward dog before giving himself a shake. I don't care what Odin says—he's a doodle. I think whoever sold him the dog played him. Still, he's adorable and wags his tail, happy to see us.

We enter the house, Odin takes my jacket, and we kick off our shoes, leaving them on the boot tray next to the door. Then we stand there, surrounded by nervous excitement—at least I am. All my bravado faded during the drive.

"Something to drink?" he offers.

"Water would be great. Thanks."

He pours two glasses and gives me one. With his free hand, he clasps mine and leads me over to the couch. It's rich, worn, brown leather. We sink into the soft cushions, me in the corner, and him next to me. I down my water in a few long chugs, nerves or dehydration making me thirsty.

"You're too far away." He sets his still full tumbler down on the wooden trunk that serves as his coffee table.

"I'm right here." I rest my hand on his arm.

"Not close enough." He tugs me onto his lap. "Better."

Gazing down at him from this new angle, I slide my hands

through his waves. Long hair on guys has never been my thing, but I like the wild mess, more benign neglect than a willful attempt at style.

His fingers grip and flex on my hips.

"I like this." I tug on a strand.

"My hair?"

Nodding, I tip his head back. He lets me.

I pet his facial hair. "And the beard."

His almost-too-wide-for-his-face mouth curves with amusement. "You sound surprised."

"I am."

"Bearded hillbilly not your type?" His smile fades.

"I don't think I have one."

"What about Norse gods and superheroes?" He bites his bottom lip.

My eyes flash to his.

"You called me Vegetable Thor in the woods."

My lids close automatically, my body shielding me from the embarrassment of having to face him.

"It beats the Jolly Green Giant." I feel his laughter shake his chest.

Bravely, I open my eyes. "I never said you were . . ." Did I think it, though? Yes.

"No, you didn't, but others have. I'm not that tall."

"Or green," I reassure him.

"Sadly, only my thumbs." He sticks them both up to show me.

Without thought, I lift his hand to my chest, and the energy between us switches from flirty nonsense to charged.

CHAPTER TWENTY-SEVEN
ODIN

I'm not certain who initiates the kiss, but her hands find their way back into my hair, and mine rest on the round swell of her chest. Straddling me, she's in control, swaying in a rhythm on my lap, grinding her hips over my thickening cock. The friction creates a sweet agony.

I tug the neck of her shirt to allow my mouth more access to her skin. My fingers skate above the waist of her jeans, brushing against her softness. Breathless moans fill her kisses as my own breathing goes shallow, my hands cupping and squeezing her breasts through her bra.

Breaking our connection, she asks, "Should I take off my shirt?"

"Only if you want to." Restraint leaves my voice ragged.

"Or you could do it." She lifts her arms and waits.

Her tee hits the floor in a flash, leaving her in only a cream, lace bra.

"Are you sure you want to do this?" I whisper into her shoulder as I drag my mouth over her warm skin. "I want to be clear you want this as much as I do. I'll stop if you ask me to. Just say the word."

Gripping my jaw, she tilts my head up and confirms I'm looking at her before she answers. "I'm sure. Don't stop. Please, for the love of all that is holy and good in the world, do not stop."

I brush my mouth against hers before sliding my tongue inside. She moans and grinds her hips.

"I want to make you feel good. Tell me what you like." I nip her bottom lip and tug gently while my hands guide her into a rhythm.

"Take off your pants, Odin."

Chuckling against her neck, I take a moment to appreciate a woman who's direct.

"I'm serious." Her tone emphasizes her words.

"I don't doubt that. Wrap your arms around my neck." When she complies, I slide my hands under her ass and stand. "Hold on."

With her legs embracing my hips and her arms coiled around my shoulders, I march down the hall to my bedroom. I built the simple frame from reclaimed wood I found on the property. Nothing fancy, but the king mattress will give us more room than the couch.

I set her down on her feet and kneel to remove her jeans and then her socks. Standing back up, I admire her body, highlighted only by her bra and underwear. Using the tips of my fingers, I trace the fabric. She shivers and tries to cover her chest.

"Don't be shy. Don't deny me the beauty of your body." I drag her underwear down her legs, leaving a trail of kisses in my wake.

"So sexy," she whisper-moans as her eyes flutter.

She wiggles out of her bra and tosses it somewhere behind me.

"Your turn." She slips her fingers under the hem of my shirt.

I help her out by reaching behind my neck and yanking it over my head. Moving on to my jeans, I quickly unzip and drop them to the floor along with my boxers. Her audible inhalation tells me she likes what she sees.

My chest rises and falls as we stare at each other, drinking in the new knowledge that comes with seeing someone naked for the first time.

"Climb on the bed," I tell her, my voice stern and commanding.

Contemplating me, she tips her head to the side before sitting down and sliding back to the pillows.

While she did what I told her, I suspect she prefers a balance when it comes to being in control and relinquishing it. I'm happy to test this theory.

I crawl over her, encouraging her to open her legs for me so I can kneel between them. My erection bobs at attention and I give it a slow stroke as she observes me.

"You have condoms, right?" Her voice is raspy with need, and it's beyond sexy.

"Patience, darlin'. Remember this is a multi-course meal, and we've only just begun."

"Sweet lord." She tilts her head into the pillows. "You're going to be the death of me."

"I promise my goal is the exact opposite. I want you to feel alive."

Her eyes close and she softly whimpers.

I kiss a path from her shoulder down, lavishing each breast with attention before continuing down past her navel to the soft curls at the apex of her thighs. Using my tongue and hands, I learn the topography of her pleasure until she's tightening around my fingers, bucking and pulsing with an orgasm.

I've always been amazed by and more than a little jealous of a woman's ability to have multiple orgasms back to back with a tiny refractory time. Easing up on the pressure of my tongue, I give her a moment to catch her breath before going for round two.

When she's flushed and molten from her pleasure, I kiss each hip a final time in reverence. "Thank you."

She barely lifts her head from the pillows. "Why are you thanking me? I'm the one having all the orgasms."

"And I'm grateful you shared them with me." I lick my bottom lip, savoring her.

"You gave me the orgasms—you should take credit."

"I wish I could, but that was all you." I kneel and slide open the drawer of my nightstand for a condom.

"I think I came so hard I lost brain cells." Her eyes close again as she shakes her head.

"Your body created the pleasure. I merely provided the right stimulation."

She slowly peels open one eye and then the other.

Reaching for the silver packet in my hand, she strokes me with the other. "We could continue discussing this, or we could continue having sex. Your choice."

A deep groan escapes me as she tightens her grip around the swollen head of my penis. She deftly opens the condom and sheathes my length.

I can't remember the last time I had sex and I know this won't be an epic marathon, but I'm reassured by the thought that this is only the first of many times we'll be having sex.

"Do you want to be on top? I'll last longer," I admit.

When she straddles me and slides onto me, my head lolls back with the agonizing gratification of finally being inside her. Dark waves of her hair surround us as we discover our rhythm, and her inner walls grip me when her third orgasm shakes her body. As I hit the peak, I flip us so I'm on top, chasing sensation as I come in wave after wave of pleasure.

Panting and satiated, I roll to the side to discreetly dispose of the condom before scooping Daphne into my arms and kissing her.

"Thank you," I tell her again.

"Mmm," she softly hums. "You're welcome."

* * *

Daphne's still asleep, her lips slightly parted. She smells of spring and the tender flowers of a pea vine, and the antique, stained-glass window above my bed throws a rainbow across her back.

I give myself permission to stare, taking notice of the details I've only skimmed over before.

Her typical expression around me varies between deer in headlights and suspicious. She senses I'm up to no good but can't put her finger on why. I came clean about the apples today, as a peace offering. Telling myself I'm withholding the truth to protect her is a waste of time. Even I don't believe the lie anymore.

In rest, the line between her brows disappears and the furrows of her forehead relax. There are exactly eleven freckles on her nose. I counted.

Saying she has brown hair lacks imagination. The strands are a blend of auburn, gold, chestnut, and molasses threads.

The sheet has slipped off her left shoulder, exposing a tattoo of a butterfly chrysalis. At first glance, I thought it was a bean. Given I'm a man with a few vegetable tattoos of my own, it wasn't an odd assumption.

In the strong afternoon light streaming through the panes of glass, I can tell the skin beneath the pale green is raised like an old scar. I want to trace the texture of it with my tongue, tasting her skin, savoring the flavor of her. Instead, I use the pad of my finger to outline the ink.

She stirs and twists her neck to face me. Without moving the hair out of her face, she murmurs, "It's a chrysalis."

Now that she's awake, I kiss her tattoo.

Wiggling her arm free from the sheets, she brushes enough strands away to reveal her eyes. "'She is a new creature: old things are passed away; behold, all things are becoming new.' Corinthians."

"Another scripture quote?"

A little wary, she blinks at me before nodding. "One of my favorites."

"Why not the butterfly?" I ask, my mouth still against her shoulder.

"At the time I got it, I had no idea who I'd become. I wanted to capture the promise of going through a major change and coming out the other side a better, more beautiful version of myself."

"That's deep. How old were you when you got it?"

"Eighteen. One of my first acts of rebellion." She smiles—sleepy, smug, and perfect.

"And the scar underneath? What's the story behind it?" I trace the outline.

"It isn't a happy story." She rolls over, blocking my view of her back. "I was getting punished for something. I can't remember what, but it was bad enough for my father to use his belt. His grip slipped and the buckle hit my shoulder."

I recognize the detachment from trauma in her flat, distant voice.

"Fuck." *How hard was he hitting his child?*

"Pretty much. I forgave both him and my mother for their actions when I cut all ties. Forgiveness doesn't have to equal connection." The rims of her eyes redden with unshed tears.

Pulling Daphne close, I kiss the top of her head, wanting to protect her and soothe away the bad memories of her childhood.

CHAPTER TWENTY-EIGHT
DAPHNE

*O*ther than a few bathroom runs and his trip to the kitchen for water and snacks, we've spent hours exploring each other's bodies and talking while we recuperate from having sex. I definitely am never kicking him out of bed for crumbs.

He asked about my scar and for the first time, I told the true story. In the past, if anyone asked, I'd make up an outrageous story about barbed-wire or a clumsy curling-iron incident, something to satisfy the curiosity enough to change the subject. With Odin, I wanted him to know the truth.

The smell of sex permeates the room and my skin. Odin's scent is all over me. We're both sticky and in need of a shower.

He joins me and we go for round three, kissing under the spray of hot water. After, we soap each other up and he washes my hair.

Wrapped in a thick towel, I watch him change into clean clothes, mourning the loss of skin with each new item he dons.

Reluctantly, I get dressed too.

The afternoon light is fading when we finally come up for air and dinner. While something delicious simmers away on the stove, we're sprawled on his couch, our bodies continually touching and seeking out the other.

"Have you ever been to a contra dance?" Odin breaks the quiet that has settled between us.

"I've never heard of it. Is it like contraband?" I twist my neck so I can see his face from my spot resting my head in his lap. He's been playing with my hair, and it's almost lulling me back to sleep.

"There's a band playing live music. Think square dancing, but with more waltzing." He makes a show of dipping forward and sweeping his right arm across his chest while swinging his left arm out to the side.

The idea of him dancing makes me giggle.

"What's funny?" He scowls.

I sit upright and poke him in the bicep. "You."

"I dance," he replies, defensive.

I lift my eyebrows in challenge. "Really? I can't imagine it."

"Nannie Ida insisted we all learn the basics. It's her 100th birthday and she's requested the family hold a dance. You should come with me."

"Like a ball? Do we need fancy clothes?" I own nothing fit for a party involving waltzing. Given my lack of budget, I can't afford to buy something new, but maybe I could drive to Merryville to check out the thrift stores in hopes of finding something somewhere between prom and mother-of-the-bride that isn't a wedding dress. Showing up to his grandmother's party in a bridal gown might give the wrong message.

He snorts. "The Hills don't know fancy. Most of the men will be in clean jeans and a collared shirt—pressed by their wives. A skirt or dress is fine. Nothing with sequins or lace—this isn't a prom."

Sometimes, I swear he reads my mind.

"I never went to prom, or to a formal dance of any kind."

"Me neither." He grins.

I purse my lips and contemplate flat-out saying no. If I don't go,

I'll miss the sight of Odin dancing. Something in the center of my chest tells me I might regret not having that visual for the rest of my life.

"Stop thinking up excuses why you can't go. You won't even be partnered with me for much of the dancing. Like I said, this isn't prom."

His words puzzle me. "If you don't need me to be your partner, why do you want me to go as your date?"

Holding my gaze, he narrows his eyes, dark lashes nearly joining to cover his warm brown eyes. "First off, I never said—"

I cut him off before he can finish saying this wouldn't be a date.

"I get it. You need to bring someone, and I'm the easy choice." I should've said respectable. "Not that I'm easy. I mean—"

"You done?" He doesn't let me finish my sentence.

Ignoring his interruption, I continue. "I didn't mean to imply you think I'm easy. I meant I'm respectable and the kind of woman you can bring to your great-grandmother's birthday party without scandal or feeding the local gossip mill."

"Nope, obviously not done." He crosses his arms and lifts his chin. "Give me a hand signal when you're finished."

My jaw tightens. "All I'm saying is I appreciate the offer, but I'm sure there are plenty of other women who'd be happy to go to the dance with you. Bet they know how to do-si-do and fro-di-fro. No need to feel obligated to ask me because we've had sex."

Rubbing his beard-covered jaw with the palm of his hand, he observes me, probably waiting for me to continue speaking, only I've said all I need to say. We enter another stretch of silence, this one more uncomfortable than before.

"Is it the idea of going to my family's party or of spending an evening dancing that has you more uncomfortable?" His knowing gaze pierces me.

"Pfft. I'm not uncomfortable."

"Are you sure?" His lips curve a tiny bit.

I go to shrug my shoulders and find my arms locked, hands on opposite elbows.

"Words weren't necessary when your body language was clear as a mountain stream."

Loosening my viselike grip, I swing my arms and wiggle my shoulders, all loosey-goosey.

"Which is it? Me or being around a bunch of hillbillies?"

His misperception about himself is weird and bothersome. "Quit putting words in my mouth."

Crossing his arms, he mirrors my former pose.

"Fine. It's the dancing, okay? I don't know how to dance." I grimace at the heat settling over my cheeks.

"Nothing to know for a contra. There'll be a caller who tells the dancers what to do."

"Sounds complicated."

"It is and it isn't. Think Simon Says with a fiddle and no winner."

"I'm not sure if that makes it better."

Meeting my eyes, reassuringly, he tells me, "I can help."

"How?"

"I'll teach you. If you can count, you can dance. Easy. Follow after me: one, two, three, four."

"Don't patronize me."

"You'll be fine. You don't need to know the Tennessee waltz or any other formal dances, and we already know you're more than capable of abiding by rules if you put your mind to it." He extends his hand and wiggles his fingers. "First rule is to always follow the caller."

Gently, he cups my hand, placing it on top of his and stands, pulling me off the couch. "Ready? We'll begin with something simple. This is an allemande. All you do is hold hands and walk. Think you can handle it?"

I narrow my eyes. "Seems easy enough."

He slowly moves in a circle around me and because we're connected, I follow.

"Good. Ready for a do-si-do?"

"No." Images of him lifting me and spinning me around come to mind.

Laughing, he releases his clasp and steps right in front of me. "It's a fancy term for walking in a clockwise circle around each other."

I remain in place as he demonstrates. "That's it? I'm disappointed."

"I told you, you have nothing to worry about." He places a quick peck on my lips.

"Show me more."

He obliges me with spins and twirls in addition to bowing.

The old-fashioned formalness of the moves make Odin feel like he's from another time period. I can see his ancestor living in this house, lit by candle or firelight, dancing while someone else plays a fiddle. There's something romantic about the image.

We dance and laugh until I'm a breathless heap on the couch. He sits next to me, a happy smile on his flushed face.

"Thank you. That was fun."

"You're welcome. Glad you enjoyed yourself. Still nervous about the party?" He picks up my legs and swings them over his lap.

"Is the rest of your family as wonderful as you?"

His happy energy disappears.

"I'm the black sheep," he says flatly. "The prodigal son without the triumphant welcome upon my return."

"Aren't you the one who was called when your cousin was hustling pool at Genie's?"

"Only because Joe knows me well, which isn't a great character reference."

I persist. "He must think you're responsible enough to take care of Gracie. Why not call your aunt?"

His brows draw together. "Samantha wouldn't be . . ." He pauses.

"Sympathetic, let's say, to getting that phone call. More likely to make things much worse for Gracie. As it was, her sister Willa arrived as I was escorting her out of the bar."

"You're not proving me wrong." I give him a satisfied grin. "If anything, you've solidified my opinion."

"Willa had her own wild streak. Ran away from home as a teenager. I'd already been gone a couple years."

"Sounds like the Hills have a reputation for being wild teens."

"Bad apples fallen from the same family tree."

"What about as grown-ups?" I ask, still curious.

"Some of us settle down sooner than others." He shrugs, dismissing my attempt to pry for more and muttering something too quiet for me to hear.

I give him a sharp look.

"Stop making me out to be some sort of hero. There was a long span of my life where I was the last person you'd call if you needed a hand, a favor, or a friend. Looking back at my early twenties, I don't have many bridges left intact."

Silently, I wait him out.

"Every generation of Hill men has a black sheep, and the general consensus among the family is I'm the lucky bastard this go-around. Samantha's husband, my father's brother, was—is? Who knows if he's even still alive—the black sheep for their generation. Left his wife and four daughters behind in Green Valley and hasn't been heard from since."

"Sounds like a real piece of work." I'm mad on their behalf.

"The difference between my uncle and me is he stayed gone like last week's garbage. I came back."

"Isn't the same true for your cousin Willa?"

He reluctantly agrees. "I guess our roots are here. Anyway, enough about me and my messed-up family. Where's home for you?"

Ignoring the bigger question, I go for the simple answer. "You already know this—I live in the ranger cabins."

I cringe at the memory of him finding me in the woods, high on Benadryl and smelling of skunk.

"That's not what I asked. Where is your soul's home? Where do you feel most like yourself?"

I blink at him and then close my lids, trying to imagine the feeling he described. Forests and rock-strewn streams come to mind, but I can't decide on one particular place. After a few seconds, I open my eyes and refocus on him.

He waits for my answer with lifted brows.

"I'm not sure. I've moved around a lot, never staying in one place for a long time."

"Maybe you haven't found your dirt yet."

"Right now, I'd say the Smokies, but it's a big area. Two years ago, I might've said Yellowstone. Before that, the Grand Canyon."

He considers me, dragging his thumb along the patch of skin between his bottom lip and the edge of his beard.

I feel like I've failed an important test. "Can I give my answer another time?"

"It's no big deal. Not everyone thinks the way I do. Most people who manage to leave this area never come back. Teachers encourage their best and brightest students to go off to college, probably knowing once the kids get a taste of the world, they'll have a better life outside of Appalachia. I imagine people lost money when I decided to return."

"What do you mean?" He speaks in riddles and clues. I want to piece him together and solve the puzzle of Odin.

"I blew out of town at seventeen, an angry tornado, weaving a random path of destruction wherever I landed. Didn't give a damn about anything or anyone, only cared about getting away from here. I burned my bridges and left nothing but ashes and scorched earth behind me." He sweeps his hand over his jaw and then scratches near his temple. "Funny thing about that metaphor."

"What's that?" My voice remains calm, but inside I'm hopeful he'll reveal more about himself.

"Have you ever seen a forest after a fire?"

I nod. "Fire training is part of ranger academy."

"Of course. Then you know soil becomes more fertile after a fire. A burn will clear out the crowded undergrowth, sparing some of the mature trees. Scorched earth doesn't mean nothing will ever grow again. In fact, it's a good thing."

"Unlike a lava flow."

"Exactly. A devastating eruption destroys all life in its path."

"Be a fire, not a volcano."

He nods, a small, knowing smile curling his lips. "I thought I was a volcano. I wanted to leave destruction in my wake so I could never return to the same place."

"And instead?"

"I came back." He gives another one of his dismissive shrugs.

"And?" I prompt again.

"I rediscovered myself in the ashes of my former life. Not in my childhood—those deep roots and giant trunks remain—but in the life I thought I wanted, which turned out to be nothing but kindling for the blaze that nearly incinerated my existence."

Our eyes lock. He's telling me everything, and yet I know nothing more than I did a moment ago.

His attention slips over my shoulder. "Did you know a few years ago there was a huge fire in the Smokies? Thousands of acres burned."

"I remember hearing about it. I was in Montana then—or was it Arizona?" My years blur together unless I can place myself by location.

"Do you know what came after the fire?"

There are several answers I could give, but I sense all of them will be wrong.

"Morels."

"The mushroom?"

"Exactly. One of the best seasons in recent memory. Huge, glorious morels pushed their caps through the blackened, ash-coated soil. The flavor was incredible, like nothing I've tasted before or since."

"You talk about fungi the way some men speak about women."

His eyes light up. "A man should have more than one passion in life."

He pounces, playfully pressing me into the couch cushions, pinning me with his hips as he lays a row of hot, open-mouthed kisses down my neck.

I decide in this moment I could get burned by Odin Hill and be okay.

Whatever pain and heartache I'd face would be worth having him look at me like I'm his.

CHAPTER TWENTY-NINE
DAPHNE

*O*n Wednesday after work, I go hunting for something to wear for the dance. After checking all possible sources for dresses in Green Valley, I'm expanding my search. All roads lead to Merryville. Literally, every local route seems to meet around the town like spokes on a wheel. I guess this is where the term hub comes from in describing a place.

Compared to Green Valley, whose main street only houses a few shops, Merryville is brimming with two thrift stores and a consignment shop. If I can't find something here, I'll be forced to drive to Knoxville.

Lucky me combining two things I loathe: cities and shopping.

If I were getting married, serving as a bridesmaid, or going to prom, I'd be set for shiny, sparkly gowns. However, since I'm doing none of those things in the foreseeable future, I strike out on finding a dress for the party. In the parking lot outside the consignment store, I text 911 to Kacey in frustration. It's almost dinner time and I'm hoping to catch her at work.

A minute or so later, she calls me.

"What's the emergency?"

"Hi to you, too. I need help."

I hear the crunching sound of loud chewing. "Sorry, eating salad at my desk."

"You could've finished swallowing before calling me."

"911 is the emergency code, only to be used in actual emergencies."

"I need something to wear to a dance-slash-birthday party. You know this is out of my wheelhouse. Help me?" I plead.

"Whoa, hold on—you're going to a party?"

"For a centenarian. It's not going to be a rager." I'm assuming as much, but I suppose I could be wrong.

"Who do you know who's that old?"

"Odin's great-grandmother."

"Daphne!"

"Yes?"

"What have I told you about burying the important information?"

"The key point here is I have to have something dance-ish and you know my wardrobe is ninety percent jeans and T-shirts. The other ten percent is uniforms."

"Stop. You're going to a party with Odin? A family birthday?"

"That's what I said."

"This is serious."

"I know. What am I going to wear? Dress? Skirt?"

She groans. "I mean with him."

If I tell her I've had sex with him, her head might explode. Given the time crunch, I decide to save that revelation for later.

"I think I'm going to be a buffer between him and his family. Nannie Ida is insisting he brings a date."

"Pfft." She blows a long raspberry into the phone. "He's a grown man and can do what he wants. I think it's an excuse."

"I'm trying not to get my hopes up," I confess, my voice soft.

She remains quiet for a moment. "I'm happy you have hopes, high or low. You deserve only the best after your childhood. If the sexy farmer wants to plow your fields and harvest your crops, I'm over the moon for you."

Kacey is one of the few people who knows the full story of my past. Isaac and I had a class with her freshman year, and she's been in my life ever since.

Laughing at her ridiculousness, I ask, "Are those supposed to be euphemisms for sex?"

"If your mind goes there, I'm going to say yes." She giggles.

"Stop. You're terrible."

"Fine. So, what are you wearing?"

Exasperated, I sigh. "No idea. I'm sitting in the parking lot of a consignment store. This is the third place I've looked, and so far, nothing appeals to me."

"You should've called me earlier. I can ship you something."

"Why didn't I think of that? Oh, probably because you're a giraffe and I'm a wombat. Everything you own will be too long on me."

"I have the perfect dress. It's short on me, so it will fit the average wombat." She snorts. "Please don't ever put yourself down. You're beautiful and sexy and Odin Hill wants you."

"I wasn't putting myself down. It's just the truth. I have a low center of gravity because my legs are short. Don't dis the wombats—they're adorable."

My phone vibrates with a text. Glancing at the screen, I see Isaac's name.

"Speak of the devil. Guess who texted me?"

"Odin?"

"No, Isaac. I haven't spoken to him in months. Have you?"

"It's been a while. Last I heard he and the boyfriend were getting serious."

"Same. I'm happy for him."

"Doesn't that complicate things for you?"

"We'll cross that bridge when we come to it." Like the item at the bottom of a to-do list, I know I'll avoid dealing with it until I absolutely have to. I need to get off this call before she asks too many questions. "Thanks for sending the dress."

"When's the dance?"

"Saturday."

"I'll overnight it tomorrow with a backup option in case it doesn't work."

"You're the best."

"Take pictures. Since you never had prom, here's your moment." She laughs again.

"Thanks, Mom."

"Love you."

As soon as we end the call, I open the text from Isaac. He's asking when I'm free to chat. I miss him, but this week is busy and I suggest we catch up next week.

He doesn't respond right away.

Relieved I can call off the search, I set my phone in the cupholder. I feel a little guilty for driving an NPS vehicle to Merryville when I'm not on official business, but I was kind of desperate.

I haven't had time to figure out my next car or how I'm going to afford it. My insurance totaled my car, and the cash value is lower than the deductible. Their suggestion that I could buy it back and repair it made me laugh until I hung up on them. I'm not sure even the Winstons are talented enough to de-bear a car interior. It's still sitting in the campground as a warning.

As I start the engine, I glance around. Leaning against a Mercedes SUV parked on the other side of an empty spot, a man watches me through the passenger window. He waves, and I return the gesture. Trying to place him, I plaster on my friendly-but-placid work smile. He mimes rolling down the window.

He's casually dressed, but his clothes look expensive and too fancy for a strip mall consignment parking lot. Something about him makes me wary, and I touch the lock button for the doors before I do anything else.

Would someone be crazy enough to carjack a government vehicle? Probably.

He says something, but I can't understand him. Maybe he's lost and thinks I'll know the area. Rangers are notoriously helpful people.

I lower the passenger window, but only a quarter of the way. Safety first.

"Are you with the park service?" he asks, more brusque than friendly, likely from the city.

I'm out of uniform but there's a big sticker on the door right in front of him. "Sure am."

"Oh, good."

"Can I help you?"

"I hope so. The locals around here are useless. Can't understand half of what they're saying."

He doesn't use the word hillbilly, but it's implied by the way he says locals.

My eyebrows rise but I remain silent. Guess he takes this as encouragement, because he keeps speaking.

"I want to hire a guide for backcountry foraging, but no one will take me up on it even though you can tell they're all dirt poor around here and could use the money. Can you recommend anyone who has half a brain and is willing to do an honest day's work? Do rangers take side jobs?"

I don't like his entitled attitude or his choice of words. "Sorry, I can't help you. I wouldn't advise going into the mountains this time of year if you're not an experienced hiker. We can have severe storms, even snow."

When I don't say anything more, he frowns. "That's all you've got? Thanks for nothing."

"You're welcome. Have a nice day." I push the button to raise the window.

What an odd, snarly man. Anyone I know who took him into the backcountry would probably leave him there. Stranger danger is real.

People "around here" don't like outsiders because of men like him. He'd be better off driving his fancy car right back to whatever city he came from.

* * *

Gaia stops by my desk under the guise of discussing my work on the social media accounts. She's happy with the engagement, reminding me to respond to any questions if possible. Overall, the project has been positive and not nearly as torturous as I thought it would be, other than the few bots and trolls who have found the account and like to post negative comments. Some people need to go for long hikes away from society.

"Now that you've been here six months, any feedback and ideas for our interpretation programming?" she asks.

"How long do you have?" I joke. "I have so many thoughts, I don't know where to begin."

"What's your number one goal?"

"Mostly, I want girls to be excited about the junior ranger program and maybe studying to become rangers themselves. Women played a huge role in the early formation of the parks, especially the GSM. I want to honor and celebrate their legacy with more role models and mentorships."

"We definitely want to encourage more girls to sign up for the junior ranger program in the spring. Same with the internship programs in the summer. Let's brainstorm on how to expand our application process to attract more diversity—more women, more minorities. Would be great if we could have more languages spoken in the information center for visitors."

I write down her suggestions on a notepad next to my keyboard. "Agree."

"We can coordinate with Ranger Walker and her team over at the living museum. We have a lot of visitor overlap between the two sites, so it's important to work on these initiatives together."

As our talk winds down, she peeks around the partitions to see if Jay and Griffin are at their computers.

"Both of them are out in the field this afternoon," I remind her.

"Oh, right. Good."

"Something else you need to chat about?"

She glances over my shoulder at my sparse desk. Like my cabin, I don't have a lot of personal touches. "I know I'm your boss, but I wanted to check in with you about how you're doing outside of work. I hope I'm not crossing the line, but I've noticed you haven't been around as much. Everything okay?"

I'm not ready to discuss Odin yet. Our relationship has morphed from adversarial to . . . I'm not sure. Gaia knows I had dinner with him, and I feel that's all the information I'm willing to share.

"I'm good. Great. Fantastic." I emphasize this with two thumbs up.

She observes me for a moment or two. "Happy to hear it. If you ever need a friend, I'm around."

"Thank you."

"Being a ranger can be lonely. Especially as a woman. It can be easy to feel isolated. I've been there."

I realize I haven't given much thought to Gaia's social life. It's rare for her to open up to me about personal stuff.

"We should grab dinner soon. I owe you on that raincheck. Burgers and pie at Daisy's next week?"

Her eyes crinkle in the corners with her smile. "I'd like that."

"I'll drive."

We both laugh.

"Fine, but I'm buying."

"Deal."

I'm lucky to have her as my boss and would be foolish to refuse her friendship.

* * *

Thankfully, my package from Kacey arrives Saturday morning.

As soon as my shift is over, I'm out the door and headed for home. I don't have a lot of time to get ready, and I'm praying she sent me something good.

Not knowing what to expect from a centennial birthday party is giving me anxiety.

Tearing open the package, I see two tissue wrapped bundles. I asked for her help, so I should trust her instincts.

I try on the first item: a short black dress.

Hell no.

The plunging V goes so low my boobs and my bra are exposed. I think maybe I have it on backward, but swapping it front to back isn't an improvement. The short skirt barely falls to mid-thigh.

Nothing about this outfit feels like me.

What was she thinking?

The second choice is a fluffy, pale pink cardigan over a deep plum maxi dress and a coordinating pink silk scrunchie to hold back my hair.

With the cardigan, I look like a kindergarten teacher. This is a job interview outfit.

After removing the sweater, I tug the scrunchie out and toss it on the dresser. Better. I feel more like myself. I'd be even happier in leggings instead of the dress.

Honestly, I'd rather wear my uniform pants or jeans.

Taking a second look at myself in the mirror on the back of my bedroom door, I decide the long dress is actually okay. The tiered skirt could work for dancing, and the square neckline reveals some skin but stays out of areola-revealing territory. I actually like the color.

Bonus: the skirt is long enough and full enough, I can wear boots underneath.

We have a winner.

I shower, shave all the important bits, and lather enough lotion into my skin to make it shiny and glowing. Next is my hair. I watched a YouTube video on a half-up, half-down style that I think I can handle. Better than a pink scrunchie.

Makeup I keep to a minimum because that's all I know how to do in spite of watching tutorials online.

"Good enough," I tell my reflection. "As long as I don't fall down, we'll call this night a success."

Ready or not, Odin will be here to pick me up any minute.

With a calming breath, I grab my dressy coat from the closet. The deep pockets can hold my keys, wallet and a lipstick.

Here we go.

CHAPTER THIRTY
DAPHNE

"*Y*ou're especially beautiful tonight." Odin kisses my cheek, then sneaks a soft peck on my lips.

I feel my cheeks warm. "And you're as handsome as ever."

He's in a dark green and black plaid shirt and dark jeans, simple clothes he somehow makes sexier by wearing them. His hair is less wild than usual, but with the way he's running his hands through it, I doubt it will remain tamed.

"Stop fidgeting." His hand rests on mine and creates a cease-fire in the thumb war I've been waging against myself.

The gesture reminds me of my mother, who always did the same thing during church. Apparently, stillness is closer to the Lord than wiggling, even when you're five.

I slip my fingers beneath my thighs like I did when I was little. "Sorry."

"There's no reason to be nervous. Half the people at this thing will be too busy avoiding the other half. The rest of them will be judging and whispering about everyone else. Then there are the ones who will be God-blessing everyone's hearts out of pure spite because their own are cold and black." His lips curl with amusement.

His words don't soothe my nerves. "Sounds awful."

"Nah. The food's always good, there will be cake, and the dancing will be fun."

"So says you." I sound grim and not at all like someone going to a party.

"I do. An added bonus is some of the cousins still make moonshine, and there will be a jar or two passed around out of view of Nannie Ida."

"She doesn't approve of drinking?"

"Not at all. Her daddy served time during Prohibition and she's been a teetotaler her entire life."

"You're family's so . . . colorful." I'm not sure what to say, but that seems closest to a compliment.

"We can play a game of guessing what different folks served time for if you get bored. Some of the answers are hilarious, even for Hills."

"Will your cousins Willa and Gracie be here?"

He dismisses my question with a shrug. "Nah, they avoid all things having to do with this side of the family."

"And Ida gives them a pass?"

"She does on account of my uncle abandoning the family. Kind of a get-out-of-jail-free card."

We bounce along a dirt road for a mile or two until it ends in a wide field, vehicles of all makes creating messy rows in the makeshift parking area. A couple of boys, probably no older than ten, direct traffic, which explains the haphazard angles and lack of organization.

Across the open space sits an enormous barn, its exterior weathered and gray with age. I scan the area for a farmhouse or cabin but find none. Trees crowd together at the edges of the field, rising up the slope of the mountains surrounding us.

"Who lives here?" I ask, unbuckling my seatbelt when Odin shuts off the truck's engine.

"No one. House burned down a couple of decades ago and there wasn't any point in rebuilding."

"Why not?"

"Did you see the road we drove in on? Imagine it when it rains or snows—impassable. This property is the most isolated and the farthest from town, and most folks don't want to live in a place without cell service, internet, or electricity."

He climbs down from the cab and closes the door.

The hills have already blocked the late afternoon sun, casting the valley floor in a soft light absent of long shadows. Tall grasses, uncrushed by vehicles, gently sway in a breeze. From the soft rush, I know somewhere close by is running water, maybe even a waterfall. Seems like a pretty perfect spot for a hermit.

Following him around to the hood of the truck, I continue my train of thought. "I'm surprised you don't want to live out here."

He sweeps his gaze from me to the mountains and back. "It is beautiful, but I enjoy having electricity and being able to stream my entertainment."

"Softened by modern conveniences." I tsk. Not sure if it's the location or the butterflies in my belly having taken over my decision-making skills, but I feel happy, almost giddy as I tuck my arm around his elbow.

He stiffens for a second before his warm palm comes to rest on the back of my hand. Pleased he didn't pull away, I sneak a glance up at his face.

He's staring down at me, a new softness to his expression. "Thanks for coming with me."

I sneak a quick kiss. "I'm happy to be here with you."

Inside the barn, the band is playing and I feel like I've stepped into a Jane Austen novel, except instead of fancy empire-waist ball-gowns and tails, most folks are wearing casual attire. Odin was right about the dark wash jeans starched within an inch of rigor mortis, and most women wear dresses of various degrees of fanciness. I'm neither over nor underdressed, falling somewhere in the middle between *That's a nice housecoat* and *Are you going clubbing after this?*

The interior is a wide-open post-and-beam structure without stalls or other walls dividing the large space. A small hayloft spans the width of one end, and the four-person band I heard from outside is set up in the shadows beneath. Comprised of a mandolin player, a fiddler, a guitarist, and a banjo player, the group forms a half-circle, and off to one side stands a man with a microphone.

"He's the caller for the dances." Odin leans close and answers my unasked question. "Think of him as Simon in Simon Says."

"Right. Okay." I straighten my spine and roll my shoulders back.

"Relax. Your face looks like you're walking through a haunted house and something scary is going to happen at any second."

I force myself to grin. "Better?"

"Worse, actually." He squeezes my hand in the crook of his elbow. "Let's find the grub before these miscreants eat all the best stuff."

"Shouldn't we find Nannie Ida and wish her a happy birthday first?"

"We could." He eyes the long line snaking toward the buffet tables laden with food, most of which appears to be homemade.

"Are you nervous to see her?" I pause, allowing my brain to come up with a worse alternative. "Or are you worried about introducing me?"

"Neither." He steps in front of me, blocking my view of the room so I can only see him. "Remember how I said I'm the black sheep?"

I confirm I do with a dip of my chin.

"Consider this a room full of rockin' chairs and me a cat with a long tail." He gazes over my head. "I've avoided most of these gatherings over the past three years. A lot of these folks will be expecting to be entertained either by gossip or scandal."

"Ignore them. We'll wish Ida a happy birthday, elbow our way to the food, and then find a corner to hide in until the dancing begins."

"I like the way you think." He ducks his head to kiss me, in front of his family and the band, who, in reality, may also be family.

I'm convinced everyone here is related by blood or by marriage except me. I'm the outlier, the one thing that is different than the others. I can feel it in their stares and hear it in their whispers. I don't belong here. They all know it. I know it.

Odin's warm fingers slide between mine as he weaves his way through the gathering. Most people say hello as we pass. Like petulant toddlers, a few turn their heads, deliberately pretending they can't see us. *Bless their hearts.* I want to yell at them and ask what's wrong with them for not seeing the good in Odin. They must be broken on the inside.

A couple in their fifties walks straight toward us, happy smiles on both their faces. The woman has blond hair and familiar warm, caramel eyes. The man is an older version of Odin, right down to the happy grin he's wearing.

He slaps Odin on the shoulder and says, "I guess I owe your momma fifty bucks."

Meanwhile, the woman I'm going out on a limb to guess is his mom, gazes at me with friendly curiosity. "Oh stop, Ray. I won't make you pay up. I'm always happy to see my son."

"I told you I was comin' and I kept my word." Odin gives my fingers a squeeze, "I'd like you to meet my folks, Ray and Shannon Hill. This is Daphne Baum. Originally from Idaho, she's a ranger over at Cades Cove. Been in the area for about six months. Doesn't have kin around here."

The three of us gawk at him, me most of all.

"Thanks for sharing my bio, Odin." I extend my hand to his mother. "It's nice to meet you."

"Oh, you too, darlin'." She gives me a warmer grin. "You don't know how wonderful it is to meet you."

Her enthusiasm is a little overwhelming. I shake his dad's hand too.

"Have you said hello to Ida yet?" his mom asks. "Better do it now before the locusts descend on the food."

Odin flashes me a smug look as if to say *See? I told you.*

"We have to find your grandmother. She's around here some-where. I promised I'd fix her a plate." Ray's already on the move and Shannon follows behind him, giving us a wave before the crowd swallows them.

We join a shorter line than the one at the buffet. "What's this for?"

"It's the receiving line to say hello."

I peer around him, surprised to see people formally queued up to greet the birthday girl.

"This doesn't seem very fun for Ida, sitting here while people parade by her, saying the same thing over and over again." I whisper my thoughts near Odin's shoulder so the others don't overhear.

He laughs. "She's a hundred. Sitting and pretending to listen are two of her favorite pastimes."

I gaze up at Odin to check on his reaction to me meeting his parents. From his rambling and his mom's response, I'm guessing he doesn't introduce many new people to his family.

"Your mom and dad seem nice." I offer a general compliment to test the waters.

"They're good people." His fingers find mine again and he entwines them together. "Mom will be calling tomorrow to get the full scoop on you."

"Really? I thought you gave her a pretty thorough rundown." I squeeze his hand.

"I, uh . . . I guess I did." He chuckles softly. "Sorry about that. I'm not used to introducing people to my parents. I mean, women." He rambles and then stops as he blows out a frustrated breath. "You know what I mean. I wanted you to meet them, and I'm glad you did."

"I do. I'm glad too." I rest my other hand on his bicep. "Thank you."

I look up and see we've reached the front of the line.

"Odin? That you? I'm so happy you're here." The tiny woman wears an elaborately decorated paper tiara tucked behind thin, white braids wrapped around her head like a headband. She grins up at him, the lines on her face like a map of city streets. She holds up both of her thin hands for him to grasp before turning her attention to me. "Is this beautiful woman the girlfriend you've been telling me about?"

Girlfriend.

The sound in the room goes all tinny as I try the word on for size. Surprisingly, it fits comfortably. Meeting the parents. Being called girlfriend. This is a big night and I'm okay.

"Nannie Ida, this is Daphne Baum—Ranger Baum."

Since Odin still holds both of her hands in one of his, I give a small wave, unsure if I should also curtsey.

"Because my favorite great-grandson is sweet on you, I'll forgive you for working at the park. What do you do there, dear?"

She doesn't miss a thing. I share about the talks I give and the visitor center. She listens, or pretends to, while seated on an antique chair that strongly resembles a throne.

"Come back and find me after you get some food. I requested stack cakes with apple butter, twenty cakes with five layers each. Have you ever had stack cake before, Daphne?"

"I don't think I have."

She releases Odin's hands and pats my forearm. "You don't know what you're missing. Nothing like them. Nothing compares."

With one promise to come back and another one to dance, we wander away from the crowd gathered around the birthday girl.

"I feel like I've just had an audience with the queen."

"In many ways, you have." His hand on my elbow guides me to our next destination.

"She loves you. You probably are her favorite."

"And you're basing this declaration on what exactly?" He strokes his beard, which I now notice he's trimmed recently.

"Human observation."

"All right, then."

"I have no evidence to the contrary," I declare.

"I'm the black sheep, remember?" he says, keeping his voice low lest someone overhear him and realize who he is.

"Which means you're different, and different means special."

He scoffs and scowls.

In the corner opposite the band is another group of tables lined with pies and cakes of all kinds. Little kids play in the area, running circles in a game of tag. Smartypants keeping close to the desserts—they know it's the best spot in the place. The adults aren't paying attention because they're kids being kids, and as I watch, two littler ones swipe cupcakes from the far side of the table, away from the eyes of authority.

I poke Odin's side and point at the horde. "Which one of them is the black sheep for their generation?"

"What are you talking about? They're little kids."

"You said every generation has one. If it's by birth order or whatever made up bullshit you were told, we can ask them to line up for easier identification. We'll bribe them with sweets."

"You're crazy." Briefly closing his eyes, he reopens them to give me a stern look. "I know what you're trying to do."

"I'm sampling the population. One black sheep per generation, and I'm guessing said sheep must also be male. We can cut all the girls from the sample, even though from what I've been told, they can be as wild and rebellious as the boys. That leaves us with . . ." I pause to count. "Eleven possibilities. My money is on the really little one with a cupcake in his left hand and his right index finger in his ear. He's got trouble written all over him even though he's no higher than the corn in July." My Southern accent returns at the end of my speech.

Glancing around, I hope no one else heard it and feels insulted. It truly is terrible.

A woman behind us has clearly been listening because she taps me on the shoulder and says, "I believe the old saying is 'knee-high to a June bug'."

"Thank you." I give her a warm smile.

Odin turns to see who is speaking and his face lights up. "Hi, Lena."

"Hey, Odin." She hugs him. "Good to see you. Figured you'd find a way to skip tonight's circus."

She hugged him, penetrated his force-field with no visible resistance. *Or did I just imagine that?*

He bestows his genuine smile on her. "I'd say the same about you. Lena Walker, this is Ranger Daphne Baum. I've been wanting to introduce the two of you."

She quickly scans my face. "Nice to meet you. You're the new full-timer at Cades Cove, right?"

I smile and shake her hand. "And you're at the farm museum? I can't believe we haven't met before now."

"Lena runs the farming operations. She knows more about native plants and heirloom crops than anyone else." Pride coats Odin's words.

"Anyone except Ida Hill. She's a walking encyclopedia. She knows things even Google doesn't." She beams up at him.

"Lena's been studying with Ida for the last five years," Odin says.

"Six, but who's counting?"

They have a deep connection I haven't witnessed him share with anyone else.

"Are you one of the Hill cousins, too?" My curiosity is piqued.

"Oh, no. I'm not a relative . . . as far as we know." She's beautiful with high cheekbones and straight, almost-black hair kind of like Kacey's, and she's wearing a brightly patterned top with jeans. I'm jealous and simultaneously in admiration of her for doing her own thing. "Odin and I share a mutual obsession with horticulture."

My gaze shifts from Lena to Odin, and I wonder if they've ever been involved. What are the odds of a woman loving weird heirloom plants as much as he does? Still, there isn't any awkward tension or simmering bitterness between them. If they were together, they appear to have ended amicably.

"How are the apple grafts doing? Still optimistic they'll take?" he asks.

"So far, so good." She crosses her fingers. "How's the spore cultivation going?"

"Good, good. I've had some success with the shiitake logs. You should come by the farm and check out my progress. I have some turkey tails in the dehydrator, too."

Oh, he's talking about mushrooms—the fungus among us. If I've learned anything, once he gets started, this could be a long conversation. Letting my attention wander as they chat, I spot Jay and Olive across the room.

"I'm going to go say hello." I point at my friend and colleague. "If you get to the front of the line before I get back, will you make a plate for me?"

Odin agrees and I tell Lena it was nice to meet her.

"Come visit the farm. I'd be happy to show you around."

Located just over the North Carolina border but still part of the GSM park, the living museum is staffed with historians who maintain the collection of original structures. Like in Cades Cove, the park pulled buildings from other locations to recreate a farm.

I remember Odin's words about erasing history and retelling it to fit the park's narrative.

Jay and Olive stand off to the side. Olive wears a flowy, navy maxi dress that highlights her blue eyes and dark hair, and Jay's wearing a black collared shirt and jeans. They could be on an album cover.

Jay's brow furrows when he spots me. "Daphne? What are you doing here?"

"I was coming over to ask you both the same thing." I smile warmly at Olive.

"I dragged him along." She points at the band. "Porter Walker invited me as part of my traditional Appalachian music project."

"Any relation to Lena?"

"Probably. You know her? Isn't she the best?" Olive gushes. "I think she's the coolest woman I've ever met."

My attention flits to where Odin is chatting with her.

"Who are you here with?" Jay follows my eyes. "No. Seriously?"

Olive stands on her toes to see better. "Odin Hill? The hot farmer?!"

Jay's head jerks back in surprise. "The guy who walks his pig on a leash? *He's* hot?"

She pats his chest. "Calm down. You're more handsome."

On paper, they don't make sense, but in reality, they're perfect together. Introverts need love too, and if our resident nerdy ornithologist can find his soulmate, there's hope for all lonely hearts.

CHAPTER THIRTY-ONE
ODIN

"This ain't my funeral, so why are we all standing around instead of dancing?" Nannie Ida stomps her cane on the worn boards of the old barn floor.

Conversations around us begin to die down, but a few folks continue their chatter, unaware or unconcerned the guest of honor is speaking.

"Odin, whistle for me, will you?"

"Sure thing." I place my pinkies in the corners of my mouth and release a shrill sound, one that's impossible to ignore or talk over.

"I taught you well." She pats my arm, her fingers bony and skin papery with age.

"You sure did. Anything else I can do for you?" I crouch next to her chair so she doesn't have to crane her neck to see my face.

"I can handle it from here."

Another pat before she turns her attention to the room, everyone collectively holding their breath as they wait for her to speak.

"Now that you're listening . . ." She gives me a smug grin. "Like I said, save the jabbering and reminiscing for when I'm dead. I reckon you won't have to wait too long."

A few people murmur about her outliving all of us before she stops them with a swipe of her hand.

"Hush with your foolishness. Porter?" She points the tip of her cane at the band.

"Yes, ma'am?" He straightens his spine and stands taller.

"Somebody paying you to play your fiddle tonight?"

"Yes, ma'am."

"Well?" She gives him a stare that could freeze a pond with ducks still on it.

With a nod, he picks up his bow and tucks the instrument under his chin.

"Any requests?" he asks.

"You know what I like."

He nods again before turning his back to us and whispering something to his bandmates, and then the opening notes of a waltz float over the crowd.

Still squatting next to Ida's chair, I hold out my hand. "May I have this dance?"

Her rheumy eyes are full of steel and intolerance for bullshit as they stare back at me.

"Isn't there someone else you'd rather partner with? Go ask your girlfriend to dance. I'll sit here and keep the time with my stick." She gives her hand-carved cane a few good thumps in time with the beat to prove her point.

Watching Daphne from across the room, I slide my fingers through my hair and curse softly.

"The last thing I want is a girlfriend," I remind her. I'm not saying that because I'm only into sleeping around without the trappings of commitment. Since returning to Green Valley, I've avoided all socializing. After years of living in cities, surrounded by people, I'm done. I think I've reached the maximum number of social connections for one lifetime.

"Everyone needs love in their life, Odin. 'Bout time you let someone into your heart."

"Daphne and I are . . ." I let the sentence go unfinished. Honestly, I don't know. She's at this party with me as . . . what? A date? A human shield? Friendly foil to my family's meddling? All true, but she's more to me.

I like her. I like spending time with her, talking with her, and having sex with her. Why do we have to put labels on people, trying to control them by claiming them as ours?

Ida giggles, sounding decades younger than she is. "Lord help you, son. Love's made you stupid. You've been struck with Cupid's arrow. Hold on to her if you can. Now, get over there and ask her to dance before one of your cousins swoops in and steals her."

I bristle at the thought of anyone else with Daphne.

"I love you, Nannie." Leaning down, I place a soft kiss on her cheek.

"Save the declarations for your sweetheart." She pokes me with the business end of her stick. "Quit stalling."

I don't bother telling her it's too soon for me to be in love with Daphne. We're only getting to know each other. We've spent a small bit of time together, but there's no point in arguing with Ida. Once she's made up her mind, she'll never be convinced she's wrong.

The caller announces the dance as couples make their way to the center of the room in front of the band. Non-dancers shuffle to the side or take seats at the round tables along the edges, though Nannie Ida's view remains unobstructed. No one is stupid enough to block her from seeing the action.

In the shifting crowd, I lose track of Daphne. Half-tempted to stand on a chair for a better vantage point, I finally locate her off to the side, with the other wallflowers.

I get the feeling she's more comfortable being an observer, not because she's shy but because she's unsure of how to join. Her expression holds cautious delight and wonder, excitement about the dancing and dread at being asked.

I'm not a therapist, but I'm good at reading people. Maybe I missed my calling of studying psychology, though working in a commercial kitchen probably taught me more about people than any book or lecture could.

Squeezing myself through the narrow gaps behind chairs, I forge the shortest path between the birthday girl's throne and Daphne.

"May I?" I extend my hand, palm up so the invitation is clear.

"Go ahead. I'm good to watch from here." Without even glancing at me, she refuses my offer.

"Nope. The fun is had in the doing." Before she can concoct an excuse, I slip my hand around her waist and give her a gentle nudge. She gives in more easily than her posture promised. Once she's beside me, I tip my head closer to hers. "You'll do fine. We practiced. Remember, contra is just Simon Says to music."

"What if I mess up?" Her forehead wrinkles with worry.

"Everyone does. We laugh it off and keep going. Dancing isn't about being perfect." I give her a reassuring squeeze.

Near the dance floor, she hesitates again. "I don't want to embarrass you."

"Impossible." I lead her to the line of women and squeeze her in between two cousins. "Just listen to the caller and follow what these ladies do."

I take my place in the row facing them, the caller claps his hands and the dance begins.

At first, Daphne's eyes are wide and nervous like a spooked colt. After a few turns and do-si-dos, though, her smile returns. Her steps aren't perfect and her grip is tentative, but she isn't the worst dancer in the room, not by a long mile.

Seeing her laughing and happy gives me a warm feeling in my chest.

Nannie Ida might be right.

CHAPTER THIRTY-TWO
DAPHNE

*O*utside the barn, I inhale the crisp air and stare at the bazillion stars sprinkled throughout the Milky Way, visible in the clear sky.

My brain feels like it's on the loopy-de-loop ride at the fair, and I don't know why or how to stop it.

Could be the dancing, all those reels and swings with their turns and spins.

Could be too much sugar from the extra piece of cake I ate. Turns out stack cake is an irresistible combination of cake and pancakes with apple butter spread between the layers. It was Odin's slice and he said I could have it, because he's nice even if he swears he isn't.

I remember the moonshine one of his cousins gave me in an adorably tiny glass jar with a slice of apple on the rim like a garnish . . . and the second or third jars that followed. I can't recall if those had apple slices.

Or . . . the source of my discombobulation could be Odin himself. The man is dangerous with his disarming smiles and happy energy.

He's not at all who I believed him to be—a weirdo scofflaw with a pig.

"At least Patsy doesn't have a bad attitude. Good piggy." For some reason, I begin singing, "This little piggy went to market, this little doggo stayed home. This farmer was a demigod, that one gave a dog a bone. Knick-knack-paddy-whack, something, something, and we all fall down."

I hear giggling close by and whirl around to find the source, only to realize the sound is coming from me. "Whoa. Is this what an out-of-body experience feels like? I should go inside and sit down."

My feet don't cooperate and tangle themselves together, causing me to sway.

As I hear deep, masculine laughter, a steady hand anchors around my waist, keeping me from pitching forward. "You okay?"

The surprise contact shocks me, and I manage to flip myself around so I'm staring up at the sky. I'm basically a ballroom dancer in a low dip, or a fish on dry land with my mouth agape. Breathing is difficult.

When I try to reply, my words get stuck in my throat, mainly because my head is tossed back at such an angle that I'm staring at the treetops upside down.

Using core muscles I rarely engage, I lift myself enough to speak and realize Odin is the one with the strong hand and excellent balance preventing me from hitting the ground. "Why are you dipping me?"

His eyebrows furrow together. "Are you drunk?"

"Maybe?" The effort to support my head is too much, and I let gravity win this battle. Bad idea. What should be solid earth shifts and undulates wherever my gaze lands. Even the barn wobbles on its foundation.

Better to close my eyes.

My lids meet, and everything goes toes over nose.

Nope. Definitely worse.

I peek between my lashes; the world is still gyrating like an over-zealous male stripper in a gold thong. Just as I'm resigning myself to this topsy-turvy existence and the very real possibility of vomiting,

I'm once again vertical with my feet on the ground and my stomach back in its rightful place.

"Hey," Odin whispers, lifting my chin with his finger. "Can you focus?"

"You know I." My words come out in the reverse order of what I intended, making me sound like Yoda. Still nauseated, I'm certain I'm sporting the same green skin hue as the wise one. "I know you."

"You do. The question is, do you know yourself?" His mouth does that thing where it curves with amusement and knowing and smugness, like he finds me immensely entertaining in a reality-show-trainwreck kind of way.

In an effort to stop his smirking ways, I use both index fingers to smoosh his smile down into a frown. I rhymed in my head and it makes me laugh.

The hand not holding my waist defends his mouth from my prodding.

"How much did you drink, Daphne?" He glares at something over my head.

"Moonshine with apple slices—a cocktail and a snack all in one."

"I know *what* you had. I was asking how many." His sigh is rather loud.

"You're not my boyfriend, so don't sound disappointment."

"Disappointed."

"That's what I said." I take a blind step back and the heel of my boot sinks into the soft dirt, causing my balance to shift.

"Okay, let's get you home before you fall and hurt yourself." He extends his arms to catch my shoulders. Gently facing me in the opposite direction, he begins marching us forward.

I'm disappointed—no, relieved he didn't decide to carry me.

"You act all mean and cynical, but you're a big softie, Odin Hill." I attempt to crane my neck to look at his face, but he adjusts his grip.

"Eyes forward, Ranger Baum." He's all Mister Stern and Bossy. I hate how much I love him—hate how much I love *it,* that is. No, actually, I think I was right the first time.

"Oh, we're using formal titles now, Chef?" My smirk is triumphant even if he can't see it.

His huff of warm air sweeps across my shoulders, causing me to shiver.

He pauses mid-step. "Damn it. Where's your coat?"

"Didn't have one."

"You did. It was dark green with a collar and black buttons."

"Sounds like mine." I attempt to keep walking, but I'm held in place by his grip. *How many people does it take to qualify as a conga line?* Maybe if I step to the left and then to the right, I can trick him into dancing our way out of here.

With a resigned sigh, he releases me. "Let's get you to the truck. Can you promise to stay put while I go back inside and search for it?"

"For what?"

"Your coat. Jesus, I want to punch those idiots and their moonshine."

"You can't punch a liquid. I mean, you could, but it wouldn't be very unsatisfying. Have you thought about freezing it instead? Depending on alcohol level, it might never freeze solid. Could be similar to punching a Jell-O mold. Slightly more therapeutic than water, but again, I doubt it's going to give you any satisfaction. And another thing, you shouldn't resort to violence to express your emotions. Boy howdy is that unhealthy. Almost as bad as bottling everything up. Did you know—"

His hand covering the lower half of my face interrupts my word flow. "Will you please stop talking for a minute?"

I open my mouth, forgetting for a second I can't verbalize my answer with his palm against my lips. I nod instead.

"Have you ever had moonshine before?" His voice is full of genuine concern.

"Nope."

"Didn't think so." With a gentle touch, he brushes my hair away from my face before kissing me softly on the lips.

His beard tickles and makes me giggle. "This might be the grain alcohol speaking, but it wants me to tell you we love you."

I swear he says it back, but the words are too quiet for me to hear clearly.

"What did you say?" Trying to read his lips this time, I squint at him in the darkness.

"Come on, let's get you home." He settles me inside the cab of his truck and then disappears into the night.

I rest my head on the window, imagining Odin telling me he loves me.

Despite my initial best efforts to see the bad in him, I know he's a good man, a decent and kind person.

And I love him.

CHAPTER THIRTY-THREE
ODIN

*I*f an "I love you" is said for the first time but not remembered, does it still count?

What if the words come not only from the woman you're falling in love with but are also expressed on behalf of an inanimate object—are they negated?

No and yes.

This is how I reason away Daphne's declaration from last night, because I sure as hell don't love moonshine back. I'm still pissed at my cousins. Bunch of idiot noggin-knockers with their apple pie moonshine.

By the time I got back to my truck last night, she was sound asleep. I roused her enough to buckle her seatbelt and tuck the wool coat around her like a blanket.

I didn't want to take her to the ranger cabins in case she got sick in the night, so I brought her home with me, carried her inside, and switched out her dress for my T-shirt before tucking her under the covers.

At first light, I'm out of bed and dressed, quietly sneaking out of the room so I don't disturb her. I have a pint jar of Ida's cure-all in the fridge for when Daphne wakes up. I suspect she's going to have one mean hangover.

Keeping to my morning routine, I let Roman out and check on Patsy while he does his business. She comes out of her house to greet me, eats her breakfast, and then the three of us wander around the yard and gardens while I drink my first cup of coffee of the day.

Behind the greenhouse is my new project. I've taken grafts from the hidden trees and given some to Lena for preservation. Eventually, the old orchard will stop producing and I don't want to lose those varieties. It will be a couple of years before any of these saplings produce fruit, but I'm here for the long haul.

Coffee finished, I whistle for the animals and they follow me back to the house. Roman gets his breakfast while Patsy claims her bed on the porch for a post-meal nap. After refilling my cup, I join her, sitting in my favorite chair.

For countless mornings, we've followed this same routine. Like the post office, we don't let snow, sleet, or rain deter us.

Today is different. Daphne's presence changes everything. I listen for sounds of her stirring, curious to know how she slept and if she has a headache. Images of her in my bed, wearing only my T-shirt leave me with a different kind of wanting.

Time has a funny way of contracting and expanding. August seems like years ago, and the last month has also seemed to last only a few days. When it comes to Daphne, I either feel like I've known her forever or like our meeting at the farmers' market was yesterday.

Do I believe in love at first sight? No.

Do I believe two people are fated to be together? No.

However, I know it is possible to wake up one morning and know with absolute certainty you're in love with someone.

Impatient for her to wake up so I can tell her that, I make my way to the bedroom and discover the bed empty.

"Daphne?" I call out, a weird dread pooling in my chest as I think she might've left while I was in the orchard. Logically, I know it isn't possible. I would've seen or heard a car coming up the road, and Roman would've reacted, barking to alert me to the invasion.

Her dress still lies on the chair where I put it last night—she couldn't have gotten far in an old T-shirt.

"Bathroom," she responds from down the hall.

Lifting my gaze to the ceiling, I roll my eyes at my worry.

While I stand in the middle of my bedroom, she dashes past me and leaps into the bed, pulling the thick quilt and blankets up to her chin.

"Brr," she mumbles into the covers. "Why is winter a thing?"

I refrain from pointing out we're in the middle of fall. Instead, I ask, "How are you feeling?"

She shifts the sheets to expose her mouth. "Rough around the edges, but I think I'll live."

"Coffee?"

She frowns. "I'm not sure."

"Food?"

"Maybe?"

I sit on the side of the mattress and hand her the glass of water from the little table next to her side of the bed.

I let that thought marinate for a moment and decide I like the idea of her claiming the other half of my bed.

"You're doing the thing again." She returns the half-full glass back to me.

"What's that?"

"Being kind and taking care of me."

I shrug off her accusation. "I'm basically treating you like a houseplant by watering you."

"Odin."

"Yes?"

"The end of the evening is a little blurry. Too many spins plus too much moonshine isn't a good combination."

My lips press together as I try to contain my amusement at her silly ramblings.

"You have a terrible poker face." She flips the quilt over her head, muffling her words. "What did I do?"

"Nothing to feel guilt or shame over."

The top of her head and then her eyes reappear. "Your answer indicates something was said, or done. I didn't get sick, did I?

"No."

"I woke up in your shirt."

"I put you in it last night. Your dress was too pretty to sleep in."

"You liked my dress?" Her brow furrows.

"Sure. You were the most beautiful woman at the party, though I prefer you as you are now—in my bed and mostly naked." In the soft morning light, she glows. No filter needed.

"You could be naked in it with me." She pats the pillow next to her head.

"I wanted to let you sleep off the moonshine."

Her warm brown eyes widen before she ducks beneath the covers again.

"Darlin'?" I peel back the layers of fabric until I expose her face.

"I remember being outside the barn with you. We were dancing and singing. No, I was. You were dipping me." She gazes out the window. "I may have said something I shouldn't have."

"Look at me." I wait for her to meet my eyes before I continue. "I promise you didn't."

The truth stretches between us, connecting us to our individual memories of last night, both of us holding our breath, waiting for either confirmation or denial.

Searching her face for doubt I don't find, I bring her wrist to my mouth and press my lips against her pulse. I'm stalling, an unfamiliar nervousness quickening my heart rate. Expressing my emotions and sharing my feelings with another human is new for me. With a steadying breath, I decide I'm willing to brave the unknown with her.

Still holding her wrist, I sit up before speaking. "The words you said last night were something I've been thinking about for a while now. I worried it was too soon to say I love you, but I do. I'm falling in love with you, Daphne."

Her inhalation catches in her throat and the rims of her eyes fill with tears. "You love me?"

"I love you."

She hasn't repeated her declaration. I'm on the edge of panic and ready to backpedal. Maybe she didn't mean it. Perhaps it was simply drunken babbling signifying nothing more than random thoughts.

"I love you, Odin."

Relief carries me away on a current of happiness. Scooping her into my arms, I lavish kisses on her mouth and neck. The oversized shirt is discarded along with my clothes as we strip each other bare. Our lovemaking is frenzied, tangled layers of love and lust. I make sure she orgasms before me, holding back until her body achieves its release. Right before I come, I kiss her, repeating "I love you" between each breath until my mind goes blank with pleasure.

As we lie sprawled across my bed, Daphne's head on my chest, our breaths slowly returning to normal, I stare at the ceiling and wonder how I got so lucky.

A shower follows before we crawl back into bed to eat the simple breakfast I prepared.

Sipping a cup of coffee, I ask about her plans for the day and week.

"Even though I don't go to church anymore, I like to take Sundays off to do nothing whenever I can. During the season, I'm always working. What about you?"

"The only thing I want to do is be here with you." I kiss her shoulder.

She bites into a piece of toast. "Sounds like heaven."

Daphne's phone pings repeatedly with new texts.

"Do you want to check your messages?"

"No." She casts a dirty look at the device on the table a few feet away.

Two more notifications quickly follow.

"Could be a work emergency." I lean over her to reach for the phone and hand it to her.

"Even more reason to ignore it." Despite the statement, she reluctantly accepts it, and her eyes widen as she reads the texts. "I have to get back to the park."

"Is everything okay?" I've never heard this tone in her voice. Fear coils itself around my spine.

"I'm not sure. Can you give me a ride?" She's on the move, locating her bra on the floor and then pulling her dress over her head.

"Of course. Let me put Patsy in her pen and I'll meet you outside."

* * *

We don't say much on the drive over to Cades Cove. She's staring out the window, lost in thought, and I don't want to pry. If she wants to tell me, she will. Occasionally, she'll tap out a message on her phone.

"Where am I going?" I ask once we're on the loop road.

"Visitor center."

When we arrive, I scan the area for signs of an emergency. There's no smoke in the air. I don't see a fire engine or ambulance or panic in the eyes of the people milling around. Appears everything is fine.

"Am I dropping you off, or should I stay?" I pull into a turnout and pause.

"Stay. Please." She grips my hand. "I love you, remember that. Nothing changes how I feel."

"Okay." More confused than ever, I park the truck. "I love you too."

She gives me a soft kiss but doesn't allow me to deepen it before she's opening her door and jumping out of the cab.

I exit a few seconds behind her.

Daphne runs across the parking area and into the arms of a guy dressed in an expensive black coat and boots straight from the streets of Manhattan. He stands out like lipstick on a pig—not that I'd ever apply makeup to Patsy. Simply put, I'd notice him even if he weren't hugging Daphne.

When he sets her down, she grins and simultaneously swipes away tears from her cheeks. It's impossible to ignore the happiness surrounding them like a bubble, the love in his eyes as he gazes at her apparent even from ten feet away where I'm observing their tender moment like a creeper.

Jealousy constricts my chest like a jacket that's too small. My lungs can't fully expand to inhale.

Whoever this man is, I don't like him. Moreover, I don't like how Daphne beams at him like he's the sun, the moon, and the best birthday cake wish come true.

Unhappy with my current state and unwilling to stand around as an outsider to this love-fest, I turn on my heel to return to the truck.

"Odin?" Daphne's voice halts my steps. "Come meet Isaac."

Her friend. Of course. Relief eases the bindings around my lungs.

"Hi. Odin Hill." My voice is friendly as I extend my hand to shake his.

"Nice to meet you. You look familiar." He gives me a warm smile. "Isaac Baum."

If he's lived in New York long enough, he may have dined in one of my restaurants. *Wouldn't that make for a small world?*

"Isaac surprised me." Daphne's fingers twist into her hair—her nervous tell.

"Baum? Are you related? I thought you said you were friends."

The two of them both freeze like they've encountered a hostile animal in the woods.

257

He gawks at her, which she ignores by keeping her focus on me.

"Daphne?" I try to get her attention by reaching for her hand. "You didn't mention you have a brother."

"We aren't siblings—or cousins. We aren't related by blood." The words tumble from her mouth.

I force a chuckle, like I'm in on the joke even though I have no idea what's going on. "Funny coincidence you have the same last name."

Isaac gives her a sharp look. "Daphne. You didn't tell him?"

"Tell me what?" If I had them, my hackles would be up.

He frowns at me, pity in his eyes. "Technically, Daphne is my wife."

CHAPTER THIRTY-FOUR
DAPHNE

*T*he happiness I feel upon seeing Isaac fades as soon as he tells Odin we're married.

I want to cry and smack Isaac.

"On paper only," I clarify. "We haven't seen each other in almost a year."

Odin's expression darkens. "Married? Maybe you should've mentioned you have a husband."

I hate the hurt in his eyes and knowing I caused it.

Isaac puts his hand on my shoulder. "It's a marriage of convenience, in name only."

I shake off his touch and try to catch Odin's attention.

"Serious enough for you to take his name." He won't look at me. "Whatever game this is, I don't want any part of it."

"Odin, stop. Please listen to us." I grab his elbow, thinking that will prevent him from leaving.

"I'm sorry we sprung this on you." Isaac gives him a sympathetic smile. "I needed to get in touch with Daphne."

"You flew all the way down here because I didn't return your texts for a few days?"

"Did you read them?" Isaac counters.

"I meant to respond. I've been busy." My gaze cuts to Odin, who has lightning-bolt-throwing eyes.

Isaac sighs. "I had business in Atlanta so I decided to rent a car and drive up here with the papers. What a beautiful area, by the way. I swear I drove through the part of Georgia where *Deliverance* was set, and I was expecting toothless hillbillies with banjos."

Odin bristles. I want to kick Isaac.

"Well, on that note, I'll leave the two of you to catch up. I need to get back to the holler and get the possums skinned for supper," Odin drawls in a thick Appalachian accent.

I'm too stunned to follow him as he stomps away.

"Whoa. Your boyfriend is pissed. He's also super-hot. Do you really eat possum down here? What does it taste like? Everything exotic always ends up tasting like chicken. Have you ever noticed that?" He laughs like this is all hysterical.

"Isaac, if you don't shut up, I'll never speak to you again."

"What? The hillbilly thing was clearly a joke. He's mad because I brought up *Deliverance,* right? He wasn't serious."

Closing my eyes, I count my inhalations and exhalations. Once I'm certain I won't tackle him to the ground and kick his ass like I did when we were seven, I turn my attention to him.

"Give me the papers and I'll sign them. You have a long drive back to Atlanta tonight."

"They're in the car." He sounds wary and he should be. "My flight isn't until tomorrow afternoon, so I thought you could show me around and we could go to dinner if there's anywhere decent around here to eat."

I'm already striding over to the nondescript black sedan. He jogs to keep up.

"I'm sorry if my jokes insulted your friend. Stereotypes exist because they're based on the truth."

"Don't say sorry to me. You should've apologized to Odin."

"Who names their kid Odin?" His brow furrows. "What's his last name again?"

"Hill."

"Wait a Hotlanta second—that was *Odin Hill*? The Michelin-starred chef? No way." His expression crumbles. "And I made a hillbilly joke. I am a huge asshole."

I tuck my chin and gaze up at him. "Yep."

He places both hands on the top of his head and bends at the waist. "I'm never going to live this down, am I?"

"Not if I can help it." I'm not ready to let him off the hook.

He groans, loudly. "How am I ever going to look him in the eye?"

"As long as you apologize, I don't think he's the kind to hold a grudge."

Isaac stands up, his expression quickly morphing from despair to hope. "Do you think he'd invite us over for dinner? Has he cooked for you? Was it incredible? I can't believe you're dating a famous chef. You don't like eighty percent of food."

"I love you, but you've lost your mind. I'm still mad at you." I glower at him. "He's not a chef anymore. He does live in a holler and runs a small farm."

"I'd read somewhere he walked away after Tony Beard died. I figured he was laying low until he opened up a new restaurant."

"I don't think that's going to happen. Seems pretty content with his life."

Isaac's hazel eyes meet mine. "Please tell him I'm sorry. Beg for his forgiveness. Offer him sexual favors."

I scoff. "If anyone needs his forgiveness, it will be me. Did you have to tell him we're married?"

He hands me the papers and a pen. "Sign these and I won't be your husband anymore."

I don't expect the stab of loss to be so sharp. My hand hovers over the paper, holding the pen. "It's really over, isn't it? The end of our beginning."

"I owe you my life, Daphne. I don't know what would've happened to me if we didn't run away."

Real tears sting my eyes as I sign my name. "Same."

He envelops me in a hug for the millionth time in our years of friendship. "I'll always love you."

I squeeze him as tight as I can. "Me too. I love you right back. Give me some time to smooth things over with Odin and then come visit again. I've missed you."

"Maybe we could have a family Thanksgiving together like the old days."

I sigh. "You're going to be insufferable about him, aren't you?"

"Probably." He kisses the top of my head and then releases me from his embrace. "I feel terrible for causing you trouble. You deserve every happiness in the world. I hope you find it with Odin."

"Thank you. When's your wedding?" I watch as he slides our divorce papers into a folder and tucks it inside his messenger bag on the front seat.

He grins at me over the roof of the car. "We're eloping to Tahiti in December."

"Of course you are. Send me pictures."

I wave as he drives away.

My past and present have been on a collision course for a while, but I didn't anticipate such a spectacular crash. I'm emotionally drained by the last hour.

I really need to find Odin and tell him the whole truth.

If he's speaking to me.

CHAPTER THIRTY-FIVE
DAPHNE

*D*riving up the long unpaved road, I spot Odin sitting in his chair on the porch. Patsy and Roman stand near the steps, two sentries guarding their master. The afternoon is bright but chilly, and I'm surprised to find him outside.

I park the NPS vehicle next to his truck. Near the tailgate, I pause, unsure if he even wants to see me.

He stands and leans against one of the posts. "Hi. Wasn't expecting you."

"Can we talk?"

"Where's your husband?" He stares down at me, his tone not exactly friendly.

I close my eyes, willing the tears to subside. "He left. I signed the divorce papers, and I'm not married anymore. I can explain if you let me."

He bobs his head once. "Want something to drink?"

"Water?" I'm not sure why it comes out as a question.

"Be right back." He leaves me standing in the yard while he goes inside.

A few hours ago, we were lying in bed, basking in the feeling of saying I love you for the first time. I wish we'd never left. I wish I'd never checked my texts.

I climb the steps to the porch and take a seat in the chair next to Odin's. Patsy sniffs my hand and Roman climbs into my lap. At least they still like me.

Odin returns with two glasses of water.

As soon as he sits, I begin talking. "Remember when I said I grew up pretty conservatively?"

"I do. You've always been vague about your past. You never talk about your family, and I assumed you're estranged. Didn't pry because if anyone can understand, it would be me."

Not surprisingly, he's sympathetic. The man has the biggest heart even if he won't admit it.

"I may have downplayed my upbringing. My family is part of an ultra-conservative religious sect in Idaho."

His brows draw together. "Like one of those cults the FBI investigates and someone makes a documentary about?"

"Yes, probably."

"Whoa." He doesn't hide his shock.

"I know." Briefly, I meet his eyes before returning my stare to my hands in my lap. "I told you I left home at eighteen for college. That's true but also not the whole truth."

"You lied?"

"Not exactly." I cringe, hating how easily I slipped into the gray area between truth and lies with him.

"Did you run away?"

"I was legally an adult, so technically, no, but Isaac and I left home together. My family doesn't believe in education for girls. We were homeschooled, mostly in domestic arts, and then when we turned eighteen, we were expected to get married and start a family of our own."

"That's when you married Isaac?"

"Kind of."

He squints at me. "I'm going to need you to clarify more."

"He wasn't supposed to be my betrothed even though we'd grown up together and were friendly. Boys had to prove themselves in the community before taking a wife. Most girls my age married older men who were already established and could afford to provide for a wife and children."

Odin grimaces. "Like an arranged marriage?"

"I guess. My parents had to approve any suitor."

"They were okay with an older man dating their teenage daughter?" His anger simmers in his eyes.

"No dating," I clarify. "More of a formal courtship, with chaperones."

His mouth drops open. "Are you from the past? Like a time traveler?"

His disbelief makes me laugh.

"No, this is still happening today."

"Next you'll tell me about sister-wives," he jokes, uneasy.

I stare at him blankly.

"You're kidding."

My smile betrays my serious expression. "No sister-wives for us."

"That's a relief. Please continue." He flicks his hand to encourage me.

"The man who came forward to court me was nice enough, but the only thing we had in common was talking about the weather and our church."

"How did you manage to convince them to let you marry Isaac?"

"I didn't. They would never have listened to my opinion because I'm a woman. Isaac came up with a plan to help us protect each other."

"Why would he need protection?"

I ignore his question for now. "If we married each other, it would legally be bigamy for me to marry my betrothed."

"Smart."

"We went to the courthouse in town, got a license, and found a justice of the peace who would perform a civil ceremony. Our hope was our families would honor the marriage, even if it wasn't done in the church."

"And did they?"

I shake my head. "My father and the elders declared it invalid in the eyes of God and they wanted us to have it annulled. Even when I said I didn't love the other man and that I loved Isaac, they wouldn't respect our vows. My mother warned if I took him as my husband, she'd turn her back on me and I'd be shunned."

"Harsh."

I shrug, refusing to let that wound reopen. "They played right into our plan. It all went exactly as we imagined."

Confused, he blinks at me. "Your goal was to be an outcast?"

"I wanted freedom. If they had approved of the union, leaving would've been even more difficult."

Comprehension sparks in his gaze. "But if they threw you out, you'd be free."

"Exactly."

"Why stay married? Why not get divorced, or get it annulled as soon as you were out on your own?"

"Isaac and I were all each other had in the world. It felt safe to have that slip of paper from the government. If we separated, I worried my father would find out and force me to return home—not that any man would want to marry a divorced woman who wasn't a virgin."

"So you and he . . ." He doesn't have to finish his question for me to know what he's asking.

"Never."

"But you were married."

"Isaac's gay."

He stares across the field at the mountains. "That's why he wanted to escape, too."

"Exactly."

"And people call us Appalachian hillbillies backward. Your families make mine almost seem normal."

"You're welcome."

"Still doesn't explain why you're still legally married to him."

"Honestly, it never felt like a real marriage. We stood in front of a random guy and said some words, he signed a piece of paper and the state of Idaho declared us husband and wife. I love Isaac with my whole heart . . . like a brother. He's been my best friend, and for a long time, he was my only friend. By being married, we got an on-campus apartment in college, and I could be on his health plan when I only worked part-time for the NPS. There were a lot of benefits."

"When was the last time you lived in the same place? No one was suspicious?"

"No one ever asked. As a park ranger, I have to go where the jobs are."

"I can't believe you're married and didn't tell me."

"Fake married."

"Legally married," he corrects me.

"Not anymore."

"Why get divorced now?"

"Isaac is in love and wants to propose to his boyfriend. They're eloping to Tahiti. That's why he came here—I needed to sign our divorce papers."

"Where is he now?" Odin's shoulders finally relax.

"I told him to find a hotel, back in Atlanta."

"You made him drive four hours for a hotel?" he asks in disbelief.

"If he stayed anywhere near here, I'd be tempted to go yell at him some more."

He pauses for a moment. "I understand why you got married. If you signed the papers, then as of today, you're divorced. That's all I need to know." He reaches for my hand and entwines our fingers before kissing my knuckles.

"I'm not mad at him for showing up. I'm happy to officially end the marriage."

"Then what has you so upset?" His concerned eyes search mine.

"His hillbilly comments were out of line. I don't know what came over him. He was shunned by his family and ostracized for being gay —he should know better. I'm embarrassed he'd even joke about that."

Odin squeezes my hand. "Don't be upset on my behalf. I've spent my whole life as the butt of a joke. Even when I worked in the top kitchens in New York, I had to deal with ignorance and stereotypes."

"Yeah, he changed his tune when he figured out who you are."

"Who am I?" He cocks his head to the side.

Oops. I've just outed myself for snooping.

"Former fancy pants chef? That's what Isaac said, something about having a star. He has a major foodie crush on you." I give an exaggerated shrug to defend my innocence.

"He shared all this with you this afternoon?" Doubt is written all over his face.

"Okay, fine. I looked you up online when we first met." I'm disappointed in how easily I fold.

Odin lifts his brow in surprise. "You did? Why?"

"Curiosity. Suspicion. Boredom."

"Interesting. And what did you find out about me?" He's not angry; if anything, he's amused.

"I freaked out when I saw how many results there were for your name. I only read one headline." I cringe and use my water as a distraction, taking long gulps until the glass is empty.

"Let me guess—it had something to do with me and Tony. Was it the one about me sleeping with his widow or my arrest on drug charges?"

"You slept with his widow?" I fail to hide my shock.

"No, we had dinner together after the funeral. The paps framed the shot so it appeared to be only the two us. And the drug charges? They were dropped, but it made for an excellent click-bait headline, which is why it continues to circulate on various websites. Don't believe what you read online."

"I didn't."

"Your investigation into my illegal park activities wasn't inspired by reading that headline, was it?" He leans forward until his elbows rest on his knees.

I scrunch up my eyes and pinch my index finger and thumb together with a tiny gap. "Maybe a little bit. Can you forgive me?"

"Already done." He gazes at me with love in his eyes.

I exhale with relief. "How are you so understanding?"

"Because I know your true character and I love you. Love means accepting imperfections in ourselves and others. We're all worthy of love."

"I love you." I mean it with my whole heart.

"And I love you." He rises and lifts me from my chair. He wraps his arms around my waist, and I circle my arms over his shoulders. Our gazes interlock. His is full of love, and a little lust. "Any other confessions, or can we return to our earlier plans of spending the day in bed together?"

"Prepare yourself—I think Isaac's going to invite himself to Thanksgiving. I told him maybe next year."

"Can't wait." He kisses the corner of my jaw. "If he asks what we're having, tell him possum."

CHAPTER THIRTY-SIX
ODIN

*D*aphne's revelations about her upbringing and marriage to Isaac surprised me but didn't change how I feel about her. We all carry a lifetime of secrets within ourselves. Today I'm going to reveal another one of mine.

* * *

When I turn onto the logging road, she frowns. "I've already been to the orchard."

"Our destination is different today."

Unlike the sunny October day I first brought her out here, the mid-November afternoon is freezing and damp. Fog clings to the trees in droplets. The contrast between the types of weather makes the span of time between the two dates feel longer than it appears on the calendar.

Roman bounces around in his crate, excited, and Patsy snorts and sniffs the air. She knows where we're going and why.

"Yes, I'm a farmer. Yes, I forage for wild edibles. However, this is where I make my money."

"In an old filbert grove? How many hazelnuts can you get off of these old trees? The going price must be exceptionally high if you're making money."

"It's not what's above the surface that matters as much as what's below it." I point to the ground. "Do you know what's beneath your feet?"

"Grass, soil, roots, rocks, insects, for starters, magma if you want to get really deep." She stares at the tip of my mud-covered boot.

"I really do love you even when you're being snarky." I kiss her temple close to the ribbed edge of her knit hat.

"I think you love me even more because of my snark."

That's true and I won't bother denying it.

"Between your foot and the magma, what else do we have?"

"Dead things?"

"Also, probably true."

"Where are you going with this? Is there a body buried here?" She lifts one foot and then the other, peering at the dirt.

"Could be. Unmarked graves exist all over these mountains. Sometimes the headstones get removed or stolen, but the grave remains."

"I knew that. People love visiting the cemeteries in the park and reading the epitaphs. I find them depressing. Too many children died as babies or at an early age."

"Life in the Smokies was hard. Still is today."

"Especially when your boyfriend drags you outside in the cold to play a guessing game of 'What's beneath my feet?' Buried treasure? Archeological artifacts? Who can say?" She gives an exaggerated shrug.

I make a buzzer noise. "Wrong answer."

"What's the right answer?" She blows on her gloved hands.

"Mycelium."

"Mushrooms? We're out here because of fungus?"

"More like the fungi motherboard or brains. Mycelium is . . ."

"I'm aware it is the vegetative part of the colony and that there are two thousand different species of fungus in the Smokies."

"I'm so proud of you, but I bet you didn't know about these." I release Patsy and Roman from their leashes. Always well behaved, Patsy takes her time strolling into the grove. Roman, however, is the opposite, running in looping circles.

"What's he doing?" she asks, eyes trained on the dog.

"Watch."

Patsy keeps her snout near the ground, slowly ambling from trunk to trunk. Roman begins digging, his tail wagging.

"Did he find a bone?" She takes a step forward, but I stop her.

"I hope not. Wait."

Patsy's snorting grows louder.

"Is she okay?"

I appreciate the genuine concern in her voice.

"She's happier than a pig in shit right now."

Roman's head is almost hidden in the hole he's dug when he pops up and trots over to me.

"Drop it," I command, and he obeys.

Out of his mouth falls a beautiful, bulbous black truffle. After rewarding him with a handful of treats, I pick it up and show it to her.

Daphne recoils. "Ew. Is that dung?"

"Why would you think that?" I'm confused.

"David Attenborough narrated a nature documentary about dung beetles, and they roll wildebeest scat that looks identical to what you're holding in your hand right now."

"You're serious." I laugh as I brush loose dirt away from the culinary treasure.

"I am. You should watch it sometime. It's a triumph of will in the face of seemingly insurmountable challenge." She side-eyes my movements.

I carefully toss the brown lump in my palm, weighing it. "I'm not sure of the market price for wildebeest shit, but this beauty is worth six hundred dollars, probably more."

Her mouth drops open. "No way."

Patsy digs with a front leg, burying her snout in the soft earth. "Hold on a second. Unlike Roman, she won't be as gentle with her find."

I have to physically shove her out of the way and she's not happy about it. From my other pocket, I pull out a baggie with a flattened piece of banana cake. Once I slide the plastic zipper open, her attention shifts from the dirt to my hand.

"Good girl."

Behind us, Daphne laughs. "You distract her with cake? I used the same trick on Kacey at the farmers' market. I'm so going to tell her about this."

With Patsy distracted, I crouch down and finish extracting the truffle with my hands. This Périgord is even larger than the first. These are lucky finds early in the season.

I focus on Daphne again. "You can't tell your friend."

"Why not? She'd think it was hysterical."

"Because if word got out, I wouldn't be the only one out here with a Lagotto or a pig. After discovering a few truffles growing here naturally, I've been cultivating spores to expand the harvest. All of my investment could be dug up by someone else. Where there is a lot of money to be made, there will always be someone trying to profit off the hard work of others."

She blinks at me as she processes my warning. "This is a real thing? Truffle pirates?"

"I've never heard them called that before, but it fits."

A funny expression settles over her face. "There was a guy in Merryville who asked me about backcountry foraging. He wanted to hire a guide to bring him into the mountains. You don't think . . ."

"What did he look like?"

"An arrogant creep in an expensive sweater driving a Mercedes. I don't know . . . I didn't pay much attention to his face."

"He randomly approached you?"

"I was in the NPS loaner. People see it and feel compelled to talk to me. Rangers have a reputation for being friendly and helpful."

"I don't like strange men trying to pick you up in random parking lots."

"He wasn't flirting with me. Tell your jealousy to stand down. You're missing the point—what if he was a truffle pirate trying to get the dirt on your operation?"

"You're making a huge leap based on little information."

"He looked like a man who enjoys spending exorbitant amounts of money on fungus."

"No one besides me—and now you—knows this location. None of my buyers, not my family, not even my friends . . . if I had any."

"This is why you park your van at the trailhead and hike down here with a backpack and Patsy, your ever-present sidekick." She points her finger at me as pieces snap into place. "You're not a weirdo . . . you're only *playing* one, like an evil genius, supervillain running your fungus empire right under everyone's noses."

"Well, under Patsy's and Roman's noses at least. Humans don't have the olfactory power to detect the truffles under the dirt."

She gives me a blank look.

"Thanks for calling me a genius, by the way. I'll take the compliment."

"I have a question." Hurt darkens her expression. "Why didn't you tell me about the truffles before? You can trust me—I'm a ranger."

"And because of that, I assumed your loyalties would be with the park."

She frowns. "You're not wrong."

"Remember how upset you were about the apples? How you suspected me of illegal activities?"

With a dip of her chin, she confirms she does.

"I didn't know you well enough to trust you with this secret."

"Why bring me out to the orchard? Was it some kind of a test? A red herring?"

"More the latter. I'm not proud of the deception."

"What if that day I'd seen the filbert grove and asked questions?"

"I think we were both too distracted by lust to notice much of anything besides getting each other naked."

She averts her eyes for a second. "True. I was trying to figure out how we could have all the sex right then and cursing my love of pants."

I give her a confused look.

"Skirts and dresses are more conducive to quickies. Think about it."

"If it's about having sex with you, I do think about it—a lot. Probably more than is healthy."

A spark of lust brightens her warm brown eyes before it quickly dims. "Can I get a raincheck on having sex with you outside until it's warm again? I don't want to worry about important body parts getting frostbite."

"Smart." I close the distance between us and wrap my arms around her torso.

Nearby, Patsy and Roman continue snuffling the ground.

"If I don't supervise them, Patsy will follow him around and eat all the truffles he finds. While I love her, I'm not letting her have a thousand-dollar snack." I release my hold on Daphne.

"Can I help?"

"That would be great. Thank you." I squeeze her hands between both of mine. "I'll manage Patsy if you keep track of him. Tell him to drop it if he finds one."

"Got it."

While we monitor the hunters, she peppers me with questions about cultivation and the harvest. Because we're early in the season, I don't anticipate finding a large quantity of truffles today. Also, it's damn cold out. After another few minutes, I whistle and recall both animals.

"How many did we get?" Daphne hands me two lemon-sized truffles to add to my collection.

"We?" I tease as I estimate the total weight. "I'd say a couple of pounds at least."

"Impressive."

"Glad you think so. Let's get out of here and I'll make you a feast for dinner. You have to taste them to understand why they're so expensive. There's nothing quite like a fresh truffle."

Her lips purse.

I sigh. "You're not a fan of mushrooms."

"No, but I'm willing to trust you to change my mind."

"Want to bet on it?"

Her brows tug together. "Did you ever collect on our first bet? I don't remember."

"Originally I was going to use it to convince you to go to the party with me. When you went willingly, I banked it to collect at a later date."

She balks. "That isn't allowed."

"Who says? My bet, my rules." I flash her my charming grin.

She glowers. "Your charms don't work on me."

"Don't they?" I sweep her into my arms and kiss her breathless. "You did fall in love with me."

"Just a technicality."

EPILOGUE
DAPHNE

"*Y*ou'd think people would be used to seeing a pig walked on a leash," I whisper to Odin as we stroll through downtown Green Valley. Holiday lights decorate the streets, and the windows are all aglow with festive displays of the season.

"I'm guessin' it might be the red and green striped scarf tied around Patsy's neck." Even if he's laughing at me, it's still my favorite sound. "You know she doesn't get cold like you do, right?"

"How do you know?" I tip my head to the side.

"You're adorable." He touches his gloved finger to my nose. "Well, for one thing, she has a nice layer of fat to keep her warm. Think about a whale. Or bacon."

Mouth agape in shock, I cover her pointy ears. "Odin Hill! *Ixnay on the aconbay.* So rude. It's bad enough we had to walk by the store advertising Christmas hams."

Patsy snorts and shakes her head, displacing my hands.

"You do remember she's a hog, right? She doesn't understand most of what we say to her."

"Still. The only pigs we should be eating are those adorable marzipan ones with the tiny candy mushrooms we saw in the fancy shop in Asheville."

Since I'm now in on his truffle secret, I make the long drives with him to deliver the goods to his customers. I love our road trips, even if he insists on listening to foraging podcasts. With my feet on the dashboard and the man I love beside me, I feel like we could keep on driving forever, going anywhere the highways take us. We spend a lot of those hours talking about travel and where we want to go. Most of my adventures revolve around parks and natural wonders. Not surprisingly, Odin's center on food.

He's never seen the Grand Canyon in person, so after the holidays, we're going to head west to Arizona for a week of sun, the red rocks of Sedona, and southwest-style Mexican food. I cannot wait for all of it.

Odin takes Patsy's leash from my hand. "Come on, we've had enough strolling for one day. Snow's comin'."

Expecting to see flakes falling, I peer up at the flat gray sky. "How can you tell?"

"I can smell it on the wind," he states, like this is something everyone can do.

I sniff and only smell sugary goodness from Donner Bakery.

"We should buy Patsy a slice of banana cake," I suggest, pure innocence on my face.

"Nothing for you?" He tucks my hand into the crook of his elbow as he walks in the direction of the shop.

"I mean, if we're already going to be in there to purchase cake, we could at least check out the muffin selection." I sneak a peek at his face.

He gives me a closed-mouth smile. "Should probably buy a dozen."

My eyes flit over his features, like I'm considering something important. "If there's the possibility we could get snowed in, two dozen might be smarter. We could freeze them."

"Good idea." He leans down for a kiss, his nose cold against mine.

The idea of spending days together at his cabin sounds like heaven. Activities at the park have slowed way down, school visits are paused until the new year, and the farm is tucked in for winter, although Odin still has a few root vegetables in the ground. Other than making frequent visits to the filbert grove and delivering truffles to his customers, he is also enjoying the quiet of the coming winter.

Two bags of muffins in hand, we slowly meander our way back to the van. "If the snow isn't too deep, can we take a hike tomorrow?"

"Sure. Where do you want to go?"

"I want to visit my chapel."

"It's yours now, is it?" He chuckles.

"I like to think of it as my personal sanctuary. I go there when I need to think or ask for guidance. Or talk to God." My gaze shifts to my feet. "Imagine how beautiful it will be surrounded by freshly fallen powder. Magical."

He lifts my chin with the tip of a finger. "Did I ever tell you the history of the chapel? Before it was relocated to the park?"

I shake my head.

"Ida's grandfather built it for her grandmother when they settled in the area. He was a pastor." Odin's warm voice holds reverence for this revelation.

"My chapel is really Ida's?" A shiver runs down my spine at the connection.

He nods. "I like to visit it sometimes, more for the connection to my family's history and not so much for conversations or prayers."

"It's a beautiful building."

In my head, I imagine marrying Odin in the chapel. An early summer wedding when the trees are bright green and flowers fill the meadow, transforming it into a colorful carpet of blooms. The building is so small, we'd only be able to invite a dozen people to witness our vows. No need to host the hundreds of Hills. We could throw a party after at the barn, though, even have a contra dance. Maybe a Maypole, with stack cakes and a banana cake for Patsy.

When I blink away the fantasy, I find Odin staring at me, a knowing smile tugging at his mouth.

He leans close to whisper against my lips. "You know, I think the chapel would be the perfect place for a wedding someday."

I whole-heartedly agree. "Someday."

ACKNOWLEDGMENTS

To SO, we survived another book. Thank you for loving me even when I'm on deadline and surly.

To Penny Reid, once again, thank you for forming Smartypants Romance and allowing us to play in your worlds. I am grateful for your faith, encouragement, insight, patience, and most of all, your friendship.

To my readers, thanks for following me back to Tennessee and embracing this new series. To the Reiders, thank you for taking a chance on these books.

Continued gratitude for the sisterhood of Smartypants Romance authors. Thank you for your encouragement, handholding, laughter, and support.

Fiona Fischer, thank you for everything you do. Someday, we'll go back to Italy. Brooke Nowiski, thank you for all you do for Smartypants Romance. Thank you to my PA, Jennifer Beach, for holding faith in my this last year.

To my editor, Caitlin Nelson, thank you for your continued faith in my writing. To Janice Owen, thank you for proofreading. Thanks to Sara M for all her insight on the NPS.

Lots of gratitude for my street team and review crew, thanks for sticking with me when I go quiet. To the members of Daisyland, my reader group on Facebook, thank you for chatting about books and life with me.

To all the bloggers and bookstagrammers, thank you for all that you do for the book community. Thank you for continuing to support me and my books.

I love hearing from readers. Come find me on social media and say hi, or email me at daisyauthor@gmail.com.

ABOUT THE AUTHOR

Daisy Prescott is a USA Today bestselling author of small town romantic comedies. Series include Modern Love Stories, Wingmen, Love with Altitude, as well as the Park Rangers books for Smartypants Romance. Tinfoil Heart is a romantic comedy standalone set in Roswell, New Mexico with a choose your-own-adventure ending.

Daisy currently lives in a real life Stars Hollow in the Boston suburbs with her husband, their rescue dog Mulder, and an indeterminate number of imaginary house goats. When not writing, she can be found in the garden, traveling to satiate her wanderlust, lost in a good book, or on social media, usually talking about books, bearded men, and sloths.

* * *

Find Daisy online:

Mailing List: www.daisyprescott.com/mailing-list/
Facebook: www.facebook.com/daisyprescottauthorpage
Instagram: www. instagram.com/daisyprescott/
Twitter: www.twitter.com/Daisy_Prescott
Goodreads: www.goodreads.com/author/show/
7060289.Daisy_Prescott
Bookbub: https://www.bookbub.com/authors/daisy-prescott
Website: www.daisyprescott.com/

Find Smartypants Romance online:

Website: www.smartypantsromance.com

Facebook: www.facebook.com/smartypantsromance/

Goodreads: www.goodreads.com/smartypantsromance

Twitter: @smartypantsrom

Instagram: @smartypantsromance

Read on for:

1. Daisy's Booklist
2. Smartypants Romance's Booklist

ALSO BY DAISY PRESCOTT

Park Rangers:
Happy Trail
Stranger Ranger

Wingmen:
Ready to Fall
Confessions of a Reformed Tom Cat
Anything but Love
Better Love
Small Town Scandal
Wingmen Babypalooza
The Last Wingman

Love with Altitude:
Next to You
Crazy Over you
Wild for You
Up to You

Modern Love Stories:

We Were Here

Geoducks Are for Lovers

Wanderlust

Want a reading list?

Book List

To keep up with my latest news and upcoming releases, sign up for my mailing list:

Subscribe Now

Green Valley Chronicles

The Donner Bakery Series

Baking Me Crazy by Karla Sorensen (#1)

Stud Muffin by Jiffy Kate (#2)

No Whisk, No Reward by Ellie Kay (#3)

Beef Cake by Jiffy Kate (#4)

Batter of Wits by Karla Sorensen (#5)

The Green Valley Library Series

Love in Due Time by L.B. Dunbar (#1)

Crime and Periodicals by Nora Everly (#2)

Prose Before Bros by Cathy Yardley (#3)

Shelf Awareness by Katie Ashley (#4)

Carpentry and Cocktails by Nora Everly (#5)

Love in Deed by L.B. Dunbar (#6)

Scorned Women's Society Series

My Bare Lady by Piper Sheldon (#1)

The Treble with Men by Piper Sheldon (#2)

Park Ranger Series

Happy Trail by Daisy Prescott (#1)

Stranger Ranger by Daisy Prescott (#2)

The Leffersbee Series